SERPENT EGG RAPTURE

SERPENT EGG RAPTURE

ROBB HOFF

Hydra Publications

Cover Photography by Bob Willcutt

Cover Design by Tom Jones

Cover Model Emily Billingsley

ISBN: 978-1-937979-63-8

Hydra Publications

Goshen, Kentucky 40026

www.hydrapublications.com

For all of those who embraced that fateful offer they just couldn't refuse: to live the life of lovers like no other lovers have ever lived this life.

PART I

CLUTCH OF COSMIC EGGS

SIX OF ONE

Since Sirena left her husband of twenty-two years for Uriel last summer, she dreaded separation from her newfound soulmate. The consummation of their coupled destiny had so enraptured her that every second they were apart felt like the universe was collapsing inside of her.

"Turn left in five hundred feet," instructed the female voice of her phone map app. "Take Church Road for one-point-three miles to your destination."

Sirena slowed on the two-lane highway and signaled when she saw the street sign posted ahead. She glanced into the rearview mirror then turned onto the gravel road that was too narrow for two cars traveling in opposite directions.

This can't be right, she thought.

Her glance into the mirror reminded her of the other reason why she dreaded separation from Uriel: fear of retaliation by her ex-husband Earl. Even though their recently finalized divorce seemed amicable enough, Sirena knew too well of the volatility that lurked behind her ex's middle-aged veneer of dutiful Christian family man. She believed that he could kill her if he ever had the chance to do so with impunity.

Sirena had ensured she wasn't followed during the hour drive from her home in Maysville, Kentucky to this destination near the ancient site of the Great Serpent Mound, but she felt a different dread spike through her, now that she found herself alone in such a remote location about to meet a man she didn't know.

What if this is a set up to lure me out here to the middle of nowhere? she wondered.

"Stop it," she scolded herself aloud. "This is all legit. The man's car just wouldn't start. That's all."

Sirena had texted her employers at the Institute of Artifactual Research about the change in her plans. The artifact collector she was scheduled to meet at a hotel in nearby Seaman, Ohio couldn't start his car. He changed their meeting place to this new location some ten miles from the hotel. She texted the address to her employer, and her colleagues had texted back to her that the change was duly noted.

Sirena breathed easier with the knowledge that The Institute knew her whereabouts, but as she ventured farther and slower along the potholed, narrow road that snaked between a creek ravine to her left and treed, hilly terrain on her right, she wanted to update her employer about her progress. She braked to a stop then retrieved her phone from the console beside her. She raised her sunglasses, only to notice the map was gone from the screen and the signal icon indicated no reception.

"Damn," she muttered, returning her sunglasses over her eyes when she realized she hadn't downloaded the map to her phone.

Sirena set her phone down before she glanced in the rearview mirror again. With no one behind her, she pulled forward, steering around a pothole that consumed nearly half of the road.

It's less than two miles on this road, she reminded herself. *It can't be too much farther.*

Sirena was already perturbed by the change in meeting location, and now this aggravation of dropped phone service irked her further. She hoped even more that her appointment would be brief but understood that her employers at The Institute expected details about the clutch of the so-called "Cosmic Eggs" discovered during an excavation by the collector. The Institute had provided her with background information about the man and his discovery in their *Camazotz Nexus* file.

Once Sirena cleared two switchbacks that coiled through the surrounding forest, a dirt driveway opened to her right. She skidded to a stop in the gravel then peered down the drive. A hoary-headed old man clad in blue denim bib overalls stood in front of a car parked between a trailer and a shed at the end of the driveway. The man was surrounded by pecking chickens. He waved first then motioned for her to drive toward him.

Sirena was relieved that the old man seemed harmless enough. With her fear now allayed, she prepared herself for the prospect of a prolonged visit. She turned onto the bumpy dirt lane and bounced along it until the hens near the old man scattered. She tightened her close-lipped smile before she reached the man and parked.

"I'm Sirena," she introduced herself once she exited her SUV, tossing her bronze-swirled balayage of brunette hair from her shoulders. "Sirena Martell."

"Pleased to make your acquaintance," came the man's raspy sputter. "Name is Enoch."

"So very nice to meet you, Enoch," Sirena cooed as she scooched her smile to the side of her mouth and tilted her head when she noticed the wrought-iron patio table behind the man. "Enoch is quite a strong, biblical name. I'm not sure I ever met anyone named Enoch."

"Surely you have!" the man heaved through a rickety laugh. "You probably just don't remember me yet.

"But you're right. Enoch is strong and biblical. It's also quite rare. Its meaning tends to get lost in translation."

Sirena flinched when Enoch lunged toward her with his gnarled, trembling hand extended. She watched him squint against his reflection in her mirrored sunglasses as he staggered closer to her. His musty breath preceded a twisted grin that exposed a mouthful of crooked, brown teeth.

Sirena stepped back from him as she clutched her notebook against her sweatered chest, hoping he would lower his hand. She noticed the soiled undershirt beneath his overalls then tried to gauge his age based on the weathered face, losing her measure when she met the dazzle of his glacial blue eyes. She finally relented and took his cracked leathery hand, realizing just how ancient the man before her truly seemed.

"How old are you?" she blurted, surprising herself that she allowed expression to the thought.

"Why, I'm older than Methuselah," Enoch wheezed with a wink then abruptly disengaged the handshake between them to lift a colorful woven garment from the top of the patio table.

Sirena again stepped back from Enoch when he lurched toward her, unfurling the fabric patterned with ovals and geometric stripes amidst the array of bright colors.

"Now behold the clutch of cosmic eggs beneath this sacred huipil," he croaked, then he folded the garment over his arm and gestured toward the open, pulp-paper egg carton at the center of the table.

"Sacred *what?*" Sirena knotted her brow when she asked her question.

"Huipil," Enoch repeated. "Pronounced *WEE-PEEL* but spelled H-U-I-P-I-L. It's known as a Guatemalan blouse today, but this one is rare and magical Mayan garb. Its legend supposed that the wearer destined for its fateful fit will find protection within its skin-tight grip against her flesh like it is a sacred shield against pure evil."

"Mayan haute couture," Sirena remarked then snickered as she lowered her chin to peer above the frame of her sunglasses at the huipil. "That is amazing, though, and that odd design is certainly...busy."

"Let's make a deal, Miss Martell," Enoch offered with a shaky wave of his hand. "I'll throw in this huipil, just in case it's your glass slipper, so to speak, and you can still pick the cosmic egg that you're destined to possess."

"Glass slippers, Guatemalan glam, and cosmic eggs," Sirena sneered at him in reply. "What more could a girl ask for?"

"Perhaps your egg will hatch your wildest dream," suggested Enoch, "whether it's a rapturous fantasy that seals your ecstasy forever or a nightmare that dooms you to eternal torment."

Sirena lifted the sunglasses from her face to prop them atop her head before she stepped to the table and set her notebook on its wrought iron surface.

"Sounds like an offer I really can't refuse," she said past her scowl. "The Institute folks said you'd only let them have one of these eggs. Since it's not like I get to keep it anyway, I'm just here to pick the egg I think they're destined to possess, not me."

"Perhaps," came Enoch's gruff reply. "But either way, do choose wisely."

Sirena leaned forward to inspect the egg-shaped objects.

She felt reluctant to try to connect with one more than the others of the dozen but remained resolute to pick the egg she felt best suited the interests of The Institute. She paused in her observation once she recognized the alignment of the eggs in the carton–solid jade eggs of varied colors were alternated with painted stone eggs bearing symbols and images.

"What's this supposed to be?" Sirena's voice boomed as she sprang upright, wedging her palms against her high, jeans-gripped hips and glaring at Enoch. "Some kind of rock egg tic-tac-toe?"

"This is no game here," began Enoch before he pointed his quivering finger at the carton of eggs. "These six polished eggs are jade, or jadeite, rather. The colors are key to the power they project. You have Olmec Blue, Galactic Black, Translucent Ice, Speckled Green, Emerald Green, and Swirled Gray."

"What about these other eggs?" Sirena asked, then she leaned over the table to put her fingertip to the point of one of the eggs that appeared to portray a red-and-green feathered serpentine form with the face of a bearded man. "Are these painted ones with the images made of solid stone?"

"That is the egg of Kukulkan on his raft of serpents," Enoch informed Sirena without answering her question. "This side of the egg represents the unified entity of divinity and underworld in the transfiguration of the snake scales into feathers. The sinister becomes celestial."

"The sinister becomes celestial," Sirena repeated then smirked at Enoch. "Sounds like my soulmate."

"Or perhaps the other way around," Enoch chuckled before he returned his attention to the image depicted. "Notice that the feathered serpent is crowned with the white face of the bearded Mayan culture hero, Kukulkan.

"Legend has it that this god-man materialized in the ancient Mayan world then vanished from Earth as though he never really died. But before he disappeared, he promised to return again one day so that he could anoint the world with cosmic rapture."

"I don't quite understand what that means," Sirena snapped as she straightened and again glared at him.

"It's the translation," Enoch grinned in reply.

"What translation?" Sirena now squinted at him. "The translation of the egg image, you mean?"

"Aw, you know," the man bellowed hoarsely. "*Translation*. Some believe that the biblical Enoch never did actually die. They think that he was taken to heaven directly by God while he was still alive with the expectation of his return to earth one day, kind of like Kukulkan just vanished from the Mayans with a Second Coming promised in the offing."

"It's just too bad nobody seems to notice I'm back."

Sirena further twisted her face in her wordless contemplation of the odd old man. She flipped her hair from her shoulder while she surveyed the furrows of his face.

"Aw, hell honey," the man finally groaned. "It's a joke: the biblical Enoch was *translated*, meaning he was taken by God from this world without dying first to experience the supernatural realm. We around these parts of the Serpent Mound with all of this ancient history here like for our jokes to be ancient, too."

Sirena now nervously laughed. She sensed a weird aura about the man that The Institute had failed to characterize in their report about him. She warily returned her attention to the egg objects.

"Now, this one looks more like it's your egg," her voice crackled as she pointed to the image of a decrepit-looking old man with a large hooked nose. "He looks like he's about your age, plus he doesn't have a beard, and neither do you."

"Itzamná," Enoch said. "The Creator God of the ancient Mayan who ruled the universe through knowledge and sorcery. His image was renowned, but I don't really look so scraggily old, do I?"

"You're definitely on your way, *translation* or not" Sirena joked before she pursed her lips and returned her attention to the eggs.

"Thanks a lot," Enoch laughed.

"What about that one there with the younger looking man with no beard?" Sirena blurted her question. "He looks like he's seated at the controls of a rocket or something."

"That is the egg of Votan," answered Enoch. "The image depicts the sarcophagus lid of the cosmic ruler of the seventh-century Mayan Snake House–Pacal the Great–who was supposedly a manifestation of Votan.

"It is more likely that this Votan is navigating his way between the underworld and celestial life rather than piloting some ancient alien spacecraft, but you never know. The origin of the Votan lineage, though, is likely much older than that of Kukulkan and his Aztec counterpart Quetzalcoatl, but not nearly so ancient as the Mayan pantheon god Itzamná."

"Old, older, and oldest," blurted Sirena before she leaned toward the next carved egg and peered closer. "This one's different, though, isn't it? There's somebody's head coming out of whatever it is that big bat creature is about to eat."

"Correct," uttered Enoch. "That depicts a scene from the sacred Mayan narrative–the *Popol Vuh*. One of the Hero Twins is about to be beheaded within the jaws of the death bat of the Maya underworld–the Camazotz."

"The Camazotz?" Sirena sought confirmation.

"Yes. The Camazotz."

"Well, I guess that settles it," Sirena announced as she smacked her hands together. "The Institute called the material they gave to me for this little jaunt here the *Camazotz Nexus* file, so it looks like my search has ended."

"Not so fast," Enoch countered, wagging his finger in her direction before he pointed toward the next carved and painted egg. "Take a look at this one."

Sirena leaned over the carton then squinted at the next painted egg until the image carved into it became clear. She sprang upright with her mouth agape, staring at Enoch as she took a step back from the table.

"Oh, my God," she began. "That's you on that egg, isn't it?"

"Flesh and blood," Enoch toothily smiled in reply. "Well, more or less. As you can see, I'm wearing a rather Coptic tunic there instead of these farm britches I have on now."

"My God," cried Sirena as she glanced back and forth between Enoch and his image on the egg. "That's like an exact match. How is that even possible?"

"Why don't you look at the last egg now?" he urged her without answering her question.

Sirena did what he said then immediately covered her mouth with her hands.

"Look familiar?" Enoch probed. "Simply divine perhaps?"

Sirena lowered her hands from her mouth then reached to the egg, tracing the texture of the carved gold-flecked angel wing below the face that was etched into every part of her being.

"It's Uriel," she gasped.

Sirena took the egg from the carton and brought it closer to her eyes.

"*Now* it looks like your search has ended," Enoch remarked

then smacked his hands together. "But, I tell you what I'm going to do. I'll throw in one of the jadeite eggs with your selection at no extra charge, especially since the one that picks you mirrors your essence for your own salvation or damnation, as the case may be."

Sirena peripherally detected swirling movement from the gray egg in the carton. She lowered the carved egg she held then reached with her other hand to claim the shimmering gray jadeite egg in front of her.

"This has to be some sort of trick," Sirena uttered once she palmed the gray jadeite egg in her possession. "The resemblances are way too uncanny not to be. These had to have been made recently. They just can't be ancient artifacts.

"Jesus, I could use a drink about now."

"That does remind me," Enoch began as he tucked his upturned thumbs beneath the suspenders of his overalls. "I believe your last name–*Martell*–is also the name of a fine cognac. Seems like I shared a batch of Martell cognac once upon a time in Paris, France with another old timer. That was at the site where the statue of Charlemagne and his horse now stands on the grounds of the Notre Dame cathedral. Of course, the statue wasn't there way back then."

Sirena felt her mouth grow dry and her skin tighten cold with goose bumps. Her heart bounded within her chest as she fought the vertigo that started to wobble her.

"Martell is a Huguenot name," she finally managed to say before she shakily set the two eggs on the table. "My ancestors survived the terror purge of the Catholic regime in Paris and eventually fled Europe to reach America."

"Indeed, they did," the old man wheezed in reply. "I remember the dragoons and their dragonnades well. That was not too long before I sipped that fine Martell cognac where Charlemagne now sits atop his Tencendur."

Sirena swallowed repeatedly to quell the rise of searing fluid in her throat. She peered more closely at the man to meet his radiant blue eyes.

"That's another joke, my dear," the old man said, grinning at her. "I can't really be that old, can I?"

"Why am I really here?" Sirena asked Enoch, her bottom lip quivering from the unease that now coursed through her.

"You tell me why you think you're *really* here," Enoch countered. "We should never be anywhere we are without knowing exactly why we are there. Unless of course, we are vacationing, like I was when I sipped that fine Martell cognac at the very spot where the statue of Charlemagne and his horse now stand at Notre Dame cathedral in Paris, France."

"Why do you keep mentioning that?" Sirena nearly sobbed her question.

Enoch then steadied her swirling gray jade egg to keep it from shifting upon the table surface.

"Because that was the last vacation I've had in hundreds of years," he said as he winked at her.

"I certainly didn't think I came here," Sirena began as she returned her sunglasses over her eyes, "to hear your reminiscence about cognac and Charlemagne statues."

"Touché," Enoch said. "The Institute didn't send you here just to listen to me babble about the days of yore and tell bad jokes that quite frankly get lost in translation anyway."

"They only sent me here for their egg, right?" she asked.

"And you have chosen on their behalf," confirmed Enoch.

"Yeah, but I feel like I picked the egg for me, not The Institute," remarked Sirena. "Maybe I should give mine back and pick again?"

"No, my dear," Enoch whispered as his fingers grazed her forearm. "The choice is made, but I do want you to learn more about these other eggs before you jaunt to your next destination."

Enoch then removed the egg of Kukulkan from the carton and turned it from the image of the bearded man with the feathered serpent body. On the other side of the egg, the image of a winged, naked man stood with a huge, pendant penis-like appendage between his scaly, feathered legs.

"Holy shit," Sirena blurted.

"The *shit* part of that is about right," said Enoch. "That's the unholy spawn of the whore fiend Lilith and Samyaza, who was the leader of those fallen angels known as The Watchers before the Great Flood. His name is Azazel.

"That grisly looking thing hanging halfway down his legs is an egg ovipositor, not a human male penis. He used that thing to beget his spawn of demonic human Nephilim that soon threatened the survival of all of mankind."

Enoch returned the egg of Kukulkan and Azazel to the carton then removed the next painted egg.

"This egg of Itzamná," began Enoch before he rotated the egg for Sirena to see the image of a voluptuously curvaceous woman with long, red flowing hair and large mounds of bared breasts, "also is the egg of Lilith, who forsook her rightful place as the wife and equal of the biblical Adam for her debauchery with The Watchers, first with the satanic seducer Samael then, ultimately, with Samyaza, who fathered her demonic spawn Azazel.

"She's drop-dead gorgeous," Sirena said as she studied the alluring image of Lilith.

"Look closer at the eagle hovering in the background behind Lilith," Enoch said then held the egg closer to her face.

Sirena cocked her head so that she could better view the bird in the presumed distance holding a double-headed serpent in its beak.

"Itzamná was a king of Atlantis," Enoch said to her. "He and his human wife begat four giant sons that were on the scale of Nephilim, and the Itzamná of the Mayan tradition also disappeared like Kukulkan and Enoch without undergoing death."

"Does that mean this is the egg I'm supposed to take back with me?" she managed to ask through her shaken voice.

"Not at all," Enoch answered. "Just understand that this double-headed serpent is the same as the Caduceus staff carried by Hermes to herald the message of the gods and guide the dead through their afterlife travel. Only in this Mayan precursor to that version, Hermes is a bird that embodies the transfigured form of the translated Itzamná, who founded the Yucatan peninsula at the great city of Chichen Itza and empowered the Mayans there with his legend and magic."

"And this was found here?" Sirena asked. "So far away from the Yucatan?"

"Very good question," Enoch replied. "This was unearthed below the Serpent Mound plateau of the Brush Creek crater. This is as ancient as any artifact ever unearthed. Some three-hundred-million years ago, the deposit of this very egg caused the meteoric impact that created the Serpent Mound crater. It is a time capsule, too, that once opened, will reveal the virtual rapture that is the prophesized End Time of this world."

"Good God," Sirena murmured.

"*Good God*, is right," Enoch said before he returned the egg of Itzamná to the carton and retrieved the egg of Votan.

"Can't hardly wait to see what's on the other side of this one," Sirena quipped mirthlessly.

"Perhaps it will be a familiar site," replied Enoch before he turned the egg of Votan to reveal the serpent effigy defined by the raised snake-shaped earth mound depicted upon it.

"That looks like the Serpent Mound," Sirena said.

"Right down to the egg held in the mouth at the head of the serpent," confirmed Enoch. "Hard to believe that this egg could have possibly preceded the construction of the site here, but truth is stranger than fiction in this case."

"That's really amazing," commented Sirena before she asked: "What about the Camazotz egg?"

Enoch returned the egg of Votan to the carton, then he took the Camazotz egg and turned it from the depiction of the over-sized Camazotz bat.

"Oh, dear God!" cried Sirena when the other side of the egg was exposed. "What in the hell is that?"

"That, my dear," Enoch began, "is the serpent spawn of Azazel ripping its way into this world through the unfortunate agency of this poor woman here."

"It looks like she's being crucified by giving birth," Sirena nearly wailed at the sight of the woman with her wrists strapped to the beam of a cross and her gray-masked face slumped forward in a tangle of hair.

"She is bound to a Roman cross," began Enoch, "like the one Jesus was crucified on, only this one is horizontal to the ground, as you can plainly see, instead of vertical. She is tied at her waist to the post."

Sirena cringed as she peered closer: the legs of the woman were spread apart, held at the ankles by hands on each side of her. The head of a bearded man with serpents for hair emerged face-first from her vulva.

"That's awful," said Sirena.

"I'd say she's being crucified at the very least," Enoch

conveyed. "That is Azazel holding up one of her legs by the ankle and Lilith holding the other. Poor girl."

Sirena asked, "Who is she?"

When Enoch didn't answer her question quickly, Sirena straightened to look at him before she asked again.

"Who is that woman?"

"We're not exactly sure," Enoch replied then returned the egg of Camazotz to the carton. "I was hoping The Institute might research the identity of this woman to better understand how this scene fits into the overall scheme of these eggs."

"Then I really should take that Camazotz egg to The Institute," Sirena declared.

"No," refuted Enoch. "Your eggs chose you."

Sirena pushed her sunglasses back to the top of her head as Enoch removed the egg of Enoch from the clutch. He turned the egg to its obverse, revealing the youthful couple of a man and woman who held hands as they stood surrounded by the front images of the other painted eggs in the carton, only the other eggs were winged in their airborne depiction.

"Who are those two?" Sirena asked.

"I'm fairly certain they're my parents," Enoch answered. "That is, my parents as they stood in the early twenties before fate altered their course either to consummate their union with my resurrected conception or meet their destruction and mine through destiny denied."

"I don't understand," Sirena said as she beseeched him with her eyes.

"You will soon enough," Enoch replied, then he returned the egg of Enoch to the carton and retrieved Sirena's chosen egg from the wrought iron table top. "And Uriel is the one who will set the course of the future right."

Enoch turned over the egg of Uriel on the table, which

revealed only swirling gray mist like that of the jade egg that Sirena had also plucked from the clutch of cosmic eggs. He then extended the egg of Uriel toward Sirena, who cupped her hands together to receive it from him.

Enoch then retrieved the swirling gray jade egg from the table and placed it next to the Uriel egg within her cupped palms.

"You know," Sirena began as she stared at the eggs that she held, "The Institute file didn't have anything about the eggs themselves or your unique historical personage. I'm really quite overwhelmed with information and didn't write anything down at all."

"I know, dear," Enoch smiled at her. "That why I have a file of my own to give to you and the fine folks at The Institute. It contains prints of each side of each egg and explains about the images and history, like I did for you here today."

"Thanks," she said before she closed her hands around her eggs and stepped to her SUV. "Could you open this back door for me?"

Enoch opened the back door on the passenger side of the SUV. Sirena placed the eggs in the hollow of the backseat.

"You can wrap your sacred huipil around the eggs to protect them," Enoch suggested. "Let me get it and your notebook, too."

"Okay," Sirena replied then straightened from her stoop to watch Enoch retrieve the garment and her notebook from the wrought iron table.

Upon his return, Enoch flashed his unsightly smile of crooked brown teeth.

"There's one more thing I'm going to ask you to do for me," Enoch told her as he handed the cloth and notebook to Sirena. "I finally was able to get my car started, but can you follow me to the Great Serpent Mound just in case the darn thing conks out on the way? I'm supposed to meet a group there to give them a personalized tour. Pays the bills and all."

"How long will all of that take?" Sirena asked before she dropped her notebook to the backseat floorboard then wrapped the huipil around the eggs.

"Not too long," Enoch replied. "The mound is only ten or so miles from here. I'll pay the eight bucks for you to get into the site so that you can tour around the place, too, if you like."

"I really do need to get back to Maysville," Sirena said past her sigh. "But I suppose I can follow you. Besides, it's been years since I've been there. It really is such a pretty place, if I remember right."

"Eggscellent," quipped Enoch before he reached into the front of his overalls and retrieved a manila envelope. "Here is your file about the clutch of cosmic eggs."

"I do appreciate this," Sirena said as Enoch handed the file to her. "I would've had trouble trying to describe everything you told me to The Institute folks."

Sirena placed the envelope atop the huipil in the backseat then shut the door. She paused on her way toward the driver's side of the SUV to shake Enoch's hand.

"Just follow me," Enoch said with a smile. "I'll go slow."

SERPENTDIPITY

Sirena followed Enoch's SUV down the dirt driveway. She checked her phone and noticed one bar of signal strength. She called Uriel, but the call went straight to voicemail.

"Hey, Babe," Sirena began as she turned onto the gravel road in the opposite direction from which she had arrived. "I might be a little later getting home in time for the showing tonight. This Enoch fellow wants me to follow him to the Great Serpent Mound before I leave. Go on without me if you need to, and I'll try to catch up. Love you, angel."

Sirena disconnected then returned the phone to the console beside her. She swept the bizarre encounter with Enoch and his clutch of cosmic eggs from her mind so that she could mull over the personally pressing matters that awaited her upon her return to Maysville, such as her and Uriel's mortgage application for a house they hoped to buy. They would make their offer as soon as they secured financing, but Sirena doubted that the process would go so smoothly.

Some of Earl's money would be nice, Sirena thought to herself then glanced into the rearview mirror to ensure that no one was following her on the gravel road.

As part of their divorce settlement, Sirena had agreed to let Earl keep everything, except for the SUV she was driving. This decision had not come easy. She and Earl had managed to build one hundred thousand dollars in home equity in the house they had owned together for the past ten years. There was also the two hundred thousand dollars in nest egg investment that Earl provided entirely through his employment at the power plant where he still worked.

Uriel had agreed to an arrangement with his wife similar to the one Sirena had with Earl, but he surrendered even more net worth: four hundred thousand dollars total. Neither initially wanted to abandon their rights to the personal wealth they had built separately with their spouses, but both agreed to do so once The Institute intervened upon their behalf, furnishing contracts to each of them that secured their employment over a five-year period with incremental bonuses over the course of the contract that totaled one million dollars between the two.

Sirena did the math again in her head to determine how much she and Uriel would earn after their first year with The Institute. Now that she was turning fifty years old at the end of the year and Uriel was already fifty, the quick influx of money seemed important for both of them to financially secure their future.

As Sirena continued to follow Enoch, she allowed herself to recall how furious Earl was with her when he first saw her again after she had left him virtually overnight. That encounter happened during a conference with attorneys before The Institute had offered their employment contract to her and Uriel. She understood that Earl's adamancy to contest all possible points of the divorce would painfully prolong the process, so when The Institute did come to her and Uriel's financial rescue in order to expedite the divorce, she and Uriel were only too happy to go to work for them.

It was The Institute, after all, that had put her and Uriel on the collision course of fate that revealed to them that they truly were soulmates of the deepest connection whose bond with each other was beyond worldly restriction and convention.

Sixty days after she filed for divorce with Earl, the dissolution was granted. The same happened with Uriel. Both had grown children over eighteen years old, so there was no other obstacle for her and Uriel to begin their lives together anew in the bliss the two of them found in each other's arms and hearts.

Now that the divorce was just finalized a week ago, Sirena did feel more at ease about Earl's state of mind, but the thought of his retaliation still flashed into her consciousness at times.

"I've got to learn to let that one go," Sirena said aloud to herself. "Earl will be Earl and that's all. He's no threat to me."

As Sirena continued to follow Enoch, she realized once again that The Institute wanted her and Uriel to be together as much as they themselves wanted to live their lives together. The Institute even had provided financial assistance to help them move in together at the Maysville location, which was more than a two-hour drive from their previous residences.

Sirena abandoned her train of thought when Enoch turned onto paved highway and a clearing from the forest revealed how suddenly dark the sky had grown in the early afternoon hour. She turned on her headlights as she followed Enoch, whose speed had increased noticeably.

Don't leave me behind, she thought as she increased her speed to match his.

The entry to the Great Serpent Mound historic site soon

appeared. Sirena followed Enoch into the entrance past the unattended booth where a sign instructed visitors to pay inside of the museum on site. She then pulled into a parking spot farther down from the spot where Enoch parked.

"Come on!" implored Enoch as he lunged toward her, grabbing her arm when she opened her door. "We're running out of time! Take your phone!"

"What?" Sirena yelled before she could stop Enoch from virtually pulling her out of her SUV, but she did manage to grab her phone as Enoch yanked her from the car and kicked the door shut.

"We've got to go!" Enoch blared above the suddenly howling wind that raced against them as the greenish billow of the squall line in the distance rushed toward the plateau. "You've got to go up that observation tower there!"

Enoch pointed to a metal-platformed staircase that rose some twenty-five feet above the ground beside an inconspicuous coil of earthen mound. He then flung open the back door and snatched the huipil from the backseat. He pulled its opening over Sirena's head as she struggled to move her arms through the garment.

Sirena's head popped through the huipil opening, then she yelled: "Are you crazy? What if there's lightning?"

"Let's hope so!" Enoch yelled back. "But don't worry! The huipil will protect you!"

"What?" she tried to protest, but he pulled her forward to the steps and practically shoved her up them.

"Record this on your phone!" she thought she heard Enoch's voice cut through a buffeting gust.

Sirena paused to look back at Enoch, but he motioned for her to continue to rise. By the time she hustled up the narrow board steps to reach the platform and turn back around to find

Enoch, she saw that he was running toward the tail of the Great Serpent Mound effigy, which she could now survey in its totality from her elevated position.

The first flash of lightning spidered in front of Sirena. She turned toward the barreling storm that raced toward her from the direction at the head of the earthen serpent, which appeared to have a glowing grayish egg in its mouth. She fumbled with her phone but managed to start recording before the grounds beside her ruptured.

"Dear God!" she blared before she again turned toward Enoch with her phone recording, only to discover that he had leapt onto the tail of the serpent and was stomping on it, like he was performing some kind of berserk dance.

Sirena shrieked when she saw the earthen snake tail tear from the ground. She then gaped at the sight of Enoch running up the tail toward the coiling folds that formed the body of the serpent. As Enoch ran, the serpent body tore from its roots to flail and slither behind him.

"Oh, my God!" screamed Sirena, then the lightning deafeningly detonated ahead of Enoch into the glowing gray egg at the snake's mouth.

Sirena turned her phone toward the upheaval. She squinted through the platform rails into the gale to glimpse Enoch sprinting toward the serpent head, where an unnatural glow penetrated the downpour. She watched him fling himself to the gray egg in front of the open mouth of the serpent. She clung to the platform floor with one hand while continuing to record with her phone in her other hand, screaming as she kept her eyes as open as she could against the onslaught of howling wind and pelting rain.

Sirena then witnessed Enoch and the egg launch into the air above the plateau edge. She stopped screaming when the head of the snake ripped itself free from the earth and the body of the serpent itself undulated midair behind the head in pursuit of Enoch and the glowing egg. She gaped at the sight of Enoch and the snake swallowed by the bruised sky as the body of the snake behind him transformed into a twisting funnel that the squall line soon sucked up into its own billowing darkness. The entire mass then veered in its flight from the plateau.

With the squall line gone, calm and sunlight almost instantly reclaimed the sky. Sirena could now see that storm had stripped the ancient serpentine effigy from the ground. The Great Serpent Mound was gone. Somehow, Enoch had conjured the earthen effigy to life.

"Oh, my God," Sirena gasped, pulling herself to a shaky stance upon the platform as she continued to record the silent scene with her phone.

What just happened?

LOST IN TRANSLATION

Sirena stared vacantly at the Ohio River bluff vista that snaked past the picture window of her upstairs living room. She arrived at her home in Maysville, Kentucky still wet and distraught from the outburst at the Great Serpent Mound, but Uriel had acted quickly to soothe her.

"Would you like another bourbon?" he asked as he pulled her closer to him in their repose on their pleather couch.

"No," Sirena declined, turning down the thick collar of her robe before she rested her cheek against his chest. "Just hold me like this and let me collect my thoughts before we call The Institute back."

Sirena sighed and once again replayed the shocking scene at Serpent Mound. She had wanted to call Uriel and The Institute immediately afterwards, but her phone was dead by the time she reached the bottom of the observation tower at the site. To make matters even more distressing for her, she couldn't charge her phone during the drive back to Maysville because she had left her car-adapter charger at home.

Sirena also anguished over the phone recording of Enoch's unearthly ascension. She hoped that she had not really seen the old man and the serpent effigy ripped from the plateau to vanish within the stormy sky. She prayed that her mind had played some kind of spectacular trick on her, but only time would tell. She had to wait for her phone to recharge enough to view the recording.

"You know," Uriel said softly to her as he threaded his fingers through her drying hair, "a twist like this was bound to happen sooner or later. I mean, the way our destiny together was such a collision course, and what we learned about who we really are and what we can do when we merge our soulmate selves–how can things not get strange fast?"

"Shhhh," she mouthed before she nuzzled against his chest, allowing the high-proof bourbon to ease her into the memory of her true self that Uriel reawakened in her virtually overnight.

For the first time since she left the hysteria at Serpent Mound, Sirena felt flushed again with the consummation of her new life with Uriel. The transfiguration she experienced with him before they both divorced their spouses was unadulterated rapture for her, revealing her true self to her and the essence of a reality that only her and her soulmate could fully fathom by being together. That is why she left Earl, even though the price of her soulmate transfiguration had come with a dear cost for her beyond just the removal of her ex-husband from her life.

From the start, Sirena feared eventual retaliation by Earl, but she hoped that he would exercise better judgment for the sake of their three adult children, the youngest of which was a freshman in college and the only one of the three who would still speak to her since the separation and subsequent divorce.

That part of the process had blindsided Sirena. She never expected her two older children to despise her quite like this.

Both daughters berated her when she told them that she intended to divorce their father for a new life with another man. Their venom for her stunned her. She expected tears and hugs. Instead, she suffered obscene tirades, and her oldest daughter even shoved her before her son intervened to intercept a punch headed for Sirena's face.

The collateral damage with her children still saddened her despite her rapturous life with Uriel. As much as she hoped for reconciliation with them at some point in the future, she could only control how she felt about the parts of her life that were now fully in front her. That pressure of immediacy made her feel somewhat vulnerable. She realized that if Uriel ever abandoned her, she might lose her mind without any hope for recovery.

But the warmth and desire that overcame her at the mere thought of Uriel quelled any inkling of doubt that surfaced within her about her future with him. He was her soulmate, now and forever. She knew it, and he proved it to her every time he met her eyes. He had rescued the vibrant woman within her as she approached fifty years of age. She had sacrificed so much of the past decades of her life for others that the empowering revival of herself in her connection with Uriel had restored her identity, including her craving for sensuality.

"Alpha and Omega," she said as she lifted her face from Uriel's chest to inch upward and kiss his lips. "I guess our transfiguration awaits us again, my love."

"Indeed," Uriel smiled at her. "Only this time around it sure sounds like we'll have to be versed even more in all things Mayan. I've been reading through both the *Camazotz Nexus* file from The Institute and the stuff Enoch gave to you at the Serpent Mound."

"It definitely seems a lot more Mayan intensive than

anything we experienced before," Sirena agreed as she straightened herself on the sofa to turn and face Uriel, crossing her legs. "I suppose our first splash into the Mayan underworld was just a quick dip compared to what might await us in the near future."

"It sure does sound like it," Uriel said, smiling thinly at her.

Sirena became versed in some aspects of Mayan mythology during her initial consummation with Uriel. That union hurtled them both across an otherworldly mindscape that climaxed with epiphany and rapture beyond anything she had ever thought imaginable. Both marvelous and terrifying, the ecstasy she shared with Uriel in her heart, mind, and body transfigured her into the woman she always knew she really was–the woman she always wanted to be but never could manage to become through her own efforts alone.

"Your phone should be charged now," Uriel said to her, meeting her gaze.

"Well, then," she sighed as he stood from the couch, "let's call The Institute, not that anything they do is really going to help us."

"What's that supposed to mean?" Uriel asked.

"They nearly got you killed the last time things got anywhere close to this weird," Sirena said, raising an eyebrow toward him. "And they criminally stalked me. Who knows what kind of danger they'll put us in this time?"

"I know," Uriel acknowledged, lowering his eyes. "But they ended up being right about everything. We would've never discovered each other if it weren't for The Institute, and now, they provide us with our income."

"So, this is nothing but a job now." remarked Sirena. "Are you saying we're forced to do this now just for financial survival?"

"No," Uriel countered as he met her narrowing eyes. "We can do any other kind of work for money to live on. This is about purpose—our vocation together. We can travel the world now. Visit all of the places and do all of the things that were denied to us and our true nature while we fulfilled our commitment to marriage and raising our children into the world. Now that our work there is all but done, we are finally together again."

"But," she blurted, "we're not really free to be ourselves together. I'm not sure I want this arrangement with The Institute, and what I witnessed at Serpent Mound scares me to death, Uriel."

"I understand how shook up you are, but we should at least hear them out on this," Uriel tried to reassure her as she stood to face him. "Then we can decide together what we should do in the future as far as The Institute is concerned. Okay?"

Sirena pursed her lips as she peered into his eyes. She wedged her palms against her hips and shifted her weight to one side. Her widening eyes pooled with brewing tears, and her lips began to tremble. She made sure Uriel knew that she feared the potential treachery that could await them if they agreed to participate in any intrigue coordinated by The Institute.

"I don't know how much more really weird shit I can take," Sirena nearly sobbed before Uriel embraced her.

Their previous encounter with The Institute altered their lives forever by forcing them both to forsake their previous lives. As painful as their decision was for their loved ones, it was clear to both of them that there was no other way for them to continue to live without each other. The Institute had subjected them to this revelation when they opened the portal of the impossible, delivering a phantom "Cosmic Egg" from a performance by the artist Salvador Dali in New York in 1965 into their lives some fifty years later as a very real egg in which life and death crawled through its fractured shell to brand both Sirena and Uriel with the *Cosmic Egg Rapture* knowledge of their true selves.

Once again, The Institute hung their lives in the balance in the unlikely form of an egg, only this time it wasn't an actual egg preserved for a half century, like the Dali egg had been. This time the egg shaping their lives was a clutch of stone and jade eggs that seemed even more foreboding and far more unreal to Sirena than the Dali phantom egg because of the menacing messenger who called himself Enoch.

"I know how hard all of this still is, baby," Uriel comforted her before he relinquished his embrace of her and interlocked his fingers with hers.

The pout left Sirena's mouth as she leaned her head back. Her lips spread open slightly in her expectation of his mouth and tongue.

"I want you inside me right now," she almost moaned as her lips spread apart wider. "I want you to absolutely ravish me until I..."

The ring of the house phone stopped Sirena from finishing her invitation to Uriel. Sirena shut her eyes, clenched her mouth, and freed her fingers from his hands. The phone rang again, but Uriel didn't move to answer it. Sirena opened her eyes and sighed. She met his plaintive stare.

"Go," she said. "So much for them waiting for us to call."

Uriel hustled into the kitchen to retrieve the cordless land-line phone. He glanced at the number and location displayed.

"It's them," he announced before he answered the call. "Pronto."

Uriel returned to the living room, only to meet Sirena's blank expression.

"Let me put you on speaker," he said to the caller then pressed the button to activate the speaker phone function. "Sirena is right here with me, Thoth."

"Oh, Sirena, you poor thing," came the gruff voice of Thoth. "I hope you're all right. I know how much this must have shaken you up. We've been watching the newscasts from the Serpent Mound today, and we're beside ourselves to try to figure out what really happened. We're all of a consensus here, though, that this wasn't damage caused by a tornado, like the reports are saying."

"Believe me," Sirena began, "What you saw on TV was not damage from a tornado. I wanted to call Uriel and you guys to tell you all about it, but my mobile died without any way to recharge it."

"So, what happened to Enoch?" Thoth asked her.

"Let me show you," Sirena said before she turned to Uriel. "Would you get my phone for me, please?"

Uriel nodded before he left the room, then Sirena began to recount the chaos that unfolded at Serpent Mound.

"Enoch asked me to follow him to the Serpent Mound because of his car problems," she started. "When we got there, it began to storm. He told me to go to the top of the observation tower there and video what I saw."

"Hey, babe," Uriel interrupted upon his return to the room. "There's something more wrong with your phone than just the battery. It still won't turn on at all."

"Oh, no," groaned Sirena, snatching the phone from him then unsuccessfully attempting to power it. "This can't be. I wonder if all the rain killed it for good."

"What's wrong?" Thoth asked.

"I'm afraid I won't be able to show you what happened just

yet," replied Sirena. "I can't get my phone to work, and I don't think the recording auto-saved anywhere else."

"Well, then just tell us what happened," Thoth told her.

"Once I reached the top of the tower," resumed Sirena, "Enoch climbs up onto the tail of the snake and starts stomping really hard. There's thunder and lightning, wind and rain everywhere, then all of the sudden, Enoch takes off running along the shape of the serpent, following its coils as the snake itself starts to lift from the ground and slither up into the air behind him."

"You mean Enoch tore the serpent from the site, not a tornado?" asked Thoth.

"That's exactly what I mean," Sirena confirmed. "Enoch sprinted the whole length of the snake until he reached the opened mouth, where the glowing shape of a huge gray egg hovered above the ground. That's when Enoch jumped onto the egg, and it took off into the sky like some kind of freaking UFO."

"What do you mean by *UFO* exactly?" asked Thoth.

"I mean the egg launched into the air like some kind of space travel vehicle," Sirena calmly answered. "And Enoch was holding onto the glowing egg as it shot into the sky with the serpent shape whipping behind him in pursuit."

"That's incredible," remarked Thoth.

"I'd really like for someone there at The Institute to tell me exactly what it was that I witnessed," Sirena requested. "And I also want to know exactly who this Enoch fellow was."

"Enoch is an antiquities expert," came Thoth's curt reply. "Among other things."

"I think you guys are holding out some information," voiced Sirena. "I had no inkling that the brain trust there at The Institute would be sending me to meet the actual Enoch of biblical fame in his translated self of the eternally undead."

"Pardon me." Thoth chuckled. "What do you mean exactly by that?"

"You know I mean exactly what I said," Sirena snapped back. "Don't even try to bullshit me. You knew who you were sending me to meet."

"Perhaps I can shed some light on this," another voice emerged over the speaker phone. "This is O. Cyrus. Hello Sirena, and you, too, Uriel."

"Cheers, O. Cyrus," Uriel acknowledged him, but Sirena remained silent.

"It's quite remarkable to us, Sirena," O. Cyrus began, "that you believe you encountered the actual Enoch of biblical and Apocryphal legend. The Institute has done more than just ponder the possibility of this before we asked you to meet with him on our behalf. We might never be able to verify this Enoch character you met is the actual biblical entity, but this turn of events at the Serpent Mound certainly adds to our working thesis, if you will."

"I have no doubt that the bizarre old man I met today was the real, translated Enoch brought back to this world just for the occasion," claimed Sirena. "Especially after his dramatic exit."

"What exactly made you think that you encountered the real Enoch, Sirena?" O. Cyrus asked.

"I saw him *translated* right into the heavens before my very eyes," declared Sirena. "But even before that, I was convinced he was the real Enoch by what his stone eggs depicted and everything he said about them. You'll feel the same way as soon as you see and read everything that Uriel e-mailed to you."

"We've already had the opportunity to review Enoch's photos and notes about the eggs," came a different, third voice. "This is Horace, by the way."

"Hello, Horace," said Sirena. "And by the way, Enoch left

his eggs at the house where we met. They're probably still there if you want to go get them, except for the two I have, of course. I'm sure the likeness of Uriel on the egg I chose didn't escape you."

"We did notice the likeness of Uriel on the egg you picked," confirmed Horace. "But I will have to tell you that we had to make this call now rather than wait for you two to call us back. There is one egg that has piqued our interest more than the others due to events that occurred simultaneously with the ascension of Enoch and the Serpent Mound snake."

"Oh?" blurted Sirena.

"Yes," returned the voice of Thoth. "It's the egg that shows the parents of Enoch surrounded by the other eggs bearing wings."

"Why is that?" asked Uriel.

"Because that egg seems most germane to the transfiguration that awaits you next," answered Thoth. "That will all soon become evident as soon as our video conference is underway. There is a serious time crunch involved with the video we need to share with you. I think you will find what you're about to see to be most remarkable, even if it does turn out to be as horrifying as we think."

"We really shouldn't preface what they're about to see," Horace chided Thoth. "That is a breach of Institute protocol in matters like this. Let them decide for themselves about what they watch, Thoth."

"I disagree," countered O. Cyrus. "I think they do need to prepare themselves for what could be very heart-wrenching for them to watch. Plus, they both need to know that the two unfortunate incidents that are depicted in the video transpired at exactly the same time that Enoch and the serpent ascended into the heavens."

"Let's just tell them to brace themselves for what they are about to see and be done with it," Horace remarked.

"Oh, my God!" blared Sirena. "This doesn't have anything to do with our children, does it?"

"No, no, no," the voices of all three men sounded before Thoth's voice boomed over the others. "This has nothing whatsoever to do with either of your kids. This is about Enoch and the contingencies that affect his existence as a being translated from this world into a realm that allows him access unlike any other mortal has ever known."

"It's really going to be better if we just show the video to you now without further explanations," Horace said.

"I'll set up the laptop," Uriel began as he met Sirena's unsteady eyes, "so we can watch whatever it is you have for us."

CAMAZOTZ

Uriel handed the phone to Sirena before he left the living room. Sirena then sat on the sofa, squished her back into the soft pleather, and crossed her arms against the thickness of her robe.

"I just want to know one thing first," Sirena said.

"What is that?" Thoth replied with his question.

"Why did I have to be the one to witness that insanity at the Serpent Mound?" she asked.

"We're actually still looking into an aspect of that," Horace answered. "But we'll tell you as soon as we know for sure."

"What Horace won't tell you right now," O. Cyrus blurted. "Is that Enoch specifically requested that you meet him. It wasn't our idea."

"Damn it, O. Cyrus!" blared Horace. "You shouldn't tell her that, not until we know more about what that means."

"Why would he ask for me?" Sirena nearly cried. "What could that even mean?"

"It means that you are central to all of this," Thoth

answered. "Please, just watch the videos we stream to you, then we'll explain more and give you the details of your itinerary."

"I still want to know more about what we're going to watch," demanded Sirena as she reached into her robe pocket and retrieved the stone egg of Uriel that she chose from Enoch's clutch of cosmic eggs.

"Me, too," added Uriel upon his return to the living room with the laptop in hand.

Sirena watched Uriel set the laptop on the glass surface of the coffee table in front of the couch, then she turned toward him, extending the stone egg for him to take. Uriel knelt before her and took the egg.

"I have no idea what this egg will do," acknowledged Sirena. "But it has to be yours, Uriel."

Uriel studied his likeness on the egg and traced the gold-flecked wings before he rotated the egg to see the gray swirl of emptiness on the other side.

"You keep it safe for me for now," Uriel said, smiling as he handed the egg back to Sirena.

Uriel switched his attention from the egg to the laptop in preparation for the video call with the three associates from The Institute. Once the laptop was ready, he motioned for Sirena to slide down the sofa backrest some until she appeared on screen to his satisfaction. He then maneuvered himself beside her and leaned forward to activate the video call.

"I'm calling you right now, gentlemen," Uriel announced.

The image of the three middle-aged bald men filled the computer screen.

"Here we all are!" bellowed Thoth. "Great to see you two again."

"Wish we could say the same," muttered Sirena before Uriel nudged her with his elbow as he took his place beside her.

"Surely, it's not all that bad to see us again, is it Sirena dear?" Thoth chuckled in response.

"I still have a bad taste in my mouth," began Sirena. "from when you nearly killed Uriel with that damn Salvador Dali egg, and you had me under some kind of spell believing I'm a Nephilim half-breed destined to roam the earth with my archangel soulmate."

"And the latter part of that is such a bad thing?" asked Horace.

"Since he's so handsome with so much vitality," Sirena resumed as she glanced to meet Uriel's eyes and reached for his hand, "I guess it's all right. I won't begrudge you too much for dragging me into all of this mess."

"You sure won't hear me complaining," chimed Uriel as he met Sirena's affectionate gaze.

"It's just wonderful to see an authentic pair of soulmates find each other like you two have," Thoth commented before he changed the subject. "But your coupling is not just for you two to enjoy each other's company. You have work to do, and Institute work at that."

"Indeed," added Horace.

"The two people you are about watch," resumed Thoth, "are the parents for the modern incarnation of Enoch, but they were unable to conceive him for him to return to earth as a human-born baby."

"Or so we believe," O. Cyrus added, "in this version of the present."

"Stop it!" yelled Horace. "You shouldn't condition their viewing of these videos like this! They have to make up their own minds about what they see first before we tell them about the people involved or condition their beliefs with any other information. This is Institute protocol!"

"That is true, I suppose," admitted Thoth.

"But Sirena and Uriel really should know what they could be up against," countered O. Cyrus. "They might be able to gain more from what they're about to watch."

"You know," Uriel said through a robust sigh, "it seems to me like you three want us to think that you don't really know exactly what you're going to show to us and, yet, you seem to imply that you know exactly what it is we're about to see."

"Exactly," concurred Sirena. "And I really don't appreciate all of the duplicity."

"Please!" cried Thoth. "This isn't duplicity we're dealing in! This is spiritual warfare! We're in the midst of a cosmic crisis much larger than any of us, whether we're merely human or divine. You have to understand that both of you are endowed with an essence so powerful that you might be the only two on the face of this earth who can save humanity from forces so dark and evil that their power only grows when you doubt the truth and dodge the responsibilities of defeating this evil."

"Just great!" blasted Sirena in reply. "If I was going to be stuck doing a bunch of crap that I didn't want to do, I would've never forsaken my husband and children. I could've been trapped in that ordinary marital bliss just fine. At least it would've been a misery that didn't require all of this convoluted noise."

Uriel scowled at her at first before he brought his hands to his head and grabbed fistfuls of hair in each. He lowered his head as he clenched his eyes shut and his face flushed red.

"You weren't the only one who gave up everything for us to be together," he reminded her.

"I'm so sorry," Sirena nearly sobbed. "I didn't mean that the way it sounded. I love you, Uriel. I only want to be with you and nobody else. It's just that I want us to do what we want to do together because it's our wish, not the bidding of some deranged organization who thinks they're out saving the world from evil."

Uriel dropped his hands from his head and reeled toward Sirena. He glared at her, but his expression softened when he saw the hurt on her face.

"I didn't mean to say I regret anything that has brought us together," she implored him to understand as she brushed his cheek with hers. "I love you so much. I just want to be with you every minute of every day. That's all."

"I never want you to regret what we've done," he whispered into her mouth. "*NEVER*. Do you understand that? I couldn't live with myself if what we've done destroys you."

She grabbed the back of his neck and pulled him to her until his mouth met hers and they kissed. Her soft moans leaked past her lips as their kiss protracted in length and intensity. Only when Thoth loudly cleared his throat did they throttle the passion behind their kiss.

"It's showtime, folks," announced O. Cyrus. "The woman you are about to watch is Baraka."

"So, bye for now," Thoth said before the aerial view of a kitchen filled the computer screen.

The screen in front of Uriel and Sirena went blank at first before a flickering, grainy screen telecast an aerial view of a person with their back to the camera, standing in a swirled gray robe in front of a kitchen sink. The sound of water from the faucet splattered against the sink as the person appeared to be scrubbing something unseen to the camera.

"Baraka there sure is washing the hell out of something," Sirena whispered. "I don't think it's a dish or glass or anything used in a kitchen."

"What do you think she's doing, then?" Uriel posed.

"I'd say she's cleansing."

"Cleansing?"

"Yeah," Sirena now sighed, "trying to cleanse herself of some stain so bad that she just can't get rid of it."

A gray spiral of light twisted its way from the ceiling then surrounded the woman, casting a peculiar shadow that seemed to enclose her within an oval egg shape.

"Do you see that?" Sirena whispered to Uriel with more urgency. "That egg of shadow?"

"I see it," Uriel whispered back. "What do you think that is?"

"Something is there in that kitchen with her," Sirena answered him in an even lower whisper.

Baraka jerked at the sink as though shocked by something.

"Noooooooo!" her scream filled the room as she gripped the counter in front of the sink in her descent to the floor, where she then retched and convulsed.

The violence to her body eventually subsided, then Baraka remained motionless facedown on the floor for several seconds until revived by a series of twitches.

"That was a brutal scream," remarked Sirena. "What do you think overcame her?"

"Maybe some kind of possession," ventured Uriel. "I really don't know. I've never seen anything like that gray snake light or egg shadow before."

"Oh, my God," gasped Sirena. "They said this happened at the same time as Enoch launched from the Serpent Mound. I think I know what this light and shadow is that is surrounding her. It's the snake and the egg from Serpent Mound."

Baraka struggled to kneel on the floor then groped for the edge of the counter to help her lift herself to her feet. Her long, slender fingers emerged from the robe cuff to remove a flat mirror from the counter that she then placed upon the window sill above the sink. The reflection remained obscured on the computer screen by her position in front of the sink. She reached into the sink and retrieved a steak knife, which she brought in front of her face with one hand while using the other hand to pin back her hair as she leaned toward the mirror.

"Ahhhhhhhh," Baraka groaned as she held the steak knife still concealed from view.

Her groan soon escalated into a scream that prolonged as Baraka maintained her grip of the knife and her head shook from the force that she applied to her face with it.

"Oh, my God," Sirena cried. "She's doing something to her face. Did somebody call the police for Christ's sake?"

The knife clanked when Baraka dropped it into the sink bowl, then she began to sob.

"Thoth!" Uriel shouted toward the laptop, but no reply came.

Uriel then snatched the phone still on the coffee table.

"Thoth, Horace, O. Cyrus!" Uriel shouted into the phone without a response rising from the dead air.

"Look," Sirena said to Uriel as she smacked his back.

Baraka turned toward the camera, hands covering her face and her white robe splattered red from the drizzle of her blood.

"Can't let the demon in," trembled Baraka's muffled voice. "Can't let the demon in. Please, God, help me keep the demon out."

She lowered her hands from her bloodied face. She turned away from camera view and stepped to the sink. Water again rushed from the faucet as she bent over the sink with cupped hands and repeatedly lowered her face into them. She ran her fingers through her hair, then she undid the robe sash, letting the bloodstained robe drop to the floor.

"You are an abomination in the eyes of God," screeched a

garbled, unnatural voice from Baraka, whose naked backside remained in camera view. "You deserve death and eternal torment for your sins against God. Grab your robe and wipe the blood from your face. See for yourself what you are."

Baraka stooped to retrieve the robe from the floor then brought it to the sink. She dabbed and wiped her face with the robe for some time until stopping to peer into the mirror at the kitchen window.

"Noooooo!" Baraka cried in her restored voice then sobbed. "Nooooooo!"

She finally turned from the sink with her hands covering her face. Her large, sagging breasts heaved as she continued to sob.

"That poor woman," said Sirena.

"She's in such distress," Uriel added. "I'm not sure you should keep watching this."

"I'll be all right," Sirena managed to say.

Baraka then lowered her hands from her face and cast her grief-stricken eyes upwards as if to implore some unseen source for help. Only when she slightly lowered her face was the word carved into her forehead visible to Sirena and Uriel.

"*WHORE*," Sirena read aloud. "She carved the word *WHORE* into her forehead."

"I don't think she was the one who carved it," said Uriel. "I think she's possessed by a demon that did it."

"Look at that shadow," observed Sirena. "What do those things on the side look like to you? Arms?"

"They look like wings," observed Uriel. "Webbed wings, at that. Look at how the shadow is changing its egg shape around her head, like a halo but only a halo in the form of a..."

"A bat!" cried Sirena. "The shadow around her has shifted into the shape of a bat!"

"That must be the Camazotz," mouthed Uriel.

Baraka lowered her eyes to look at herself as she held her visibly shaking hands and arms out to her side and surveyed her body. She then brought her hands to cover her mouth and stifle her sobs.

"Poor thing," Sirena lamented.

"Why do they want us to see this?" Uriel asked Sirena. "What is this telling us about what we're supposed to do?"

Before Sirena could answer, Baraka started to pace in the kitchen, mumbling and rubbing her hands together as her steps quickly turned frantic. She then stopped pacing to bolt into an adjacent room.

Uriel and Sirena continued to watch in anticipation of her return to the kitchen. They could hear noises that sounded like the thuds and crashes of thrown objects. When she finally did return, she was carrying a white five-gallon bucket without a lid. Still naked, Baraka placed the bucket on the floor beside the sink before she opened a cabinet beside the sink and retrieved a shaker of salt. The woman then took the mirror from the window sill and flung it across the kitchen. It shattered against the wall and the shards cascaded across the floor.

"Got to keep the demon out," she said as she as she shook salt where the window met the sill.

What is she doing?" Sirena whispered to Uriel.

"I believe she's spreading salt to keep evil spirits away," replied Uriel. "It's a folklore belief that salt repels them from entering a house."

Baraka then stepped to the door, now chanting: "Keep the demon out. Keep the demon out. Keep the demon out."

She stooped to the kitchen door and shook the salt shaker along the threshold, chanting louder now with a voice that started to crack and garble. She stood and desperately began to shake the salt all over herself. She dropped the shaker to the floor and smeared the salt over her body, rubbing it against the front and back of her groin.

"Oh, nooooooooo!" she screamed before her body appeared jolted by some unseen force and the bat shadow enlarged around her, spreading beneath her flailing arms like wings that lifted her from the floor itself. "Stop! Stop! Stop!"

Baraka bent her legs at the knees, but her body remained suspended. She tried to pull her arms to her chest, but the winged shadow overpowered her and kept her levitated. Only when the ringing of a telephone sounded did the winged shadow retreat and the woman collapsed to the floor, curling into a ball and sobbing. The phone continued to ring, but she did not answer it.

"Somebody is trying to help her," Sirena blurted as she gripped Uriel's forearm. "Answer the phone!"

The phone rang an abbreviated fifth time then rang no more. Baraka stopped her sobbing and jerked her head from the floor.

"This is my last chance," she managed to say before she clambered to the five-gallon bucket on the floor.

Baraka squatted over the bucket and grunted. The splatter of loose fecal matter resonated below her first before the spray of urine followed. She stood above the bucket and peered into it. She retched at the sight of her bodily fluid then knelt beside the bucket and lowered her trembling hands into the fluid gathered at the bottom. She scooped the urine and feces from the bottom of the bucket.

"Keep the demon out," she cried as she smeared the excrement mixture over her chest and along her arms.

Sirena gasped and covered her eyes. Uriel gagged but did not vomit as he continued to watch Baraka cry out to, "Keep the demon out." Sirena reopened her eyes in time to see the woman scoop more of her excrement from the bucket and apply it to her face then insert it into the orifices of her lower body.

"Keep the demon out," Baraka's words were now barely discernible as her sobbing overtook her and her body heaved with each utterance.

Baraka grabbed the bucket and held it over her head. She flipped the bucket, and the remaining excrement drizzled into her hair. She flung the bucket across the room then smeared her bodily waste into her scalp. She then brought her hands to her mouth and inserted her fingers, gagging as she rubbed the waste against her tongue, teeth, and gums.

"Keep the demon out," she managed to utter one last time before she collapsed to the kitchen floor and sprawled motionless.

The shadow appeared to writhe from her and slither across the floor before it gathered into a gray oval of light that quickly snaked upwards in its ascension from view of the camera.

Pounding came from the kitchen door followed by a blaring voice, "Police. Open the door." The pounding and verbal command repeated two more times before Baraka stirred on the floor.

"Help me," she cried with her remnant strength. "Help me."

The first kick from outside shattered the door window glass and cracked the wood jambs. The second kick split the door in two with half remaining on its hinges and the other half splintering as pieces of it flew into the kitchen.

Two police officers rushed into the house. One immediately started to drop to the floor but paused upon detecting the stench covering her. He instead stooped over her, asking her if she were all right while the other police officer remained standing with weapon drawn as he surveyed what he could see from his position.

"Is anyone else here?" shouted the policeman with weapon drawn.

"The demon is here!" Baraka managed to yell. "Azazel has come to kill me again! Destroy him before he implants his egg into her!"

With her pronouncement complete, the computer screen went blank.

STILLBORN

Sirena drew closer to Uriel, clutching his waist as she shifted herself to his lap. Uriel wrapped his arms around her, then she lowered her head to his chest and squeezed him.

"That was terrible," Uriel said. "Did you hear what she called the demon?"

"I don't want to hear that name again," Sirena answered him. "Please protect me, Uriel. Don't let me end up like that poor soul. Please."

"I'll never let you be harmed, Sirena," Uriel emphasized by squeezing her tighter than she squeezed him. "I will always be here to protect you."

"But what about when we're not together?" she asked him. "How will you protect me then?"

"I believe I've always been there for you," he said to her. "I know in my soul that's why we're together now. I'm always here for you, now and forever."

"Swear it to me," Sirena pleaded to him as she lifted her face for their eyes to meet. "Tell me that we'll love each other forever."

"I love you Sirena," he told her. "I love you like no one has ever loved another. You are my universe."

She lifted herself to meet his lips. The two kissed softly before the laptop screen brightened white then rang with the tone of the incoming video call. Sirena spun herself from Uriel's lap as he leaned forward to activate the video call. The three men from The Institute returned to the screen.

"Did you catch the names at the end of that?" O. Cyrus asked before anyone else could speak. "Azazel is depicted on the other side of the feathered-serpent Kukulkan egg that Enoch has among his clutch. He had the huge egg-implanting penis."

"Ovipositor, I believe is the technical term for it," clarified Horace.

"Just hold on a minute," snapped Uriel. "I don't want us to go into something that is going to cause more turmoil for Sirena. She's already endured enough today."

"I'm all right, Uriel," Sirena said to him. "Let them ask their questions. It's the only way we're going to find out what we have to do to make all of this end."

"What about the word, *Camazotz?*" asked O. Cyrus. "Are you familiar with that term?"

"Enoch discussed it briefly before he disappeared into the sky," replied Sirena.

"I understand it's a Mayan demon like a vampire," Uriel then said.

"Let me provide a little more background about them," began Thoth "They are tied to the ancient Mayan text–the Popol Vuh–in their attack upon one of the Mayan Hero Twins, whose head is bitten off by a Camazotz.

"We theorize in our Biblical context that the Camazotz

were minions to help slaughter the human beings in the rise of the Nephilim and their Fallen Angel fathers. Their dominion is human sacrifice for the design of the purest evil."

"So that's what the shadow was that we saw," Sirena surmised aloud.

"Precisely," confirmed O. Cyrus. "That was a Camazotz sent to terrorize the woman you saw to the point that she would be considered certifiably insane."

"So, who exactly was this woman Baraka?" asked Uriel. "And why would someone or something want to drive her that batshit crazy?"

"You may not want to hear this, Sirena" Thoth announced. "It's not something that will conjure pleasant memories for you if you're able to access the recesses of your distant memory."

"I'll be all right," Sirena reassured Uriel as she met his gaze. "Just so long as I got my man with me now."

"You sure about that?" added Horace. "This is not a very pleasant picture that we're going to paint."

"I'm fine," Sirena said then glared into the laptop camera.

"All right," began Thoth. "Here is what we think Baraka was trying to communicate and prevent from happening–the Nephilim Azazel spawning his unholy Antichrist seed. The demonic forces of the universe have attacked this woman because she was supposed to be the mother of Enoch in his return from translation for his eventual transfiguration into the archangel Metatron."

"Unfortunately," began O. Cyrus, "Baraka fell under the spell of evil as a young woman in her current incarnation and has paid the consequences for her transgression."

"Oh, shit," spewed Sirena. "We must be in deep trouble then."

"Not necessarily," countered O. Cyrus. "At least, truly deep trouble for everyone can be avoided if we are able to have you two alter a few things from the past."

"What does that mean–exactly?" Uriel asked.

"We don't know yet–exactly," began Horace as he glared at both Thoth and O. Cyrus. "Nor should we really be telling you at this point. For all that we really know, this woman you saw is just *batshit crazy*, like Uriel said. Nothing more than that."

"That is a possibility," conceded Thoth, "But from what we've been able to hypothesize thus far if we assume her actions are authentic, there is a point in time in the past when this woman was attacked by the entity Azazel, who we suspect is the procreation of the fallen angel Samyaza and the demonic whore Lilith, and not the fallen angel among The Watchers as traditionally believed."

"All available references indicate that Azazel was permanently imprisoned with The Watchers and Lilith," O. Cyrus began, "but this video suggests otherwise. If Azazel and Lilith are indeed free, this is where we will want you to intervene."

"But we have to research all of this further, at this point," added Horace. "We'll let you know more as we discover more."

"This is nuts," Sirena blurted as she repeatedly shook her head. "Enoch babbled on about this whole Azazel connection, too. There's no way we should try to do any of this, Uriel. I fear that things won't end well for us if we do."

"Maybe you're right," Uriel admitted. "But let's hear all of what our friends have to say first, then we can decide together, okay?"

Sirena folded her arms across her chest and clenched her lips. Uriel stroked her hair before he looped his finger around some strands and guided her hair behind her ear. He then kissed her ear as he rubbed the back of her neck.

"I'll be fine with whatever we decide," Uriel whispered to Sirena then kissed her cheek.

"That woman Baraka was denied the chance to meet her fated husband, who was supposed to be Enoch's father" explained O. Cyrus. "That much we do know. What we're still trying to piece together is exactly when she could have met her husband but didn't."

"Do you know where her husband is?" asked Uriel.

"You mean the husband she never had," corrected Sirena.

"That's right," Thoth confirmed. "Baraka never connected with her husband, but you are about to meet him. He is the subject of the second video we're preparing for you, which occurred at exactly the same time as the Enoch event at Serpent Mound and the video of Baraka that you just watched."

"So, what will happen to Baraka?" Sirena asked.

"She'll be institutionalized," Thoth answered her. "She'll be continuously tormented by the Camazotz surrounding her and then medicated beyond any recognition of her former self. The cycle will repeat over and over again until she finally dies. Azazel doesn't want her to be able to ever disclose his identity, which she had finally figured out."

"How old is she?" pursued Sirena. "And is she married now?"

"Fifty years old, just like you Sirena," answered O. Cyrus. "And she never married, nor did she have any children."

"That is the subject in the next video," informed Thoth. "You are about to witness the fate of the husband Baraka never had–Jared."

"Why can't you stop all of this if you know it's going to happen?" Sirena nearly shouted her question.

"We're still not entirely sure we have all of this right," Horace answered. "You can imagine the position The Institute would be put in if we were wrong about this. It could have a disastrous impact."

"So far it does seem like we're right, though," O. Cyrus interjected. "And if we're right about this video of Jared, then we should be correct about altering history as soon as we can identify the time slip you'll have to follow and what you'll have to do after you pass into it."

"We have monitored these two for quite some time," Thoth disclosed. "We held out hope that we could somehow manage to cross their paths in a way that would lead to consummation, but only recently did we discover that Baraka is barren."

"How long has she been infertile?" Sirena wanted to know. "I mean, if she never could have had Enoch, then why would any of this be possible?"

"We believe that she wasn't always infertile," disclosed Thoth. "Her infertility most likely resulted from the attack Azazel perpetrated against her during the time period of your planned transport."

"But most of this still remains speculation," commented Horace. "We really shouldn't divulge all that we know about them, but given the circumstances, I'd say it is fair for you both to know who these two people are and how they figure into the enterprise The Institute has undertaken to try to salvage what has really become the future of all of mankind."

"But why is the rebirth of Enoch so important?" asked Uriel. "I mean, what's the worst-case scenario that could happen if the old Enoch that Sirena met today is the last version of him on earth?"

"That's actually a good question," remarked Thoth. "Many understand why Enoch was important before he became trans-lated, which is to say he was removed from the face of the earth by God without actually dying, but most might not fully appreciate how Enoch ultimately is transfigured into the archangel Metatron."

"Yes," Uriel blurted. "Metatron. He who becomes the other half through his bodily ascension into Heaven while still alive."

"That is precisely the point of all of this," Horace then said. "You see, Heaven is the resting place for the dead who are but resting, like zombies, if you will, for the day of the biblical Rapture when those dead believers and the living believers are translated together for their revival with the Second Coming of The Messiah, who is destined to lead them all into the Millennium after the Battle of Armageddon."

"Look who's letting the cat all the way out of the bag, now," joked Thoth as he patted Horace on the shoulder.

"So, all of this gets bundled up into the whole Christian biblical thing again," Sirena observed aloud. "I've just never understood why the two sides couldn't just face off and let God sort out all of the rest already."

"Me either," added Uriel. "Then maybe they would let you and I live our lives together the way we want, Sirena. Shouldn't that be the purpose behind all of this? Live with and love the light of your life–your true soulmate–for all eternity."

Sirena wrapped her arm around Uriel's and pulled herself to his side before she kissed his neck.

"You really are the sweetest man I've ever known," she beamed at him. "I love you so much."

"And I absolutely adore you," Uriel returned Sirena's affection then took her head within his hands and kissed her forehead.

"It was a hard two years for me before you confessed your love for me," Sirena continued. "You've empowered me with your true love and soulful desire for my entire well-being."

"Before you two decide to race off to the bedroom," interrupted Thoth, "we really do need to continue with the briefing before you watch the second video, which I've been notified is only minutes away from activation."

"So, your attention please," added Horace.

"All right already," moaned Sirena before she winked at Uriel. "You're just going to have to let your wad stew there, big fella."

"That also would be part of the point behind all of this," resumed Thoth. "You see, if we can't reverse engineer, so to speak, the incarnation of Enoch for his eventual transfiguration into Metatron, you two might very well both cease to live."

"You mean, we'll die?" asked Uriel.

"Could die," Thoth corrected. "We're only able to project models about the future based upon the return of Enoch or his ultimate demise due to thwarted rebirth from translation. In at least a couple of those models, both of you perish."

"So, if you'd like to continue to remind us," O. Cyrus picked up the thread of Thoth, "just how enamored you are with each other, you might want to decide to cooperate with us for your own self-preservation."

"Now that sounds almost like extortion," huffed Sirena. "That makes me want to tell the three of you to go screw yourselves."

Uriel laughed at her comment. He watched all three of the men squirm from their remote location. Sirena placed her hand along his upper thigh near his groin and squeezed. He again pulled her to him then lifted her chin with his finger. As he looked into her eyes, she slid her hand to his crotch and cupped him. Her eyes widened, and she pursed her lips as she kneaded him. He leaned into her grip before he pulled her head back by her hair and thrust his tongue into her open mouth.

"Are we ready yet?" twittered Horace. "I'm afraid we're losing these two to their lust for each other."

"Hold on a second," Thoth replied. "O. Cyrus, do you see the feed notice yet?"

"We just received it," O. Cyrus nearly exclaimed. "Click the link, enter the access code and away we go."

"I need for you two to listen to me for just a minute," Thoth announced. "I mean, I'd like for Sirena and Uriel to listen to what I have to say now. We all appreciate the passion you two have for each other. We really do, and not just because it is a critical component of your unique psychic ability together. We're old but not dead, and honestly there's a part of us that would just assume to watch you two go at it right there on the couch than watch what we're going to have to witness via this video of Jared."

Uriel now had Sirena's face in his hands and thumbed her cheeks as the two embraced even tighter. Sirena dug her fingers into Uriel's back with one hand while she rubbed his crotch even harder now with the other hand. Neither had acknowledged the statement by Thoth, and both were now issuing soft moans into each other's mouth as their kissing deepened.

"If I might add," began Horace, "your passion for each other also is partly why you are so right to undertake this challenge on behalf of The Institute. You need to find a way to convey it to this man and woman–Jared and Baraka–so that they can avoid the damnable pitfalls of their young adult lives in their pasts and exalt each other in such a way that their soulmate consummation leads to the incarnation of Enoch."

Uriel removed his hands from Sirena's face then stroked her hair with one hand while he brought his other hand to hers on his crotch. The two slowed their kiss but maintained it without withdrawing their tongues from each other's mouth.

"And it's Enoch," O. Cyrus began," who is the Metatron that in angelic form must descend with the spirit of The Messiah to combine their power into the one force that can save this world. Without Enoch, there can be no Messiah."

"For God's sake, you two!" Thoth suddenly blared. "If you don't help us, it will be the end of the world!"

Sirena and Uriel both laughed into each other's mouth as they withdrew their tongues and smacked their lips in conclusion of their kiss. Uriel tried to lift her hand from his crotch, but she resisted at first, laughing harder as she searched for his mouth again with her tongue. He finally pulled her hand from him and interlocked their fingers with a firm squeeze.

"All right," Sirena throatily whispered to Uriel. "I'll stop for now, but when this is done tonight, we're not even going to make it all the way into the bedroom. We're going to make love right here on this couch then on this floor and then against the hallway wall and then the hallway floor before we ever even make it to the bedroom."

"We have the video ready," Thoth announced. "Please watch closely."

Uriel kissed Sirena on her forehead then leaned to her ear.

"It's a date," he whispered so that only she could hear.

DEAD ON ARRIVAL

Muted country music drifted in a bar where a middle-age man and a woman visibly half his age sat at the far end of the bar. The woman clutched a bowl glass filled with strawberry-colored slush. The man had his elbow propped on the counter and held a glass tumbler half-full of amber liquor near his mouth. He sipped from it then set the drink down as the woman tossed her long blonde hair over her shoulder.

"There doesn't have to be anything sexual about our arrangement, Crystal" the man's voice resounded surprisingly loud. "We just have to make sure that we can find the time to spend together on a regular basis or else the whole thing won't work."

The woman's large, hoisted breasts heaved beneath her yellow sweater when she sighed.

"You know, Jared," Crystal's voice came equally as loud as Jared's above the twanging vocals of the music, "I'm not going to rule anything out between us. I just think you're so sweet.

"Besides, my husband hasn't exactly been all over me since

we had our son, and he cheated on me when I was pregnant. I should've divorced him then, but I was too ashamed at the time to go through a divorce and all, especially since we had just married after I found out I was pregnant."

"Divorces happen," Jared said then sipped from his drink. "There's no shame in that."

"True," Crystal agreed before she sipped from her drink. "But he does make good money now with his job. It would be hard for me to rejoin the work force and earn enough of a living to provide for my son."

"You could always get half of what's his," Jared said.

"Oh, no," she replied. "I'm sure he'd kill me over something like that. I'd have to just leave town."

Jared brought his hand over his head and stretched, arching his back as he stood. He turned toward Crystal so that she could see the bulge extending from his groin to his thigh. She peered down at his waist as he kept himself thrust out toward her. She then took her glass from the counter without removing her eyes from his bulging mass.

"You know," she began, still staring at his erection, "why don't we go to your place now. I don't think we can really do what we want to do here. Do you?"

"Sounds good to me," Jared replied as he kept his waist turned toward her and motioned for the bartender to provide him with the tab for both of them. "I only live couple of miles from here. Do you want me to drive and leave your car here or would you rather follow me?"

"I'll follow you," she said as she stood and stepped into him, guiding her hand across his erection. "I'll freshen up first in the ladies' room before we go."

Jared leaned into her as she pressed against him in passing. She paused as she stuck her finger between his belt and jeans and pulled herself to him. She tip-toed and leaned her head back as he wrapped his hand around the small of her back and pulled her farther to him, grinding himself against her. She met his lips when he lowered his face to hers. She slid her tongue between his parted lips first, then he thrust his tongue against hers.

"Easy," she said as she withdrew her tongue and lips from his. "I want you to have me proper on your bed. If we keep at it like this, we'll never make it to your place."

"I can follow you into the bathroom if you like," Jared whispered in her ear. "There's only a couple of guys in here right now. There won't be anyone joining us in the ladies' room."

"Do you have protection?" she asked him.

"I have two condoms," he said. "You can straddle me. I'll hold you up. I won't lay you out on the floor or anything like that."

"Like I said," she smiled at him as she rubbed his hardness. "I'm not going to rule out anything between us, even though you really are old enough to be my father.

"Plus, we can still go back to your place for more after we're finished here."

Crystal took Jared's hand and led him behind her as she stepped away from the bar and proceeded toward the marked restrooms. He held up a finger to his pursed lips as he glanced at the bartender, who glared at him in return but did not intervene as he followed the woman to the ladies' restroom. When she pushed open the door, he glanced back at the bartender whose back was turned to them at the far end of the bar. Two other men seated at a table in the far side of the room weren't watching them. The restroom door then shut behind them.

The first series of thuds that banged from the restroom didn't draw the attention of the two customers or the bartender, but when louder, rapidly successive smacking thumps resounded from behind the bathroom door, all three men turned their attention to the direction of the sounds.

"Something wrong with the plumbing?" one of the men asked the bartender.

"That don't sound like there's any plumbing problem in there," quipped the bartender.

"Did that couple at the bar go in there?" the other man asked.

"Sure enough," replied the bartender. "The guy looked old enough to be her father."

"No doubt," the first customer said through a chuckle. "Gives us all hope, I guess."

"I just hope I don't have to clean up any kind of a mess in there," the bartender said.

"Make sure he gives you a damn good tip for use of the facilities," the second customer said. "He really ought to be paying a room rate with lodging tax on top of that."

The front door to the bar then flung open. A young man wearing a cowboy hat and boots strode into the bar. He looked around the room and nodded to the two men before he turned his attention to the bartender.

"What can I do you for?" the bartender asked as he cleaned the inside of a glass with a cloth.

"Just wondering if a long-haired blonde came through here," the man replied. "I saw her car outside."

The muffled moan protracted from the restroom before the bartender was able to loudly respond to the man:

"There's a gal in the restroom right now," the bartender began. "She just went in there, though, with a phone in her hand, talking really loud to a girlfriend or something, I suppose."

"This her strawberry daiquiri?" the man asked as he pointed to the drink on the bar.

The bartender nodded.

"What about that drink?" the man asked before he leaned over it to smell its fumes. "Bourbon?"

"That's right," the bartender said then stepped to the other end of the bar farthest from the man.

The man seated himself on the bar stool in front of the strawberry daiquiri. He traced the rim of the bowl glass with his fingertip. He glanced toward the bartender to see him kneel below the counter. The camera view showed the bartender jotting into a notepad as he checked the level of liquor in bottles.

The young man turned his attention away from the bartender when he heard the woman's muffled laughter drift from the restroom. He stared at the door for a few moments before he then spun on the barstool to face toward the two men seated at a table at the other end of the bar. One of the men had his back to him, but the other who faced him turned his eyes away from him when he made eye contact with him.

"How long she been in there?" the young man blurted as he looked toward the two seated men, but the man facing the young man started a conversation with his friend instead of answering him.

The young man briefly stared at the two of them then glanced toward the bartender, who remained hidden from his view. He then sprung from the bar stool and stepped toward the restroom. Once he reached the door to the ladies' restroom, he pressed his palms against it then held his ear to it.

"Hey!" erupted the bartender's voice from across the room. "What can I get you to drink?"

The young man spun around to face the bartender. Now both men seated at the table were also facing him.

"I'm good," he said and nodded to the bartender before he then spoke much louder. "I'm just trying to find out if my wife is in this bathroom or not."

"Your wife!" the bartender exclaimed in reply then turned his back to the man before he muttered. "Oh, shit."

The young man turned his attention to the two seated men, who were both still staring at him.

"Hey buddy," one of the men said. "Why don't you let us buy you a drink?"

"Why?" the young man asked. "You think I need one?"

"Hey," the other man laughed. "Don't we all?"

The young man returned his attention to the restroom. He stepped to the door and banged on it with the palm of his hand.

"Crystal!" he yelled once he stopped banging on the door. "Get your ass out here right now!"

He then wedged his fists against his hips as he stepped away from the door and paced in a circle in front of the restroom.

"We're going to settle up," one of the two customers said as both stood from their seats. "Too early to watch fireworks."

"I'd appreciate it if you stuck around for just a minute," the bartender said to them. "Let me get what I need really quick, and I'll be right back with your check."

The door to the ladies' restroom then opened. Crystal stepped back into the bar, her blonde hair disheveled on one side as she adjusted her blouse to straighten its wet, stained front.

"Where you been?" her husband said to her.

"What are you doing here, Jimmy?" Crystal's voice trembled. "I thought you were..."

"You thought wrong," he interrupted her. "I wanted to

know what you've been doing with your free time lately, so I took off work a little early to find out. I've been waiting for you to come back outside."

"You followed me," she spewed at him. "Why are you doing this, Jimmy?"

Crystal flinched as he brought his hand to her cheek, then he traced her jawline with his fingertip until he touched the substance below her chin. He removed his fingertip from her skin before he rubbed the substance between his fingertip and thumb. He smelled it before he scrutinized it further.

"Sticky stuff you got underneath your chin, sweetheart," he said, glaring at her, "Looks and smells like cum. You been sucking somebody's cock in the ladies' room?"

Jimmy then wiped his finger on her stained blouse along her neckline.

"Looks like you got quite the pearl necklace," he remarked before he grabbed her arm and jerked her to him. "And what happened to that yellow sweater you were wearing? You got yourself a boyfriend, Crystal?"

"Please just leave, Jimmy," her voice cracked. "Just leave right now before you do something you regret."

"Regret?" he laughed as he flung her arm from him. "The only thing I regret is marrying you and having a kid with you. I wish you both were dead."

"Please don't hurt me, Jimmy," she begged him. "I'm just messed up right now. I'm so lonely and depressed, and being a mother is so hard."

"A mother!" he scoffed at her. "Some mother you are, leaving your son home with some teenage neighbor you hardly know while you're out in a bar sucking some guy's cock in the goddamn bathroom."

"Jimmy, it's not like that," she tried to counter. "We're

working on writing. He's helping me write, so I can get my thoughts down better and maybe write a book about what I'm feeling."

"Is your writer friend still in the little girl's room?" he asked her through his scowl. "I sure would like to meet your pen-pal. Sounds like a really cool dude. I mean, here he is helping you out with your thoughts and all, and then next thing you know he's got his dick in your mouth and is shooting his wad all over your face and shirt."

"Jimmy," she cried. "Please just leave it alone. We'll talk about it at home."

"No, we won't," he replied as he gnashed his teeth. "There is no more home for you. You're going to go to your new home with your bathroom lover boy there–the emergency room, but I'd like to meet Romeo first before I send you on your way, just to make sure I approve of him."

She tried to stop him in his path to the bathroom, but he shoved her aside into the wall. He then banged on the door.

"Come on out lover boy!" he yelled then repeatedly slammed his palm against the door. "I want you to meet the husband of the woman whose mouth you just stuck your dick into."

"That's enough," the bartender told him. "Why don't you both get out of here right now, and I mean together. Go!"

"Maybe you're right," Jimmy said as he turned to face the bartender. "Maybe her and I just need to talk so we can try to work this out."

"Oh, no Jimmy," she sobbed, sliding down the wall until her bottom reached the floor. "For God's sake, no."

The bartender walked around the bar, revealing the holstered sidearm hung over his belt. Jimmy nodded in acknowledgement of the weapon before he stepped toward the bartender with his hand extended in the gesture of initiating a handshake. The bartender remained steadfast in his distance from the man.

"You just saved me a whole world of trouble, friend," Jimmy smiled in his continued approach to the bartender. "I really appreciate the fact that you cared enough to make me stop and realize what I was doing."

The bartender held one hand on his holstered gun as he extended his other to shake hands with Jimmy, but at the verge of the handshake, Jimmy stepped back and kicked the bartender in the face, dropping him to the floor. He removed the bartender's revolver from the holster and pointed it toward the two customers, who were now both standing.

"Get the fuck out of here," Jimmy said to the pair. "Unless you both want to die."

"Don't shoot, dude," one of the men said as he backpedaled from the table with his hands up.

The other man scurried around the table past the man in his dash for the front door of the bar. He flung it open and fled with his friend on his heels.

"Tell your boyfriend to come out of the bathroom!" Jimmy shouted, then he turned to Crystal, who remained slumped on the floor. "Do it right now. I want you to watch how bad I fuck him up."

"No, Jimmy," she sobbed. "Please stop."

Jimmy aimed the muzzle at the floor in front of Crystal then fired the gun. The shot splintered wood at her feet. She spun on the floor and scrambled to the bathroom.

"Come out, Jared!" she screamed as she smacked her palm against the bottom of the door. "He's going to kill me!"

Crystal curled onto the floor, her body heaving as she

sobbed. The bathroom door then opened, and Jared appeared at the threshold.

"Jesus Christ," Jimmy laughed. "You're old enough to be her grandpa. How much did you have to pay her to suck your nasty old cock."

Jared didn't reply as he stepped over Crystal and walked toward Jimmy, who steadied the barrel of the gun upon him.

"Look," Jared began as he spread his hands out. "You don't have to do this. You don't have to commit murder."

"Might be too late," Jimmy replied, pointing the gun toward the unconscious bartender on the floor. "I just kicked the living shit out of this guy, but I tell you what, Grandpa, I'll give you a fighting chance. All you have to do is fight for your life."

"Don't Jimmy," Crystal pleaded. "Leave him alone."

"I'll leave him alone once he pays the price for messing with my wife," Jimmy told her. "And you get to watch me fuck his whole world up."

Jimmy stepped back to the bartender and returned his gun to the belt holster. He then glared at Jared before he extended his right fist and charged. The first blow glanced off the side of Jared's head as he ducked but still connected enough to knock him sideways. Jared lowered his head and rushed his assailant, who sidestepped him then punched Jared in the neck. Jared threw a wild hook as he straightened up. His fist connected with Jimmy's jaw hard enough that it staggered the much younger man and knocked the cowboy hat from his head. Jared tried to jab Jimmy's face, but Jimmy dodged the punch. Jimmy then threw a hook of his own that crashed into Jared's temple.

As Jared visibly wobbled, Jimmy took one step backwards before he delivered a kick square into the center of Jared's face. Jared stumbled back into the wall but managed to remain standing. Jimmy jumped to him, placing both hands on Jared's shoulders before he launched forward with a head butt that further smashed Jared's bleeding face.

The back of Jared's head smacked against the wall. Jimmy stopped Jared from collapsing to the floor, holding him up underneath his arms as he glared at him.

"Stop it!" shrieked Crystal as she covered her head with her arms. "Stop it!"

"Stop it?" laughed Jimmy. "I'm just getting started. Take your arms off your head so you can watch what I do to your old man gigolo here next."

"Shut up, Jimmy!" Crystal screamed, her arms still covering her head.

"Come on, Crystal," Jimmy mocked her with a soothing tone to his voice. "Watch what I do to your grandpa boyfriend here. Not too long ago you had his rotten dick in your mouth. Surely you care enough about him to see what he's about to suffer."

Crystal bawled with her arms still covering her head. Her whole body heaved as Jimmy laughed.

"Come on, Crystal," Jimmy then gravely said. "You really do need to see what I do to him, what you made me do to him because you're such a stupid whore."

Jared hung lifeless within Jimmy's grip. The blood gushed from his pulverized face. Jimmy then grabbed Jared's throat with his left hand and pinned him against the wall. He then opened his other hand and thrust the butt of his palm upwards into Jared's broken nose.

"Oh, my God, Jimmy!" Crystal screamed as she uncovered her head and looked up. "You're killing him!"

Crystal pushed herself up from the floor and staggered to her husband. She tried to pull his arm from Jared's neck, but Jimmy knocked her to the floor with a punch to her head with his other hand. She hit the floor at the feet of the unconscious bartender.

"Should've thought about this before you sucked him off," Jimmy scowled at her, then he grabbed Jared by the arm and flung him to the floor.

Jared dropped face-first, splattering blood when he hit. Crystal crawled to his askew, limp body. Before she could place her hand upon him, Jimmy kicked her in the shoulder, knocking her back into the feet of the bartender.

"What else can we do for our new friend here," Jimmy sardonically asked Crystal, who sat on the floor at the feet of the bartender, sobbing as she gazed upon Jared's body.

Jimmy then dragged Jared by his hair to the nearest bar stool. He stuck Jared's head into the opening at the base of the stool and wedged his neck against the metal ring connected to the legs. He then positioned Jared's head so that the back of his neck angled upwards.

"Watch this, honey," Jimmy announced. "I'm about to curb stomp this motherfucker to death with a bar stool. You won't want to miss this. Maybe you should give your last regards to your grandpa boyfriend here before I do it? What do you say?"

Crystal stared vacantly past the scene in front of her. Jimmy laughed before he stepped behind Jared. He rubbed his chin then positioned himself with one foot on each side of Jared's limp body. With one quick motion, Jimmy lifted his right leg and stomped down, grunting from the force delivered. The sickening crack of bone preceded the jolt to Jared's body. Jimmy then grabbed Jared by his hair and dragged him by it away from the stool. He released him to drop with a blood-splattering thud in the middle of the room.

When Jimmy looked up from Jared, he smiled at Crystal as she aimed the bartender's gun at him. Jimmy looked down to his chest when the first bullet struck him. He then glared at Crystal before the second shot hit him in the forehead. He staggered toward Crystal, but she clambered away from his stumble. Jimmy then tripped over Jared and crashed to the floor between Jared and the unconscious bartender. Crystal threw the gun across the room, buried her face in her hands, and bawled.

The laptop screen went black.

PART II

SERPENT EGGS SCRAMBLED

SNAKERONICITY

"I feel sick," Sirena told Uriel, then he pulled her to him.

"I just want to know why he had to watch this," Uriel replied. "They have to have some reason for this instead of just telling us about it."

"We do," the voice of Thoth arrived with the return of the video conference. "We're not just showing gratuitous violence and derangement to you. There's a very specific purpose behind our actions here."

"Besides the fact that they both happened simultaneously with Enoch riding the serpent into the sky?" Sirena blurted.

"Yes," answered Horace. "We have had Baraka and Jared under our own type of surveillance for quite some time now, years in fact. The course of events aligned like this somehow. We're really not sure how, but they did."

"So, what is it we're supposed to learn from this?" Uriel asked.

"You've just watched the earthly demise of the earth parents for Enoch's reincarnation," said Thoth. "It's been a foregone conclusion for quite some time, but this just confirms its finality."

"It's really not quite a reincarnation proper," O. Cyrus interjected. "You see, Enoch never really died. This would have been more like his psychogenesis into the life he was supposed to have lived out up until the final days of spiritual warfare that awaits this planet and humanity."

"But I just saw the guy," Sirena remarked. "How is it he needs to be reborn from earth parents if he's already alive right now?"

"It's not only that he never died," replied Thoth. "He never had the chance to regenerate from his current life into the archangel Metatron. He would have transfigured into the life of a newborn begat by the two whose lives you have just seen destroyed by forces that are very evil and very real."

"Regenerate is the best way to describe it,' commented Horace. "The Enoch you met, Sirena, would have never existed because he would have been long since reborn of the parents Baraka and Jared. He would be about as old as your oldest–twenty-two years.

"They obviously are no longer capable of producing a child together. She is hopelessly possessed by a demonic Camazotz, and he is probably dead or at least paralyzed, I suspect."

"So, what exactly are we supposed to do about all of this?" asked Uriel.

Both Horace and O. Cyrus spoke at once until Thoth held out his hands and shushed them.

"Here's the deal," Thoth then began. "Our researchers have scripted one period of their lives in which both Baraka and Jared traveled the same itinerary through Western Europe unbeknownst to each other. They have provided details based upon accounts pieced together over time, some orally conveyed while others were actually written down."

"What do you mean by *written down*," inquired Sirena.

"Baraka aspired to be a writer," revealed Horace. "She actually authored and published a homemade fanzine for a couple years right after she graduated from high school. She wrote about musical bands in the Midwest region, most of which were groups that played alternative music not heard through customary media outlets."

"She was a very curious young lady," O. Cyrus added. "And quite talented and beautiful."

"The Baraka we just watched was far from what you're describing," Uriel observed. "I understand that we must be talking about more than a twenty-year difference, but the woman we just watched was an absolute mess. There was nothing talented or beautiful about her that I could see."

"What did happen to her?" Sirena probed. "Something awful must have happened."

"It was horrific," Thoth answered her. "Many people experience far worse than she did, mind you, but what she endured had a component of evil that penetrated her so deeply that it forever changed everything about her. It ruined her, in effect."

"Her experiences made her withdraw from the life she knew," Horace continued with the details about Baraka. "She isolated herself within a shell that she protected with a rather extreme fundamentalist Christian religious belief."

"Many of the issues we are dealing with now," Thoth now proceeded, "were very much a part of the belief she embraced with all of her might, but she clung so maniacally to the real core of lunacy at the heart of her fundamentalism that she deteriorated into a regrettably brainwashed condition."

"She couldn't escape her own mind," stated O. Cyrus. "And no one was there who could deprogram her. She became increasingly alienated from everyone except for the most fervent of believers who also revolved around the cultish brand of Christianity."

"What about the man–Jared?" asked Uriel.

"He also aspired to be a writer," Thoth said. "And he actually did become one."

'What did he write?" blurted Sirena. "Anything we might know?"

"He wrote for the very newspaper where you now live," O. Cyrus disclosed. "He also wrote for a couple of other newspapers and a magazine group for a while."

"Jared's life unraveled quite differently than Baraka's did," remarked Horace. "He was married twice, divorced, and fathered four children, none of whom maintain any more than limited contact with him for a variety of reasons."

"So, Jared was a single man about fifty years old at the time of his death tonight," Uriel observed aloud.

"If he in fact did die," qualified Thoth. "We don't know that he actually died tonight. We'll know more later."

"There's one commonality between Baraka and Jared," Horace resumed, "that far outweighs their differences."

"What's that?" Sirena finally asked after Horace paused.

"Both of them wrote about their experiences in Europe while they were there at the same time in the same places," revealed Horace.

"The synchronicity of it is really quite miraculous," added O. Cyrus. "The fact that these two young people left behind their description of what happened to them and how it impacted them is staggering."

"Their testaments really are technical guides in the most

intensely personal battle waged during spiritual warfare," Thoth remarked. "They wrote the script to which you two will refer in your travel to right the wrong that befell not just these two cursed soulmates, but all of humanity."

"You want us to go back and change history?" Uriel said.

"Yes," the three men answered in unison.

"We have coordinated for both of you to initiate your travel to Paris," revealed Thoth, "where you will be under the remote guidance of the Institute's liaison. She is a CERN expert."

"CERN?" Uriel's voice boomed. "As in the European Organization for Nuclear Research?"

"Yes," Horace replied. "We've received verification of a time slip technology that will enable your access to the exact point in time and location to intercept Baraka and Jared so that you can bring them together during their travel in Europe thirty years ago."

"But I thought Uriel and I had our own unique method of time travel?" questioned Sirena.

"You do," confirmed O. Cyrus. "And you'll be using your coupling power with each other to flip the switch, so to speak. The CERN connection is how we will get you where we want you to go together in both time and location."

"That just sounds great," Sirena couldn't help but laugh. "I can't wait to see what happens with all of this unless of course we're killed in the process and don't know the difference."

"We've taken measures to ensure your survival in this," Thoth replied. "We just hope that you can maintain your focus upon Jared and Baraka throughout their ordeal."

"But first you must know more about the writings of Jared and Baraka," mentioned O. Cyrus before he deferred to Thoth with a gesture of his hand.

"Both Baraka and Jared actually submitted copies of their

manuscripts to the Library of Congress for unpublished copy-right," Thoth further explained. "We have accessed them both and faithfully rendered them onto files for your perusal."

"Wow," Sirena blurted. "That's crazy."

"They both must've thought they had material for a book in the future," remarked Horace. "hence the copyright."

"So, what are we supposed to do first?" Uriel wanted to know.

"First you must read," Thoth answered him. "We would prefer that both of you read each account, but time constraints may limit that."

"If that is the case," prefaced O. Cyrus, "which it very well might be, then we would like for Uriel to read the material from Jared and Sirena read what Baraka wrote."

"We're preparing physical copies to send to you," informed Horace. "We know you are both from an older generation like us, and you may still prefer to handle an actual hard copy rather than view extended content like this from a screen."

"How long are these manuscripts?" Sirena asked.

"The actual manuscripts are both over fifty-thousand words," answered Thoth. "It really is like they wrote the basis for books then stopped, perhaps knowing that they weren't going to be able to finish them for whatever reasons."

"We should also mention at this point," O. Cyrus began to expound, "that staff from The Institute has also prepared alter-nate history documents for this."

"What do you mean by that?" asked Sirena. "I've never heard of anything like that."

"These two documents," began Horace, "are scripts, basi-cally, that rewrite the history that has actually occurred. What you've just watched happen to Baraka and Jared was the conclusion to two lives that went astray from a course of fate that was altered by nefarious forces and actual events."

"And these alternate history documents," chimed in O. Cyrus, "provide the pathway to right the wrong committed and thereby alter historical events so that the future following pivotal moments in time can transition into a new reality."

"The reality in which Enoch is reborn," Uriel speculated in reply. "Or reincarnated, whatever you want to call it."

"Exactly," confirmed Horace. "We probably should enlist your input at this time about what you actually prefer to read first. We've had some discussion amongst ourselves, including some of the other principals here, and the consensus was that you would first receive the copyrighted material written directly by each of them."

"But we're not so sure," O. Cyrus remarked.

"I eventually came around to concur with my colleagues here," added Thoth, "that you would be better prepared to meet the challenge and our purpose here expedited if you actually read the alternate history documents first before you read the copyrighted material."

"The primary sticking point with this, however," O. Cyrus countered, "is that you won't have any context for how events actually transpired, so you may not know when it's your cue to intervene."

"You know what eventually became of both of them," Thoth resumed, "but you won't know the specific turning points that led them to such awful ends."

"So, we need to know exactly what events turned their lives for the worse," Sirena said.

"Yes," all three men replied.

"Here," came Thoth's voice as enlarged images of one

Enoch's eggs and two still photos of a young man and woman filled the screen. "The resemblance is more than uncanny."

"Wow," Sirena marveled aloud as she leaned forward to scrutinize the depiction of Enoch's parents on the egg and the images of the two young people. "They're a match without question."

"The young man and the woman depicted on Enoch's egg and in the photos," began Thoth, "are the same two people whose lives you saw destroyed on these videos tonight."

"Even though the pair were much older in the videos," continued O. Cyrus, "it's clear to us from forensic analysis that they are, or were rather, the young couple presented on Enoch's egg and in the pictures from about thirty years ago."

"What you need to discover," Horace took his turn, "is exactly how their lives were ruined and their destiny together subverted."

"And we need to figure out what to do to change that," Uriel surmised, "and exactly when to do it. Is that it?"

"That is your upcoming future blast into the past in a nutshell," confirmed Thoth. "I've come to the belief that if you read the alternate history version first, you'd know how the script is supposed to go and would be able to intervene when you see events spiraling away from that perfected fate."

"That is also my belief," added Horace. "I actually feel like you shouldn't read the original manuscripts at all because they are both laden with personal thoughts that probably aren't quite so germane to our purpose here."

"Also," O. Cyrus began to offer his input, "the research documents are so much more polished and readable. The narrative is artfully constructed and comprehensive in scope and texture. I think you'd find that these are far more interesting and valuable to you both as readers and vested subjects."

"Sounds like you might have had something to do with the writing of the narrative, O. Cyrus," remarked Uriel. "That's fine if you did, but I think I understand why someone at The Institute would prefer for us to read the original written by Baraka and Jared. I myself am inclined to request the original first."

"Not me," Sirena declared. "I want to read how it's supposed to go so I know better what to do. I might like to read Baraka's original memoir or whatever you want to call it sometime later, but for our purposes now, I want The Institute's version of alternate history."

Thoth began to rub his chin. He glanced first at O. Cyrus, who raised his eyebrows in response, then turned to face Horace, who simply shrugged. Thoth cleared his throat before he removed his hand from his chin and stared straight into the laptop camera.

"I don't think it's wise for you two not to be reading the book from the same page," Thoth stated. "You should choose one or the other first."

"But you can always read both," O. Cyrus reminded them. "Just pick the same one to start with."

"Alternate history version first," Sirena said as she flung her hair back behind her shoulder and cocked her head toward Uriel.

"You know I'll do whatever you want," Uriel smiled at her in return then placed his hand around her thigh and squeezed.

"Let's just have them send up the alternate history version," Sirena proposed to Uriel, "so we can turn this laptop off and enjoy each other's company for the rest of the evening right here on the couch."

"We'll send the alternate history version of events to you," Thoth replied. "All of this is going to happen quite rapidly. Prepare yourself for the journey of a lifetime."

"And with that, we will bid you both a most delightful evening," added O. Cyrus.

"Good night," said Sirena before she blew the three men a kiss.

The laptop video conference then ended.

UNEGGSPECTED ARRIVALS

Sirena reached to the laptop and pressed the power button until the computer turned off. She then sighed as she turned to Uriel, who shifted his hand from her thigh to her waist. Sirena scooted closer to him, and he slid his arm around her waist as he pulled her closer to him.

"You know," began Uriel, "I can't help but think how differently the lives of those two unfortunate souls would have been if they had only met to fulfill their destiny."

"I have no doubts that their lives couldn't have ended any worse," Sirena remarked. "That part of this enterprise does have me motivated."

"Why?" asked Uriel before he removed his arm from around her waist and brought his hand to Sirena's.

"Because if they truly are soulmates," Sirena began her answer as she interlaced his fingers with his and met his eyes, "then I want to do everything within my power to empower them with the experience of being able to share their lives together in ways that only the truest of lovers can ever understand."

"You are the sweetest," Uriel smiled first then eyed her body as he brought her hand to his mouth and kissed her fingertips.

"And you're divine," her voice undulated.

Uriel pulled his lips from her fingers then brought his hands to her face as he leaned toward her.

Uriel traced her bottom lip with the tip of his tongue before he said: "Let's go to bed."

But before Sirena could answer, both recoiled from the shattering of windows downstairs in four successive impacts. The squeal of tires then tore from the street in front of the house.

"Oh, my God!" Sirena cried as Uriel covered her body with his. "Somebody's shooting at us!"

"I think they're gone," Uriel said as he met her searching gaze. "Whoever that was."

"What is going on?" Sirena's voice shook.

"I don't know," Uriel answered before he sprang from the couch. "But I need to find out!"

Sirena pushed herself from the couch as Uriel lurched from the room and bounded down the steps.

"Wait, Uriel!" she yelled.

Sirena staggered after him. She stumbled down the steps, catching herself from falling as she seized the handrail. She negotiated the remaining steps to reach the front room of the house. When she turned the corner to the threshold, she saw Uriel kneeling to the floor with a stone egg in his hand.

"Now why would someone throw one of these stone eggs through our window?" he asked without turning toward Sirena.

"I have no idea," Sirena answered, then she stepped to the emerald green jade egg on the floor. "But here's a jade egg like the ones Enoch had."

"And there's another one," Uriel said as he pointed to a speckled green jade egg.

"That one is like one of Enoch's, too," replied Sirena, then she gasped at the sight of the stone egg situated on the carpet. "Oh, my God! That's the egg of Kukulkan! How in God's name did Enoch's eggs get thrown into our house?"

"Surely they can't be the same eggs?" Uriel asked her. "Can you verify them for sure?"

Sirena sidestepped Uriel and reached to retrieve the stone egg from the floor. She observed the image of the feathered serpent god on front, then she turned the egg to reveal the winged, naked man with the enormous appendage dangling between his feathered legs.

"What the hell is going on?" exclaimed Sirena before she crouched toward Uriel and held the egg turned in front of him. "This is exactly the same egg that Enoch had! He called this image on the egg, *Azazel*."

"Azazel as in the same demonic *Azazel* that Baraka warned about in the video," Uriel said, then peered closer at the unusual image. "And that giant thing hanging down between his legs is the giant penis appendage that Horace was taking about?"

"Enoch also told me that it was some kind of egg depositor," Sirena told him. "One that would deposit his demon seed."

"*Ovipositor*, right?" Uriel inquired further.

"Yes," confirmed Sirena. "That's exactly what Enoch called it, too."

"And what about this one?" Uriel extended the other egg in his hand for her to examine.

Sirena peered closer at the egg. She immediately recognized the old man with the hooked nose and the beautiful red-haired woman on the other side of the egg.

"I just can't believe what I'm seeing!" blared Sirena. "This is

Enoch's egg with the old Mayan man on one side, and Lilith on the other!"

"The demonic Lilith, I presume," Uriel hypothesized aloud. "As in the first wife of the Adam in the Book of Genesis, who left him to fornicate with the fallen angel Samael."

"Actually," Sirena began, "Enoch said that Lilith fornicated with several of The Watchers, including Samyaza, who Enoch said impregnated her with the spawn otherwise known as Azazel."

"But why are these green jade eggs here?" Uriel asked her as he pointed toward one of them.

"Why are any of them here?" Sirena asked in reply. "I told The Institute about them, but surely they didn't get them just so that they could throw them through our window?"

"So, who did get them?" posed Uriel.

"I have no..." Sirena started, only to stop her response when she heard conversation from people approaching their house.

The rap on the front door preceded the announcement: "Police! Is everyone all right in there?"

"Coming!" Uriel called back before he whispered to Sirena and pointed to the étagère bookcase along the far wall. "Hide the eggs over there."

Sirena collected the four eggs and hustled to stash them below the bottom shelf of the bookcase. Uriel watched her until the bang came louder at the door and shook more shards of glass free from the window.

"Police!" the same voice boomed again. "Open up, please."

"Hold on a minute!" Uriel's voice exploded, then he stood and stepped toward the entry hallway.

"We're coming!" Sirena announced. "Just a second!"

Uriel reached the front door, turning the lock on the knob

before he pulled the door halfway open and thrust his face into the opening.

"We're all right," Uriel told the two uniformed police officers standing on the porch, one an extremely tall man who appeared to be roughly seven-feet tall compared to the much shorter woman next to him, whose hair was pulled tight beneath her police cap. "Someone just broke out our windows with rocks."

"We can file a complaint for you," the policeman announced as he pulled a notepad from his chest pocket and the pen clipped there.

"I don't think that's necessary," Uriel said, "but I'll check with the landlord later to see if he wants one filed for property damage. We're just lucky, I guess, that these are older multi-pane windows. There's only going to be four small panes of glass to replace."

"Still wouldn't hurt to file a report," the woman officer said, peering into the hallway. "If whoever did this isn't stopped now, they might just get braver and cause more damage. We'd be glad to come in and take a look for you to see if there's anything that might help us locate the perpetrators."

"I really don't think that will be necessary," said Sirena before she opened the door wider, showing herself to the officers.

"Well," the policeman began, "if you say so ma'am, but if you have any more problems like this, please don't hesitate to call 911."

"Will do," Uriel said. "Thank you for the unbelievably quick response, officers."

"Who called you guys, by the way?" asked Sirena as she folded her arms across her chest and peered closer at the police woman.

"Neighbor two doors down," informed the woman officer with a point down the street. "We just happened to be a block away when the call came through."

"We'll have to thank her," said Uriel. "And thanks again, officers."

"Your welcome," the policeman said, returning his notepad and pen to his shirt pocket. "That's why we're here."

"You folks have a good night," the policewoman said with a wave of her hand.

"You as well," Sirena said with a smile. "Goodnight, now."

Uriel watched the officers walk down the concrete porch steps to the platform that started the descent of steps to the street. He then shut the door, locking both the deadbolt and the knob lock. Sirena kept her arms crossed as she met Uriel's eyes.

"She looks familiar," Sirena remarked about the police woman.

"He did, too," added Uriel. "But I can't quite place him. Maybe he was a college basketball player or something."

"Weird," said Sirena, knotting her brow when she met Uriel's eyes.

"I'll cover the window as best as I can for tonight," he told her. "Why don't you take the eggs upstairs and tell our friends at The Institute what just happened. I'd like to video conference with them again tonight if possible so that we can show them the eggs and get some answers about this, especially if they know about who has the eggs if they don't."

"Okay," Sirena nodded, then she uncrossed her arms and brought her hands to Uriel's shoulders. "I love so much, you know."

"I know," he said, smiling at her as he placed his hands over hers. "I love you, too. Now and always."

"Now and always," she smiled back at him then slid her

hands from his shoulders. "Now, you get to work on covering up those windows, all right?"

"Soon as I watch your shapely exit from the room first," he grinned at her.

"Let me have the eggs," she feigned disdain. "Would it be too much trouble for you to get them for me?"

"Not at all," laughed Uriel before he returned to the front room and retrieved the eggs from beneath the bottom shelf of the étagère.

Uriel then carefully placed two eggs in each of her hands.

"You can start watching me leave now," she said, tossing her hair behind her before she began her ascent of the steps.

Sirena turned back at the top of the stairs to smile at him before she removed herself from his view. Uriel then returned to the front room. He traversed the glass-strewn carpet to the adjacent storage room where he kept his tools and supplies. He took a folded blue plastic tarp from the floor in the back of the room, utility knife from his toolbox, and a roll of duct tape from the shelf of a metal storage cabinet.

"Let me know when you want me to contact Thoth and company?" Sirena's voice drifted downstairs as he reentered the front room.

"Whenever you're ready," he raised his voice for her to hear him. "This shouldn't take more than a few minutes."

Uriel eyeballed the amount of tarp he would need to cover the four broken panes of glass in two of the room's windows then cut rough squares of the same size from a fold of the tarp with the utility knife. He then stepped to the window with the tarp pieces and tape in hand before he set them on the carpet. One by one, he taped each tarp square over each pane of broken glass.

"That should do it," he said to himself

Uriel tossed the roll of tape to the folded tarp in the middle of the floor.

"I'm setting up the video conference with them right now," Sirena hollered down the steps to him.

"All right, babe," Uriel hollered back before he glanced at his handiwork.

"I'm live with The Institute, honey," Sirena announced.

"I'm coming upstairs right now," Uriel's voice boomed as he left the room.

OVIPOSITIVE

URIEL HUSTLED UP THE STEPS TO REACH THE SECOND floor. Sirena was already seated on the couch. He plopped beside her then reached over the four eggs on the table to adjust the screen of the laptop.

"Can you guys see us all right?" Uriel asked Thoth and Horace, who both nodded and said yes. "Where's O. Cyrus?"

"We just sent him to the research department for some information about what just happened to you two," informed Horace. "Hopefully, he will have more details about what might be going on. As of right now, we're really not sure what to make of it."

"Uriel," Thoth began, "why don't you tell us what you think happened?"

"I already showed them the eggs with Azazel and Lilith," Sirena informed Uriel. "And they told me the eggs weren't there in Ohio when they sent their people to get them."

"So, who in the hell got the eggs?" boomed Uriel. "Somebody threw these eggs through the downstairs windows. It has to be somebody who knows what we're doing."

"And it has to be somebody who knew exactly where Enoch's artifacts were near the Serpent Mound," added Thoth.

"The only person we know who fits that bill," began Sirena, "is Enoch, but I saw him launched into the sky with the Serpent Mound snake hot on his tail."

"I didn't want to identify him so soon," Uriel remarked, "because he's supposed to be on our side, isn't he? I mean, after all, we're on our mission here to rescue his translated self for his final incarnation if I am to understand what this is all about. He surely must know that, too."

"We agree," concurred Thoth. "I'm personally just having a hard time believing that anyone else could've thrown the eggs beside Enoch. We're unaware at this point of anyone else in the region who could've had the wherewithal to do this, both from a material standpoint and an awareness level."

"There is some speculation that a Camazotz or their agent might have been involved in this," revealed Horace. "Confirmation of that is something that will be difficult. Perhaps O. Cyrus may turn up something in that regard when he returns."

"When you say *Camazotz*," began Sirena, "you're referring to these supernatural bats from Mayan mythology, correct?"

"Correct," confirmed Thoth. "We understand their mythological significance quite well, but we're just beginning to really wrap our minds around their kind of vampiric translation into the real world."

"Do they drive cars?" Sirena asked. "Because we definitely heard car tires screech away from the street in front of the house."

"I suppose it depends upon how the Camazotz are manifest," speculated Thoth.

"So, these things can materialize into human form?" asked Uriel.

"We're starting to believe that they do," Horace replied. "The Camazotz of the Mayan creation text are demons. One bit off the head of one of the story's hero twins when he tried to come out of hiding."

"Our overall theory about the role of these Camazotz in this," began Thoth, "is that they are at the disposal and dispatch of the unholy trinity of the fallen angel Samyaza, the demonically possessed human Lilith, and their Nephilim spawn Azazel, who could very well prove to beget the rival of the Messiah in the form of the actual Antichrist."

"Right," sighed Uriel. "And the eggs thrown into our house have Lilith and Azazel depicted on them, so maybe Enoch is trying to warn us about something that's going to happen."

"Or," Horace countered, "we might be dealing with Camazotz dispatched by Lilith and Azazel in this case. We are diligently pursuing this angle because the Camazotz is clearly depicted upon the egg with the woman giving birth to the snake-headed demon."

"But why would they throw the eggs of Azazel and Lilith through our windows instead of the Camazotz one?" Sirena asked.

"That does seem odd, doesn't it?" posed Uriel.

"Not necessarily," countered Horace. "I mean, if whoever is responsible for this does in fact have the Camazotz egg, then they might very well be saving it for future use, especially if it somehow corresponds to the actual future birth of the demon snake-headed entity from the unknown woman. At this point, we really just do not know."

"I wouldn't concern yourselves with the Camazotz egg too much at this point," suggested Thoth. "Just know that the

Camazotz depicted on Enoch's egg equates with the one you watched attach itself to Baraka in the video.

"Also understand that it was Azazel who destroyed Baraka's body and her mind, ruining her life and altering her destiny all of those years ago in Paris, we now believe. By Azazel assaulting her, he unleashed the forces of evil that thwarted the return of Enoch and the eventual transfiguration of his twin, if you will, in Metatron."

"Well," Horace began, "the archangel Metatron won't be born if we can't use our alternate history research to right the wrong committed against Baraka decades ago."

"So that's what you want from us," interjected Sirena. "You just said again that Baraka was assaulted by Azazel in Paris all those years ago. You want us to stop that from happening?"

"The files will clarify more of that for you," confirmed Thoth. "Baraka's alternate history script provides the milieu and the details of the actions that will be required of you, Sirena, to help the much younger Baraka avoid the assault upon her by Azazel."

"Sounds like so much fun," grumbled Sirena. "But at least we'll get to see some of Paris."

"And you, Uriel," Horace began. "You will find yourself embroiled in the debauchery thrust upon Jared, the poor bastard you saw beaten in that bar by the cuckolded husband."

"That brings me to one last point about the Camazotz that I forgot to mention," Thoth said. "We did not see the Camazotz shadowing Jared at any time during the beating we witnessed, unlike the Camazotz we saw surrounding and possessing Baraka. That tells us that it was already known that Jared would be killed, and his corpse would be of no use to the Camazotz or their organizers."

"So, he definitely died?" Uriel asked.

"Actually, we haven't verified his death," admitted Thoth. "But I find it hard to believe he survived."

Thoth stopped talking once O. Cyrus appeared on the screen. Horace stood from the chair beside Thoth and offered it to O. Cyrus, who then placed a file folder on the desktop and sat.

"Greetings," O. Cyrus said with muted smile before he opened the folder and removed a sheet of paper from it.

O. Cyrus glanced at the laptop screen before he held the paper up in front of the computer camera. It appeared to be terrain imagery captured via satellite. A yellow-highlighted path coursed across the satellite map.

"This is the GPS route research collected from Enoch's car," O. Cyrus announced as he pointed to the highlighted path. "We have visual confirmation that Enoch's car traveled from the Serpent Mound area to your house in Maysville, Kentucky, where it is now parked just a block away from your house."

"Oh, shit!" Sirena exclaimed. "That means whoever threw the eggs is still here!"

"Is it Enoch?" Uriel asked. "I mean, how did you get the GPS?"

"His phone is apparently in the car somewhere," answered O. Cyrus. "I tried to call him, but no one answered."

"How can it be Enoch?" Sirena blared. "He got sucked up into the storm!"

"I'm not sure," O. Cyrus replied. "Maybe he was able to return."

"Wait a minute," interjected Sirena as she sprang from her seat on the couch. "I think I just realized something. Oh, my God! I just realized something!"

"What is it?" Uriel asked and grabbed her arm.

"I hope I'm wrong about this," resumed Sirena, "but those two cops downstairs looked like the Azazel and Lilith on the eggs thrown through the window!"

The banging on the front door jolted Uriel from his seat to his feet. He and Sirena looked at each other in the pause that followed, but when the banging recommenced at the front door, they clutched each other's arms.

"What now?" Uriel voiced before he stooped to look at the three men on the computer screen. "Somebody 's knocking at the door again."

"Go see who it is," said Thoth. "We'll wait for you."

The banging at the front door came stronger and louder.

"Wait," entreated O. Cyrus, "there's more you should know before you answer the door. If that's Azazel and Lilith knocking, I believe you can throw the stone eggs at them to stop them from harming you. I suspect that's why their images are rendered on those eggs."

"If that's true," Uriel began as he leaned over the computer screen, "then why did they throw them into the house to begin with?"

"I don't think they did," O. Cyrus replied. "I think it was Enoch who threw the eggs for you to arm yourselves."

"What?" Sirena snapped. "How is that possible?"

The knocking at the door repeated with even greater urgency.

"Just take the stone eggs with you," implored O. Cyrus. "Uriel, you throw the one with Lilith depicted. Sirena, you throw the other that shows Aazael."

Sirena grabbed the two stone eggs and placed them in her robe pocket, leaving the two jade eggs on the table. Uriel grabbed her arm before they started their descent down the steps to the front entry.

"We're coming!" announced Uriel as he reached the door.

Uriel peered through the door eyehole and saw the same couple in police officer uniforms standing there again.

"It's our police officers again," he said as he turned to face Sirena.

"Why are they back?" she whispered before she put her arm around his waist. "If they really are Lilith and Azazel, they have to be very dangerous to us."

"We have the eggs," Uriel said with a shrug.

"I'm putting the one with Lilith in your pocket," Sirena told him then stuffed the egg into his back jeans pocket.

"Here we go," Uriel said as he opened the door, smiling in his greeting of the pair.

"Sorry to bother you again," the towering officer apologized. "But we were just driving by when my partner here said she observed someone up on your roof. Is it possible for us to come upstairs for a few minutes and perhaps look into your attic?"

"Oh, my God," Sirena gasped. "I didn't hear anything on the roof, did you?"

"No, I didn't hear anything," replied Uriel, then he opened the screen door and motioned for the pair to enter the house. "Come on in and have a look upstairs. We really don't want any prowlers lurking around here."

"Please follow me," Sirena offered then released Uriel and started upstairs.

"Thank you, ma'am," the policewoman said before she followed Sirena.

"After you," Uriel offered to the male officer with a wave of his hand.

"Much obliged," the policeman said as he removed his cap and followed his partner up the steps.

"You sure are tall," Uriel observed from the rear. "Exactly how tall are you?"

"I'm seven-foot four," the officer said. "But I may have shrunk over the years. Most people want to know if I played basketball, but I have to confess that I never acquired the skills or coordination to play the game very well."

"That's too bad, I guess," Uriel half-laughed. "Probably could have made a lot of money."

"The love of money is the root of all evil, so they say," the policeman replied. "Besides, I'm quite content to live a life of service for those whom I'm sworn to protect."

As the foursome all reached the living room, Sirena stepped between the couch and coffee table. She then stooped to address the three men from The Institute.

"It's the two police officers who were here before," Sirena told them. "They said they saw someone lurking around on our roof."

"Didn't realize you had company," the policewoman said. "Sorry for the interruption."

"It's all right," Uriel said. "They'll hold tight while we get this sorted out."

"I take it these men are from The Institute," the policeman said before he placed his cap on the coffee table and leaned over the laptop to peer upside down at the three men broadcast upon the screen. "The Three Initiates, is it, or is it the Three Stooges."

The woman removed her cap and flung it across the room, then she undid her bun and let her red hair flow down her back.

"Now that's much better," she sighed before she tugged at

her crotch. "Now if I can only get these pants off. They're really riding me high."

"Tell us who you are," Uriel ordered them as he stepped to Sirena and put his arm around her.

"What we are is your best chance to get out of this mess these imbeciles are about to put you both into," the man said, straightening to hover in the room at his full height. "I'm Azazel and this is the glorious whore who begat me into this world, the one-and-only Lilith."

"I'll show you how pleased I am to meet you both," she began as she undid her belt buckle and unbuttoned her pants, "as soon as we're bundled up into a ball on the floor having ourselves the orgy to end all orgies."

"Perhaps you would like to see what I can bring to the party," Azazel said before he undid his belt, unbuttoned his pants, then unzipped.

"I'm quite sure you've never seen anything like this," Lilith throatily announced. "He's endowed like God himself would be if he bothered to join us here on this bead of spinning mud."

When Azazel lowered his pants, his enormous appendage flopped free down the length of his scaly and feathered thighs.

"That gruesome cyclops there is eighteen inches of earthly salvation once it's fully engorged," Lilith said, then she turned to address Sirena directly. "Honey, that throbbing mass is as thick as a firehose, too, especially when it's loaded with eggs. It'll pound your G-spot into one squirting orgasm for hours on end. You'll be drenched in ecstasy beyond anything you thought possible."

"Shall we enjoy each other's company, Sirena?" Azazel said as he flashed a smile full of double-rowed, razor-sharp teeth.

"No," whimpered Sirena before she buried her face into Uriel's chest.

"Uriel," cooed Lilith, "I've never actually had a real archangel inside me. Fallen angels, yes, but not one who was still standing like you."

"You two need to leave right now," Uriel warned them.

"Uriel!" yelled O. Cyrus. "Don't try anything against them! They can't harm you if you don't attack them!"

"We don't want to attack you two," Azazel declared as he grabbed himself and began to stroke his ovipositor. "We want to pleasure you. We know Sirena is Nephilim. We know how they succumb to the seduction of their insatiable lust, and how they crave deviant sexual acts. It is the true nature of a Siren, after all, and you, my lovely Siren, were named Sirena for a reason."

"We understand it too well," Lilith added as she extended her hand toward Sirena. "Azazel is Nephilim, like you Sirena, and he really just can't contain himself. You and Azazel would make a perfect match, Sirena.

"No doubt that Uriel is quite athletic and robust in his intercourse with you, but Azazel is just cut from a different cloth, so to speak. When you experience his package of pure bliss inside of you, you'll finally have your deliverance again."

"Stop it," Sirena sobbed as she pressed her face harder into Uriel's chest. "Just leave me alone."

"What am I supposed to do?" Uriel asked the men from The Institute.

"Throw the stone eggs at them!" O. Cyrus yelled.

"Don't do it, Sirena" countered Azazel as he stepped to her. "We know you have the egg with my image on it. Put that egg in here, where it belongs."

Sirena peeked at Azazel as he extended the enormous ovipositor from his scaly and feathered groin. He then spread the fleshy folds at the end of his gargantuan appendage, revealing the bloody pulp inside of the organ.

"Oh, God," cried Sirena again burying her face into Uriel's chest.

"Sirena isn't the only one with an egg," Uriel said, then retrieved the egg with Lilith depicted upon it.

"Uriel, baby," cooed Lilith as she arched her back in her approach of the couch. "You know what we're saying is true. Let Azazel and Sirena have their way with each other. Those two really do belong to each other. She needs her man to be super-sized. It's just the way she is wired."

"No," Sirena sobbed into Uriel's chest. "Don't let him take me, Uriel. Please."

"Now, you and I, Uriel," resumed Lilith as she knelt into the soft material of the couch and flared her bare backside toward Uriel, "I'm sure I can satisfy your earthly self like no other woman who has ever walked this earth."

"She's simply divine, Uriel," remarked Azazel, then he flashed his smile of double-rowed teeth toward him.

"I'm your reward for agreeing to descend to earth," claimed Lilith as she leered at him, undulating her haunches. "Go ahead and stick the stone egg with my image into me then mount me and experience pleasure unlike anything you've ever known. There's a reason why all the fallen angels want me so bad, and God himself even made me for Adam."

Uriel pried Sirena from his chest and guided her behind him. He smiled at Azazel then motioned for him to step to the side.

"It's not like I can't be tempted," Uriel said. "After all, once I remembered who I really am, I had no problem leaving my wife and children for Sirena, even as I seduced her away from her husband and their family."

"That's right, lover," Lilith hissed in agreement. "You know what you want, and you get it. Once you've had me, you'll want me all of the time, and I'll give you all the rapture you can stand."

"It really is all about power," said Azazel. "We all want it, and once we truly have it, we're insatiable for the high it gives us when we exercise our divine right to rule over others with our might and our brilliance."

"Brilliance, indeed," Uriel nodded toward Azazel. "I can't tell you how many times I've pondered the stupidity that I encounter in this world, wondering why it has to be like this when it's clear there are ways to live out one's existence with the utmost gratification."

Azazel clasped his hands together as Lilith groaned, reaching behind herself to spread her haunches even farther apart.

"Sirena has taught me that," Uriel said, then he stepped toward Lilith with the stone egg extended in his hand.

"Uriel!" Sirena cried then fumbled for the egg in her robe pocket.

"Hush, now, Sirena," Uriel told her as he traced Lilith's backside with the tip of the egg. "We're all here to harmonize with each other, and if that means we all get to enjoy each other's company to the fullest physical extent possible, then so be it."

"Who are we to judge," commented Azazel as he flashed his inhuman smile and held his hands apart. "We knew the eggs were here. That's why we're here. Once you put those eggs where they belong, we're going to make our time on earth together just one everlasting orgy."

"That sounds like real rapture," Uriel replied then traced the spine of Lilith with the tip of the stone egg.

"What about us, Uriel!" shrieked Sirena as she cocked the

stone egg of Azazel in her hand and positioned herself to throw it at the giant.

"Us?" Uriel laughed, then he stopped tracing Lilith's body with the egg and turned toward Sirena. "Alpha and Omega: your transfiguration awaits you, my love."

Uriel jumped back from Lilith and fired the stone egg at her head. He recoiled even farther from her when the egg embedded into Lilith's head and began to spew sparks and smoke.

"Throw yours now!" Uriel yelled at Sirena, who screamed as she flung the stone egg at Azazel, hitting him in the chest, where the egg embedded as it also began to smolder.

Uriel grabbed Sirena and pulled her to him as he guided her from the room, then he slammed the bedroom door shut behind them. Sirena covered her ears and cowered as the screams of Azazel and Lilith pealed from the other room. The smoke from the impact of the eggs drifted beneath the door and soon spread throughout the bedroom. Uriel brought Sirena's face to his chest and shielded her mouth with his arm as he covered his own mouth with his hand.

The screaming faded into moans that soon dissipated into the trampling of feet across the room, then down the stairs. The sound of the front door and screen door opening then drifted upstairs. As the smoke started to clear the bedroom, Uriel pried Sirena's face from his chest and gripped her by her shoulders.

"Our love knows no bounds," he said to her, then he embraced her lips with his.

"Oh, Uriel," she nearly sobbed once he pulled his lips from hers. "I thought you were going to give into their temptation."

"You are my temptation," he smiled at her as he brushed her hair from her eyes. "And my salvation."

"Thank God," came her trembling reply.

The muffled voices of the three men from The Institute filtered into the bedroom from the still-active video conference on the computer.

"Our real friends await us," Uriel smiled at Sirena before he opened the bedroom door and motioned for her to go into the front room.

"You first," she said as she peered into the empty room and waited for him to lead the way.

Uriel paused at the threshold to survey the room. Azazel and Lilith were gone. There was no sign of damage from the reaction of the eggs with the pair of intruders, but Uriel and Sirena both crinkled their noses at the stench of rotten egg.

"Hello?" yelled the voice of Thoth.

"Why, hello there, my friend," Uriel cheerfully greeted Thoth as he stepped around the coffee table to position himself in front of the computer screen again.

"Thank God you're all right!" rejoiced O. Cyrus. "That was crazy!"

"Tell me about it," Uriel remarked, then he sat on the couch and motioned for Sirena to join him.

"Is Sirena all right?" came the rattled voice of Horace.

"Yes," Sirena softly replied as she sat beside Uriel.

"Sirena," Thoth gently addressed her. "I know this is a lot to absorb and a lot that we're asking you to do. Just please know how much we all truly love and respect you here at The Institute. We find you to be just a delightful beauty upon this earth, and we all strive to nurture and embrace you."

"Thanks," Sirena managed before she guardedly turned her eyes toward the three men on the screen.

"We saw what happened to those two evil creatures and recorded it," Thoth announced. "We'll research all of this and report to you what we find."

"But for now," Horace began, "we need for you to get ready for your journey to Paris."

"What about these jade eggs?" Uriel asked. "Aren't they supposed to do something?"

"I'm really not sure," answered O. Cyrus. "Perhaps they protected you somehow."

"So, what should we do with them?" asked Sirena.

"Just hold onto them for now," replied Horace.

"What is it you really want?" Sirena suddenly confronted the three men, shifting her scowl to each of them in her wait for an answer.

"All that we really want is for you two to be happy together," Thoth finally said. "We believe the world is a much better place if you two are happily together as one."

"That's really all," O. Cyrus added, "because we're really not sure any of the intervention we propose can actually work."

"And we will respect whatever decision you make with regard to your participation," concluded Horace.

"Thank you," sighed Sirena. "As long as Uriel and I are together, everything will be all right."

"We should all call it a night," announced Thoth. "Your files are there for you to read tomorrow. If you have any other questions or needs, please don't hesitate to call us tomorrow morning."

"Thank you," Sirena and Uriel both said.

"Good night," Horace and O. Cyrus both said before the video conference disconnected.

Uriel bent to turn off the computer. He crooked his arm for Sirena to take, which she did, then the two of them crossed the room to the master bedroom. Once inside the bedroom, Sirena slipped his arm from hers and turned down the comforter. She turned on the nightstand lamp then crawled into bed still wearing her robe. Uriel shut the bedroom door and locked it before he disrobed to his briefs and crawled into bed beside her. He rolled to her and kissed her cheek before he rolled back to turn off the lamp.

"Good night, my beautiful angel," Uriel whispered to her.

"Good night, my beautiful man," she replied, then the room went dark.

EGGCERPTED

Uriel staggered from the bedroom into the living room, wearing just his briefs. Sirena peered at him above her reading glasses as she paused from typing on the laptop keyboard. He stepped to the couch where she sat, then he leaned over her to kiss her forehead.

"Good morning, babe," he greeted her as he straightened.

"Try good afternoon," Sirena corrected him before she wrapped her arm around his leg and kissed his thigh.

"Really?" he asked before he stroked her hair.

"I don't think I've ever seen you sleep this much," she replied, then she released his leg and returned her attention to the laptop screen.

"Guess I needed it," he said as he stretched.

Sirena resumed typing on the keyboard.

"We have a full day of reading ahead of us," she announced to him.

"Hope that doesn't put me back to sleep," he managed to say through a yawn.

"More likely it will keep us awake with nightmares," she remarked then paused from typing to look up at him. "Just so you know, the folks at The Institute apparently decided to make a significant revision to our reading material. They've produced a manuscript that combines their two separate alternate history versions based upon the original copyrighted material written by Baraka and Jared."

"What does that mean?" asked Uriel.

"It's good in a couple ways," Sirena began to explain, "because now we only have to read one manuscript instead of two. It also means that we'll be able to read one script together instead of two scripts separately. That way we can enjoy each other's company while we do our work together."

"I actually like the sound of that," Uriel remarked as he eyed her. "I can't think of anyone else I'd rather be with all day than you."

"You're just going to have to keep your big paws off me for a while, buddy," she said smiling. "But I agree. This will be good for us to be together doing this, not just because we'll be together but probably more importantly because it will enable us to better plan for our time slip and our course of action after we reach our destination."

"I see," Uriel said before he sat beside her on the couch. "How do you want to do this, then?"

"I've already printed the combined manuscript," she informed him, "so we're good to go whenever you wake all the way up. I figure that maybe we can take turns reading this aloud. That way it might help us sharpen our attention to the content and enhance our dialogue with each other."

"Sounds like a plan," Uriel agreed. "Obviously, we'll be stopping and starting as we read this. I'm ready to go whenever you are."

"I figure we should read this right here," Sirena said. "Too many potential distractions if we try reading this in bed."

"I know I wouldn't last very long," he replied as he gripped her thigh and squeezed. "You're just way too hot for me to resist."

"If you don't keep your hands off me," she began, pulling her leg from his grip, "and put some clothes on, I'm afraid we'll never even get started."

"I understand," he said, withdrawing his hand as he stood. "Give me a minute, and we'll get this reading party of ours started."

"I've added some folders on the desktop," Sirena mentioned, "that will help us keep organized."

"Keep talking," he told her as he left the living room for the bedroom. "I'm listening."

"Thoth added some instructions to preface the latest version of the manuscript," Sirena told him. "Our time slip will start in Paris in 1987."

"Paris, France or Kentucky?" Uriel jokingly said in thick accent from the bedroom.

"France," Sirena played along with a mock accent of her own, then she resumed her serious tone. "The manuscript itself will be sent to us in parts, with the first part being the account of Baraka and Jared in Paris. The other part that we haven't received yet shifts location to Amsterdam."

"That almost sounds like we're going on a European vacation," quipped Uriel as he returned to the room dressed in sweatpants and purple t-shirt.

"It does, right?" Sirena replied.

Uriel sat beside Sirena and peered over her shoulder as she scrolled through the communication sent by Thoth. She stopped at a section on the screen then turned to address Uriel directly.

"One thing I had questions about," she started to convey to him, "was how I would be able to travel to places I've never been."

"Is that a precondition for our ability to jaunt through space and time?" Uriel asked. "I've been to the places mentioned. You haven't?"

"Not that I know of," Sirena admitted. "I asked Thoth about that, and he told me that based on research conducted by The Institute about my incarnation profile, they believe that I've been to all those places at some point in time."

"Does that create a problem," Uriel asked, "if you don't remember being there?"

"I asked Thoth that, too," sighed Sirena. "He said even though the probability was high that I've been to Europe, it wasn't a certainty because they can't prove who they think I really am."

"So, what exactly does that mean?"

"It means we won't know if we'll be able to travel to Paris or not until we open the portal through our physical connection," answered Sirena. "Our Institute friends have doubts that I can actually travel through a time slip to a place I've never been."

"That would be one hell of a way to find out we won't be able to do this, wouldn't it?" remarked Uriel.

"Kind of like making all the travel arrangements and being at the airport," began Sirena in reply, "only to find out that your passport isn't valid."

"Guess we'll be flying by the seat of our pants until then," Uriel said, flashing a thin turn of a smile toward her as she looked to him.

"I guess," she sounded skeptical. "I just hope we don't crash land."

Sirena leaned across the table to retrieve the two stacks of paper. She handed one of them to Uriel and set the other beside the laptop. Uriel took the paper and read the cover page aloud:

JARED AND BARAKA **Alternate History Revision:**
Paris Location.
The Artifactual Institute Research Department

URIEL THEN PEELED the cover page from the rest of the stack, placing it face down on the coffee table. Sirena closed the window of the communication by Thoth and opened a file that contained the exact same information as the cover page. She then arrowed down the file page and clicked the mouse to keep the cursor at that location.

"You ready for me to read, now?" Uriel asked her.

"Yep."

"All right. Here's the first page:

JARED AND BARAKA
Notre Dame Rendezvous
Paris, France

EDITOR'S NOTE: Essential backdrop before starting. Jared and Baraka are both twenty-year-old free spirits in Paris simultaneously in 1987. Jared arrived with a group of students from the college he attends in England. It is the first semester of his junior year of college. Baraka is there with three of her girlfriends for a two-week travel experience abroad. She has decided to suspend her collegiate studies for the first semester of her junior year to accept a full-time position as a flight attendant. Her new job awaits her upon her return home, but while she is in Europe, she wants to focus on the alternative music fanzine that she designs and writes.

"JE T'AIME! JE T'AIME!" Jared blared repeatedly as he careened through the Friday night throng of the Rue Montorgueil.

The crowd spread for him and his collegiate entourage in their wine-fueled carousal through the Parisian street full of pedestrians. Jared obliviously outran his fellow revelers, shouting his proclamation of love until he reached a section where the crowd thinned.

"Je t'aime!" he huffed as loud as he could before he froze in his tracks.

His wobbling eyes found her dark, disheveled hair that climbed atop her head like some kind of black iris. Her perfectly round and pale face struck him even more when she arched her wisps of eyebrows as she turned toward him from the food window line where she stood. His blurring sight then drifted down her shapely form stuffed tight within the stretched, mid-length black dress that bore the glowing imprint of an emerald-colored skeletal pattern along the front of her body.

"Where are you from?" he somehow said without slurring.

"Mars," she sneered then turned away from him.

"Small world!" Jared bellowed, stepping beside her so that she would have to acknowledge him again. "I'm due to return there soon, but how about a rendezvous with your fine self back here on earth tomorrow, ma chérie."

"Meet me at Notre Dame at noon," she said, knotting her brow and smiling at him. "Do you know where that is, ma Martian?"

"I was there today, " Jared replied as he swayed. "I'll be at the statue of Charlemagne on his horse at noon tomorrow. I mean, I won't actually be on the horse, though."

As they both laughed, one of Jared's friends caught up with him, grabbing him by the arm to steer him back into their roving pack.

"Je t'aime!" he shouted one last time in her direction before the crowd swallowed him again.

Jared's foray into the Paris night with his fellow students led to more and more wine to the extent that he awoke the next morning quite surprised to find purplish clumps scattered around him on the mattress of his hotel bed.

"Who the fuck did this?" he bellowed toward the first room-mate he saw, who watched him from the far corner of the room nearest the door.

"You did," the roommate informed him. "You got absolutely shitfaced and blew chunks all over the place in your sleep. We almost called the hotel desk to get an ambulance for you. We thought you might puke yourself to death."

With that explanation, his roommate left the room.

"Oh shit!" his voice boomed as the memory of his noon date managed to cut through his stupor. "What time is it?"

He dizzily rolled from the bed, his legs wobbling beneath him as his sneakers found the floor. He was fully dressed from the previous night but soon discovered his shirt stained by his vomit. The clock on the night table displayed 11:30. He had a half hour to clean himself and reach Notre Dame Cathedral for his rendezvous with the black-clad Martian he met the night before.

"Charlemagne," he muttered before he pulled the soiled shirt from his body and flung it to the purple-blotched sheet.

Jared flung open the top of his suitcase and grabbed a folded collared shirt, his toothbrush, and a traveler's sized tube of toothpaste, then he staggered toward the hotel door. He staggered through the hallway on his way to the shared bathroom for the hotel floor. Once inside the bathroom, he grimaced at his reflection smeared with the stain of his vomit. He pulled at hardened purple residue stuck to a clump of his hair.

"Jesus Christ," Jared muttered at the reflection of his bloodshot eyes. "You're a royal fuck up, for sure."

He twisted the faucet handle. Cold water spurted out. He brushed his teeth first before he worked to rinse the vomit crust from his hair. He splashed his face then tugged the clean shirt over top his head. His hair remained disheveled, so he wetted all of it down and ran his fingers through it from front to back to smooth it as much as possible.

Satisfied, he winked at his reflection, turning off the faucet before he stepped to the toilet. He maneuvered his erection from his underwear then hunched over the porcelain seat until he could guide the crashing deluge of urine into the toilet bowl. Emptied, he stuffed himself back into his underwear, pulled his pants back up over his waist, then stepped back in front of the mirror.

"Let's go do us a French chick, studly," Jared announced to himself, inspecting his front teeth in the reflection as he flashed his winning smile.

Jared took his toothbrush and toothpaste, then hurried back to his room. He tossed the items to his bed and left. His labored passage down the hotel steps ended with a blast of sunlight that forced him to clench his eyes shut. He squinted to maintain his path upon the sidewalk as he hustled toward the Cathedral of Notre Dame. He visited the cathedral during the day before with fellow students and remembered the way for the short distance required to reach the gargoyle-studded beacon.

I'll impress her with my knowledge of the gargoyle legend, he thought to himself as he weaved through the pedestrian traffic. *How Saint Romanus delivered the city of Rouen of the fire-breathing monster with a crucifix then burned all but the head of the beast.*

Jared searched for clarified memory of the woman he encountered last night at the food window, hoping the web stretched within his hungover mind could capture her image well enough for him to recognize her in the crowd at Notre Dame.

I'll tell her I met Charlemagne's horse, Tencendur, yesterday, Jared began to rehearse in his mind, *and handfed the beast the heart of an Infidel. We'll see what that sparks in the eyes of my Martian Mademoiselle.*

The cathedral sprang into his view. He squinted and craned his neck for definition of the gargoyles he knew were frozen in their perch. As he filtered through the throng milling about the plaza in front of the cathedral, he scanned for the verdigris statute of the coronated emperor of the Holy Roman Empire and his famous warhorse.

She emerged from behind the viridescent statue clad in the same, skeletal-patterned black dress she wore the night before.

She's wearing that same weird dress, he observed to himself.

Her eyes immediately found his once he peered toward her over top the heads of the pedestrians who remained between him and her. They locked eyes in his approach to her. His heart bounced when the tinge of a smile crimped the corner of her mouth. Her gothic noir aura aroused him. He licked his lips at the thought of unwrapping her from the black dress that clung to curves made more enticing now in the daylight than the night before. The allure of her ghostly complexion beckoned him like some otherworldly magnet as he reached her and opened his arms, engulfing her in his embrace before she gripped his waist and the two slipped their tongues into the other's mouth in a brief, but drenched French kiss.

"Bon jour," she smiled, peering up at him as he kept her within his clutch.

"Je t'aime, my Martian" Jared whispered into her ear. "I fed a real human heart to Charlemagne's whorehouse."

"Slow down, cowboy," she laughed, placing her palms against his chest and leaning back away from him. "I'm not a whore."

"I meant to say *warhorse*," he laughed in return then pulled her closer to him. "I'm still drunk from all the wine I drank last night."

"I can tell," she said as she pinched her nose. "And smell. You drink too much, maybe?"

Jared paused but retained his embrace. She slid her fingers down his chest to his stomach then leaned into him once again, lifting her face and tiptoeing to kiss his lips.

"Slow down just a little," she smiled again. "But not so much."

He smiled, pressing her body against him so she could feel how engorged he was. She raised her eyebrows toward him and traced her upper lip with the tip of her tongue as she met his lustful stare.

"I think we become great friends," she said to him. "And lovers, too, maybe?"

"I can't wait," he replied as he further tightened his embrace of her. "Let's go back to my hotel."

"But you must wait," she said past her giggle, turning slightly from him. "At least wait a little, okay?"

"I'm about ready to bust at the seams," he said too loud as he lowered his hands to her waist and squeezed her hips. "I'd like to hoist you up there to Charlemagne's lap and have my way with you right here and now."

"Not so soft, I think," she said, grimacing once she glanced at the statue above them. "We make other arrangements soon, maybe?"

Before he could tell her that he didn't want to wait any longer, a wave of gasps rolled through the crowd. A white delivery truck with the sides removed screeched to a stop in front of them in the plaza. Four musicians—a drummer and three guitarists—stood inside of the exposed truck bed. The first guitarist stepped forward and struck discordant chords that blasted through the crowd from a speaker positioned beside him. A group of skinheads then surged into view between the truck and Charlemagne statue. The group slam danced into each other as the remaining two guitarists and drummer erupted into the full fury of their cacophony. A singer in priest garb appeared on the box top of the truck. Behind the singer towered a cross of wood posts with a stepladder in front of it. The priest-posing singer then screamed his non-English lyrics into the microphone he held. His amplified voice raged even louder than the guitars and drums.

"What's he screaming?" Jared's voice roared into his French date's ear.

"He sings that the Nephilim demon Azazel told him to do this," she, in return, yelled into his ear above the jolting din. "That only the sacrifice of the young, beautiful woman chosen by Azazel himself can save the souls of the damned from an eternity of Hell."

She paused in her translation to focus on the singer when suddenly a young woman with long, wavy auburn hair climbed from the truck passenger seat to the top of the cab. The singer clasped her arm and pulled her the rest of the way to the top of the truck. The young woman wore a tight black dress that gripped the curves of her streamlined body. The skeletal pattern along the back of the dress cast the same emerald glow as the dress of Jared's French date.

"Her dress is just like yours!" Jared tried to yell above the noise so that she could hear him.

The costumed priest helped his accomplice climb the stepladder before he resumed screaming into the microphone. The skinheads in front of them continued to smash into each other with a fury to match the seething music. Jared's date then resumed speaking loudly into his ear as he leaned toward her again to hear her:

"He says women are vessels for evil. The Nephilim Azazel was born of demon-woman Lilith and fallen archangel Samyaza to destroy all beauty in this world and keep God from ending debauchery."

The young woman stepped from the stepladder onto a narrow platform that extended from the upright post of the cross. She turned around to face toward the statue of Charlemagne and his horse so that her arms could extend along the crossbar beam of the cross.

"Looks like they're about to crucify her," Jared shouted his remark before the singer set down his microphone and climbed the ladder himself.

"That is the only way," the woman yelled in his ear as both

of them watched the singer tie the woman's wrists to the cross posts with straps.

The singer pulled up the woman's dress past her red panties, exposing all of her legs and stomach then stuffing part of the end of the fabric into her mouth. He retrieved his microphone and a curled mass that he unfurled with a crack, revealing that he now held a whip as the woman shook her head back and forth to try to dislodge the dress fabric stuffed into her mouth.

"He says this woman is Baraka," his date yelled in his ear as the singer screamed into the microphone and snapped the end of the whip into her thigh, splitting her flesh and instantly drawing blood.

"He says Baraka must be skinned alive," his date continued yelling in Jared's ear as the singer whipped the woman's stomach and then her other thigh, drawing blood with each lash. "She must then be defiled for the disease of wickedness to poison the purity of her soul."

"Sounds harsh," Jared replied at the top of his lungs.

"Azazel will impregnate her with his evil instead of the good she was otherwise destined to receive," the woman hollered into his ear. "She will begat demonic possession that consumes her alive instead of giving the life of light that lives forever in the glory of the God she has forsaken. Her sacrifice is the way to earthly salvation for all of the wicked sinners who live today."

Another wave of skinheads converged in front of them as a cluster of policemen with cloche-shaped helmets emerged swinging batons into the crowd. One of the skinheads burst from the throng with a television hoisted over his head. The crowd spread around him as he slammed the TV to the stone. The music continued to blare and the crowd roar as the TV smashed and debris flew like shrapnel. The baton of one of the policemen scored a direct hit to the scalp of the skinhead who threw the TV. Blood streamed down his face as he turned toward Jared and his date, toothlessly smiling before he veered and fled from the crowd.

Sirens from approaching police vehicles wailed above the music, which then suddenly stopped. The singer dropped his microphone but whipped the woman once more, this time the lash striking her panty-covered crotch.

"This shit is for real," Jared commented, cringing as he watched the young woman thrash her head back and forth with the dress still gagging her and blood flowing from her wounds. "Somebody needs to help her."

Jared stepped forward, but his date seized his arm. The truck sped away with the woman still tied to the cross, her hands and arms outstretched, her legs crossed at the knees, and her head now hanging as the movement of the truck jolted her whole body and caused the cross to sway.

Jared's acquaintance now grabbed his hand and sprinted with him behind her. The two veered through the crowd of skinheads now brawling with the growing number of policemen. Jared took one last look at Notre Dame Cathedral behind him, suddenly remembering that he was going to tell his date about the history of gargoyles. Now all he could do was go where she was leading him as his heart bounced in his chest and he panted in pursuit.

DOUBLE EGGSPOSED

"You're going to have to take a turn," Uriel told Sirena. "That got my throat."

"Sure thing," replied Sirena. "I'll read from the computer, and you follow along with the pages."

"Will do," Uriel said, the Sirena began to read aloud:

JARED AND BARAKA
La Pagode Theater Audition
Paris, France Location

JARED RAN without any idea where he was being led as he focused upon dodging foot and car traffic in his pursuit of his date, whose hand he clenched as hard as she squeezed his. Only when they reached the Metro station at the other end of Îl de la Cité did he realize they were headed somewhere besides his hotel. He weaved behind her in her haste toward a ticket window, then she released his hand and veered toward a turnstile instead. In one fluid motion, she jumped to the turnstile, placing her palms on its flat metal top as she spread her legs into the air enough to clear the turnstile and catapult over it. Jared hesitated before he resumed his chase of her and sprinted as he neared the turnstile. He peripherally saw an attendant emerge from the ticket window booth and holler at him in French, then he also hopped the turnstile.

Jared stumbled when he landed but quickly gathered himself without breaking stride in his pursuit of her. He closed the distance between them, then she darted to a platform where a train had its doors open. She quickly stopped herself when she entered the compartment, and Jared bumped into her in his attempt to stop. The contact knocked her to the empty seat in front of them, but she managed to right herself quickly. She smiled and laughed as she turned in the seat toward him.

"You American cowboys like to play rough, no?" she managed to say as she panted.

"You sure can ran," Jared said, panting in reply. "Notre Dame was crazy. Did you know that was going to happen?"

"Here, sit," she breathed heavily as she patted the seat and the doors closed.

Jared plopped beside her, extending his feet and legs into the aisle. He put his arm behind her head and she leaned back to rest the nape of her neck on his bicep.

"What is your name?" he breathlessly asked.

"Frederique," she wheezed as the train lunged forward. "And you?"

"I'm Jared," he replied, his heart still battering his chest from the unexpected exertion.

"Lovely to meet you, Jared," she said as she grinned at him and extended her left hand above his lap.

"Lovelier to meet you," he smiled in reply, gripping her fingers instead of shaking her hand, the he guided their held hands to his thigh. "You are a vision of loveliness, especially in that sensational dress with the green skeletal glow."

"You love my dress?" she now beamed. "It is made from design of artiste Salvador Dali and fashion genius Elsa Schiaperelli."

"The black and green together," he began as he shifted their hands from his thigh to hers and traced the fabric with the tip of his index finger, "are quite seductive."

"You are attracted?" she said as she raised her eyebrows and dimpled her cheek.

"I'm so attracted," he leaned to her cheek and said so that the heat of his breath would contact her skin.

"You still have the breath of a gargoyle," she laughed at him. "I think you drink more than too much."

The Metro pulled to a stop, the compartment door opened, and two people exited in front of them as two others entered. She brought her other hand to their held hands and covered them.

"What exactly was all of that about back there at Notre Dame?" he asked her. "You did know that riot was going to happen, didn't you?"

"I confess," Frederique batted her long eyelashes at him, then the train jolted forward. "I knew. The musicians are friends of mine."

"What about the girl?" he asked. "It sure seems like the singer was hurting her for real."

"I do not know her," she said turning away from him to peer down the compartment away from them. "I think it was cute theatrics."

"But that was real blood coming out her after he whipped her," Jared replied.

"Some women like rough play," Frederique countered as she continued to peer down the train. "I think she just played her part of the theater."

"He even whipped her down there," Jared said before he guided his hand to her groin and touched her with his index fingertip. "I find it hard to believe that the woman was part of the act or even really knew what was going to happen when she allowed herself to be tied up."

"Some women like it tied up," Frederique now addressed him directly, meeting his eyes. "I find arousal that way."

"You do?" he asked as he ogled her.

"Oui," she answered him then winked. "Would you like to tie me up later?"

"Then you will be mine," he whispered into her ear then blew. "And I'll whip you, if you like."

Frederique giggled as she leaned away from him. He leaned closer to her then kissed her cheek. She turned her face toward him and shifted closer, then she placed her hand against his thigh and leaned into him with her lips spread apart. He maneuvered his arm from behind her to grip her by the back of her head. He held her head tight as he met her lips then slid his tongue into her mouth to meet hers. She massaged his thigh, and he squeezed the back of her head harder as their kiss protracted.

When the Metro stopped, Frederique pulled away from Jared.

"We must go here," she announced, jerking him by his arm as she sprang to her feet.

The door slid open. Jared lurched behind her lead. She released his arm before she sprinted down the platform, snaking her way through the awaiting Metro riders. His side almost immediately cramped as he struggled to keep her within his view and not bump into bystanders. He detected the glowing green skeletal spine of her dress design when she turned to climb stairs. He veered from the platform to follow her.

Once Jared completed his ascent, he slowed at the sight of Frederique walking toward the Metro exit. She turned, waving for him to catch up. He quickened his gait to close the distance between them. When he reached her, she grabbed the crook of his arm, and he escorted her into the open air of the street.

"Where are we going?" Jared huffed.

"To a beautiful cinema," Frederique answered without slowing or turning to face him. "It is Parisian treasure, an Arc de Triomphe for the art of film."

"So, we're going to see a movie?"

"Oui," she confirmed. "A private screening of art arranged for us by friends, but we must hurry to be on time. We must run again!"

Frederique broke into a sprint ahead of Jared. He jogged after her at first but ran faster as he noticed her pulling farther ahead of him. He felt dizzier with each thump of his feet against the sidewalk and breathed harder, wheezing as his labored breaths constricted his chest.

After crossing streets and weaving their way through pedestrian traffic, Frederique finally slowed to a walk. Jared slowed to a jog until he was close enough to her for him to walk fast to reach her.

"Can't hardly breathe," Jared wheezed as he gripped her shoulder. "Stop."

"Here," Frederique panted as she motioned to a bench. "Sit here. We rest a little."

Jared flung himself into the bench, then Frederique sat

beside him. The two panted until their breathing slowed enough for them to resume walking.

"Come," she said, pulling him from the bench by his arm. "We can walk slow from here."

Jared lifted himself from the bench with her help, then walked arm-in-arm with her. The two continued silently until Frederique stopped to tiptoe and kiss him on his cheek.

"The film will ravage you, my cowboy Martian," Frederique told him.

"What kind of film is it?" he asked.

"I believe you call it something like cinema noir because it is of darkness in the human heart and mind," she answered. "This screening is the debut. La Pagode is perfect for our date. You will see."

"La Pagode," he repeated. "That is the name of the theater?"

"Oui," she confirmed then pointed across the street and said: "It is there."

The neon blue of the vertical sign bearing the word, *Pagode*, was barely discernible from the backdrop of overhanging foliage. The entrance of subdued red displayed film posters on each side of the recess that bore the lettering *La Pagode*. As the two crossed the street, Frederique released his arm.

"This cinema is old and, how do you say, *fragile*," she began. "Careful how you touch things."

"Will it be dark inside?" he asked as they reached the sidewalk in front of the cinema.

"*Très*," she said.

"That's all that matters to me," he resumed then put his arm around her waist. "I'll be careful how I touch things, I promise."

Frederique quickly stepped to the black entrance door. Jared lowered his arm from her waist, and his fingers skimmed her pear-shaped derriere as she walked ahead of him. She stopped and nudged the door, but it remained shut. She rapped upon the door then stood with her hands on her hips. A voice wafted from the other side of the building.

"I think there's someone over there," Jared said to Frederique as he pointed past the entrance.

"*Ècoute,*" Frederique shushed him then held her finger to her mouth.

A second voice–a woman's–came louder and angry above the first. Frederique stepped out of the entry way and tiptoed toward the side of the entry, where a high wrought iron gate towered ajar. She held her hand palm outward behind her as Jared approached. He stopped, then she turned her head to the side and cupped her hand behind her ear. Jared rested his chin on her shoulder and also cupped his ear.

The unseen woman spoke English in an American accent:

"You hurt me," her voice crackled. "I had no idea you were going to whip me like that, especially where you hit me with the last one."

"There is pleasure with pain, no?" a man's voice replied in his thick French accent. "You write this in your magazine. Your readers love it, I promise, ma Cherie. You will be the star because you live life full."

"But it still stings like hell and it could've been a whole lot worse," her anger remained evident in her voice. "I might have to get more medical attention than just cleaning these cuts and putting bandages on them."

"No, no, no," the man protested. "These cuts are–how do you say–*skin only*. You are fine, a heroine for your readers and beautiful goddess for musicians. You show this world you know truth. You are there to worship, my goddess. You write of this and more."

"It does make for good copy," she replied with more ease in her tone of voice. "It might even get picked up in a larger magazine than my own fanzine."

"Some people like rough play," said the man. "That sells, no? It makes people think, excites mind and body. They want more and more. You give them more? A film star maybe?"

"What do you mean by *film star?*" she asked him.

"I show you inside," he replied. "I use this cinema for film to make, not just to show. You and I star in this film I propose for you."

"Do you mean like a porno?" her voice rose again, but this time trilled in laughter. "I'm not going to do that!"

"No, no, no," the man countered. "Not pornography. Art film. You and I make beautiful art film."

Jared lifted his chin from Frederique's shoulder and started to whisper in her ear, but she elbowed him in the ribs to quiet him. He relented to her then again wedged his chin against her shoulder and listened.

"You have all of the filming equipment here?" she asked him.

"Oui," he confirmed before he spoke louder. "It awaits only the star–the American Goddess in Paris–at La Pagode to show all the world how divine she is."

"I don't know too much about shooting film," the woman expressed with reservation.

"It will amaze," the man countered. "You show how the scene at Notre Dame happens. It is like a film that explains. How do you say, *documentary?*"

"So, you want to shoot a documentary," the woman began with more enthusiasm to her voice, "that explains and demonstrates the performance art of the music and mock crucifixion that we just did at Notre Dame."

"*Voila!*" the man cried. "With footage of event added. The title of *Baraka–American Goddess in Paris*–maybe?"

"*Baraka–American Goddess in Paris!*" Baraka squealed with delight. "That would make me famous with my friends, at least!"

"I say much more," the man added. "You are the star already. The bloom just waits the flower of your decision."

"Well, let's at least see where you want to shoot this film of yours," Baraka finally relented to the man's idea.

"No, no, no," he repeated. "Not my film, no. This film is our film, ma Cherie. I am small against the real star. And that's you, *Baraka–American Goddess in Paris*."

Baraka again laughed then came the sounds of heavy chair legs scooted across hard surface. The man joined in the laughter that traveled away from the gate. The grate of a heavy door resounded followed be a sustained creak. The door then thud shut.

"If I didn't know better," Jared began in a whisper, "that sounded like they were talking about the scene that we just saw at Notre Dame with the chick on the mock crucifix."

"Oui," Frederique replied with normal volume restored to her voice. "She is the star now. The planets are hers."

Frederique nudged the heavy gate open far enough to pass through. Jared followed her onto the walkway, then she stepped around him to shut the gate, its latch clicking shut in place. Frederique resumed entry to the property. The walkway led to a courtyard beside the theater building. Clusters of bamboo stalks sprang around overgrown greenery that hung from mature trees. A wrought iron table was situated in the center of the courtyard. Two iron chairs were positioned beside it.

"Let's sit for a moment," suggested Frederique as she pointed toward the table and chairs.

"Sure," Jared agreed before he stepped to one of the chairs and pulled it out for her to sit.

Jared helped Frederique scoot the chair forward to the table then sat in the other chair. His eyes gravitated to the high double door in front of him that hovered within the stained-glass framework surrounding it. He then noticed the pair of stone sculpture lions with their paws on globes that bookended each side of the doorway.

"This is quite a beautiful place," commented Jared.

"Quite lovely," Frederique agreed with him. "I visit this shrine much more than, say, Eiffel Tower."

"What do you think the man and woman were talking about with their film?" Jared asked her. "It sounded to me like they were going to shoot the film here right now."

"I do not know," she replied. "There is film to show soon for matinee, I know."

"What kind of film is it?"

"Art film, I should say," she began as she reached across the table to take his hand. "You hold me in the dark, won't you? I might frighten."

"I'll hold all of you," he smiled at her. "Just the idea of that makes me ready to get inside."

She squeezed his hand tighter, pulling him toward her.

"You sit next to me," she told him. "The film starts soon. I want you to touch me and kiss me now."

Jared dragged his chair in front of hers then gripped her thigh. She drew herself to him, wrapping her arm around his waist as she craned her neck to meet his lips. He met her mouth and slid his tongue inside. She hummed her soft moan past their kiss. As their embrace grew more animated, she pulled her dress length above her knees and lifted her leg to his lap. He helped guide her leg across him then gripped beneath her other leg until she straddled him in the chair. Without breaking their kiss, she tugged her dress higher up her thighs before she spread her legs farther apart across him. He slid his hand beneath her dress and fingered her silk panties.

Voices emerged from the direction of the gate beside the cinema street entrance. She stopped kissing him and flung one of her legs from his lap until she could place both of her feet on the patio. She held her finger to her mouth to keep him from speaking while she listened attentively to the barely audible exchange of voices. She finally lowered her finger from her mouth and stood, cupping her ear in the direction of the voices as their sound began to wane.

"We got company?" Jared whispered to her.

"Perhaps," she replied before she again sat in the chair next to him. "But perhaps not."

The voices dissipated into the muffled noise of the street. Frederique returned her gaze to him but remained seated without reaching to touch him again.

"Our film should start soon," she said. "I hope, at least."

"While we're waiting," Jared began, "I just want to know more about what we saw at Notre Dame and, now, the man and woman who are here at this theater. I presume the woman is the one who was strung up to the fake cross and whipped?"

"Oui," Frederique answered, "I do not know her. I have not met her, but the man I know quite well. He is a singer with underground band with name translated means something like the word, *Demonic Vampire*. "

"How do you know him?"

"I go with friends to hear the music," she explained. "Often performances but also their practicing at a flat near here. So much fun with so many of the beautiful people from jet set."

"So, he is something of a celebrity?"

"Oui," she replied. "But not so much besides Paris. Not yet, but maybe soon."

"What's his name?"

"He calls himself, *Camazotz*," she revealed. "It has meaning beyond music."

"Like what?"

"Ancient vampires from the Mayans, I think," she began to explain. "These Camazotz are bat-people creatures who live in world of darkness only to come out to attack their victims so that they can drink their blood and kill them."

"Why does this sound so familiar?" he asked himself aloud. "I believe somewhere along the line, I actually heard about these Camazotz, but I just can't place it."

"The Mayan, it is in their bible creation story, I think," Frederique continued. "They have ancient twins who are heroes for the world and their people. These twins make journey through the underworld for passage to lead the world from darkness, but Camazotz trap the twins in the darkest place."

"And the Camazotz bites off the head of one of the twins!" Jared suddenly exclaimed.

"Shhhhh," Lilith responded, holding her finger to her lips again to quiet him.

"One of the twins sticks his head out of their hiding place," Jared resumed quietly, "and the creature was waiting for him to stick his head out. Then...chomp. Off with his head."

"Oui," she giggled. "That tells the story, like vampire bat guillotine."

"But there's more, isn't there?" Jared asked her. "Seems to me like there was something about how the other twin was able to summon some power or other entity to actually return the head of his beheaded twin so that they could resume their journey together."

"I do not know of that," Frederique curtly replied. "I know only of the Camazotz. That is the name the singer calls himself, Camazotz Henri, and, also, that is the name of the band, Camazotz."

"From what I heard at Notre Dame," he began, "They sound a lot like some of the harsher music coming from the states right now. Do they have anything recorded?"

"They do have recorded music," she said. "But the live music is much better. Much of it is—how do you say it—performance art. The music is made for performance...theater, you say. Some of the act is playing the music, but, also, theater meaning for the fans who listen to perform the will of the music in acts to revive spirits that come alive among the people."

"You're saying it's like some kind of magic act," ventured Jared in reply, "that when the band plays, they summon some kind of presence to join them that overtakes the crowd of people like a spirit of some type."

"Oui," she confirmed. "It is very powerful and quite beautiful, I think."

"From what I heard outside of Notre Dame," Jared resumed. "Beautiful wouldn't quite be the way I'd describe their music. Sounded like some pretty hardcore thrash to me."

"And that is beautiful," she said, puckering her lips when she enunciated the beginning of *beautiful*. "Loud, fast, and hard. I like it like that. It's beautiful."

"When you put it that way," Jared began, "I suppose I must be a fan, too. Loud, fast, and hard certainly works for me."

She smiled at him as their eyes met. He raised his eyebrows toward her, then she did the same.

"I think I'm liking you too much" she told him.

"The feeling is mutual."

The oversized double-door behind them suddenly jolted open. A man wearing a maroon velour usher's coat stepped outside and addressed the two of them in French. Frederique nodded and replied, *Oui*, to the man before he returned inside, closing the door behind him.

"Five more minutes before we enter," she informed him as she took his hand.

"Doesn't look like they're will be too much of a crowd," he observed aloud, glancing around the overgrown courtyard.

"This is what you might call a private screening," she said as she interlocked her fingers with his. "Just the two of us inside the dark theater watching the art film on the screen."

"Oooh," his voice rippled. "Sounds thrilling. Let the darkness descend."

"The darkness most definitely will descend, mon chéri," she throatily said in return. "Then I will have my way with you."

"Is that what you do with all of the tourists you meet?" he asked past his grin. "Lure them with your beauty and wiles to this place, seduce them into fantasies of ecstasy with you, then rip out their hearts and eat it in front of them before they die?"

"Spoken like a true lover," she grinned in her reply. "Only I never eat the heart. I prefer to make my victims eat their own heart instead."

"Touché," he laughed. "I'll gladly eat my own heart if it means I get a taste of your flesh first. I would die happy, I should think."

"Careful how you wish," she said as she wagged her finger toward him. "You may get that for which you ask."

The garden shaded from sudden overcast. The stained glass surrounding the doorway sharpened in the dimmed light, and the bamboo leaves rustled with the arrival of a fleeting breeze.

"I believe it's time," voiced Frederique. "The spirit seems awakened, no?"

"*Oui*," Jared chimed before he scooted his chair and stood.

He stepped to Frederique and pulled out her chair for her.

"*Merci*," she thanked him then stood and straightened her dress.

"I noticed this earlier," Jared began as he pushed the chair back beneath the table, "that you don't carry a purse, handbag, or anything like that. Why?"

"It is part of my charm, you do not know this?" came her coquettish reply before she slid her arm around his waist.

"My mysterious Parisian," he cooed then put his arm around her.

The two eased through the garden to the few steps that rose between the lion statues to the ornate French door. They ascended together before Jared released her to pull open the door.

"*Merci beaucoup*," she thanked him as she entered.

Jared followed her into the darkened lobby, which was covered with tarps, flooring materials, and tools.

"Why, this place isn't even open," he blurted.

"There is renovation," she explained. "But no, it is not open to the public today. Just this private screening for the two of us."

"How could you possibly arrange all of this?" he asked her once he stopped and grabbed her arms.

"I have friends involved with this cinema," she said as she looked up to him. "They want to create atmosphere and excitement about their work here. I help to publicize their work and raise money for their cause to restore La Pagode to its past grandeur. The Camazotz band and Henri also work for this place. You see, we do the work of charity, no?"

"So, that might explain why the singer brought the American girl here," Jared deduced.

"Very much so," confirmed Frederique before she turned from him and sidestepped an assortment of tools piled in the center of the lobby. "The original theater is just this way. You will love it. This is where our private screening is performed."

"What do you mean by *original theater*, exactly?" Jared asked as he followed her.

"The renovation creates a second theater in the basement," she explained. "It is too early for its completion, but equipment is there now for filming about cinema and promotional work."

"Can we see that, too?"

"No," she answered. "The Camazotz singer Henri and his American goddess girlfriend have the place for themselves, I think."

"To do their documentary?"

"I suppose that's what they do," she replied. "I do not know really. I only know about the performance today at Notre Dame. Somehow, the two arrived here, perhaps by foot or auto or the Metro."

Frederique opened the door into the theater. She did not enter, though, but instead paused at the threshold peering inside.

"Smells kind of musty in there," Jared grimaced in his remark.

"That is part of renovation, too," she commented in return. "The grandeur of this place delights all of the senses."

Jared held the door open as Frederique entered the dank theater. The lack of light concealed the interior, but Frederique walked briskly down the aisle ahead of Jared, who staggered in his attempt to follow her.

"Don't go too fast," he requested of her. "My eyes haven't adjusted to the dark yet."

"So sorry," she said. "I am slower now."

Jared reached her and put his arm around her back, gripping her shoulder as the two continued along the aisle.

"Are we going all of the way to the front?" he asked.

"*Oui*," she answered. "I want you to experience our private screening together in a way that you will never forget it or me. I want your experience in Paris to be something that you never leave."

Frederique turned into the front row and proceeded midway down it before she stopped. Jared kept his hand on her shoulder as he shuffled his feet behind her. She turned to face him then reached up to drape her wrists over his shoulders. She pulled him down to her as she tiptoed to meet his lips. He gripped her behind, each cheek firmly in one of his hands as he massaged the tight flesh of her backside and drew her slender waist to him. He pressed himself against her, growing more engorged each time he lifted her slightly from the floor then set her down again. She withdrew her tongue from his mouth and pulled her face from him.

"You realize you're going to have fun sex for the next hour, don't you?" she panted as she leaned back, pressing herself harder against his hardening groin. "That is part of the screening."

"Sounds great," he groaned, searching for her lips again with his tongue as he met her pressure against him.

The screen in front of them suddenly exploded white, prompting both of them to disengage from their embrace and shield their eyes. Both turned toward the screen, squinting as they fought the glare. Scratching sounds followed before a pair of voices in French volleyed a grunted exchange.

"What are they saying?" Jared asked Frederique, who had now lowered her hand from her eyes and was watching the blank screen.

"One has said, *Where does this end go?*" she translated. "And the other said, *Try there*, are the words I heard."

"*Excuse moi*, Frederique," came one of the French voices before the face of the singer priest Henri appeared still framed in cleric garb. "Oh, I should speak in English for your friend and my friend here, also."

"Please do," came the voice of Baraka, who was behind him but unseen on the theater screen.

"So, you can hear us talk," Frederique almost shouted her question, "like we can hear you talk?"

"*Oui*," the man acknowledged. "But you do not have to speak so loud. The spy microphones we have in the cinema are quite sensitive."

"Is that legal?" Jared blurted. "I mean, putting devices like that in the theater when people are watching movies?"

"This is all testing for us now," Henri replied. "We want performance art. This is a technique we think the audience can...how do you say, Baraka?"

"Interact," she finished his sentence.

"*Oui!*" the man exclaimed. "Interact! It is fantastic idea, Frederique, no?"

"So much!" Frederique answered. "I love it! Do you see us like we see you?"

"No," the man returned. "This may change for future testing, but now this is window to see us only. You see us, but we do not see you."

"That's too bad," said Baraka. "I wouldn't mind the company about now."

"Why is that?" Jared nearly laughed in response to her

question.

"Because I want to make sure I can watch somebody watching me in case this French weirdo decides to whip out a chainsaw or something."

"No one is holding you against you will, are they?" Frederique quickly asked.

"No," admitted Baraka, "but I don't exactly trust Mr. Camazotz here to keep my best interest at heart."

"But, *je t'aime!*" he cried as he turned to face her from her position still shielded by his head. "We are artists, you and I. This is art for art sake, and love for the sake of our art together."

"We'll see," her sigh resonated. "I'm not sure I should even be here after the way you hit me with that whip on the cross."

"That was you?" blared Jared.

"Yes," Baraka answered, still hidden from view. "And I've got the welts and slashed flesh to prove it."

"That last one looked like the worst," Jared remarked as he winced. "Are you sure you are all right?"

"That one probably looked worse than it really was," Baraka conceded. "But it still stung like hell and drew blood beneath my panties. The other lashes really split open some skin. They've been cleaned with disinfectant, but I'm sure I'll be feeling them for a while."

"Sometime pleasure is pain," commented Henri as he turned toward Baraka and her concealed position.

"Right," Baraka scoffed at him. "Let me crack that whip across you a couple of times and see how much pleasure you get from the pain."

"Promises!" Henri blared above his laughter.

"So, what do you propose, Camazotz?" Frederique asked Henri. "My new friend and I were really hopeful to enjoy each other in the theater with the art film on the screen. But, now, I am not sure what we will be watching."

"You will see why this is so good," Henri said then turned around to face the camera again, revealing his smile. "This is *ménage à trois* of gargantuan size with Monsieur Azazel here to join us."

"I love these films," Frederique replied before she sat in her seat and motioned for Jared to sit beside her, which he did. "This will arouse us, no?"

"You will orgy from this," Henri smiled even wider. "Baraka agrees to perform for us with her Camazotz mask over her face. She will excite us with her pleasure, no?"

"I just need to see the five-thousand dollars first," voiced Baraka, "and as long as my face is never shown, I'm willing and more than able. I'll put on quite a fuckfest for our horny audience there."

"*Magnifique, ma chérie*," Henri said as he completely turned to her and stood. "But what I have is...how do you say, is bigger than bargain, maybe?"

"More than you bargained for," corrected Jared.

"*Oui!*" Henri erupted before he cackled. "Much, much more than you bargained for!"

Henri snapped his fingers then pointed out of view of the camera. Heavy footsteps thumped across the floor then stopped. Henri motioned with his hand for the other person to approach him, then the footsteps again thumped in his return to Henri, who took the briefcase handle from a hand that was twice the size of his own hand. The other man remained beyond view of the camera as Henri clicked the latch of the briefcase open.

"Five-thousand American dollars," Henri said with his back still facing the camera.

"I'd say that's quite a bargain for just an hour's worth of

work," came Baraka's voice. "Just as long as nobody I know ever knows about this. Lord knows I should've been paid this much for shit I've had some asshole pricks put me through."

"You shall soon see *Baraka:The American Goddess in Paris* tied to her cross with nothing worn but her Camazotz mask," said Henri before he snapped his fingers again and motioned for the other person to go to the other side of the room.

The heavy steps resounded again before the person paused then returned. Again, the huge hand emerged within camera view, this time holding a human-head form with wings that jutted from the side of the head. Henri took the mask from the man's hand then turned toward the camera. He sat down, holding the mask by its hair in front of his own face. The mask portrayed wide circular eyes with oversized pupils, a long, flared nose, and a mouthful of fangs. The wings were fixed in the position of ears. The black locks of hair appeared to be real hair.

"This artifact is precious," announced Henri. "There are only six surviving from ancient times. All six are the same: made with human skin of sacrifices before the rise of the Mayan in the Yucatan Peninsula. The hair is their hair, black and eternal like the hearts of all Camazotz."

"You mean I've got real human skin over my face!" Baraka protested. "I don't want this thing on my face! That's just way too creepy!"

"I say that, but the mask is just costume, not real skin," retracted Henri before he stepped from the camera view. "I purchased at costume shop. I must embellish a little, no? The story must seize minds and hearts, or else all is lost for us."

"Such panache!" Frederique proclaimed and applauded. "It speaks of ancient magic, like a resurrection of demonic spirit. Now, I am more excited to watch your film, Camazotz Henri."

"I shall now place the Camazotz mask upon our lovely Baraka," conveyed Henri. "Raise your head from the cross, *s'il vous plait*, and become one with the Camazotz."

"*Très bien*, Camazotz," Frederique commented as she seized Jared's hand and squeezed it. "We are here, and we are hungry. We want our bodies and souls to devour the rapture you offer us."

"I shall now bind Baraka's wrists to our blasphemous cross with these cursed leather straps made from the flesh of skinned martyrs," Henri announced, still beyond the view of the camera.

"Ouch," complained Baraka. "Not so tight."

"*Pardon moi*," returned Henri's voice. "Better now?"

"A little," Baraka answered.

Henri stood, turning his back to the camera before he stepped from view and revealed the nude, large-breasted Baraka, her wrists strapped to the beam of the cross upon which she lay, her feet dangling on each side of its post, and her face covered by the grotesque Camazotz mask.

"This is bondage cross of Roman design," Henri announced as he held his hand toward the cross supporting the supine Baraka. "It is the same type of cross for the crucified Jesus, only this one is...how do you say...horizontal to the floor, not upright into air. It has legs like table."

"Let's get this party started," Baraka muffled voice leaked past the mask. "My friends and I have to catch a train for Amsterdam tonight."

"Azazel is almost prepared," Henri announced, then he addressed Baraka. "You must submit yourself to us completely. Our domination of you releases the power that we worship."

"You freaks sure are giving me a lot of story material," Baraka managed to say past the mask. "But if I tell you to stop what you're doing, you better stop. Do you hear me?"

"Of course," Henri smiled in return before he lifted her legs by her knees and placed her feet on the post of the cross. "We have also applied the softest material to this cross for your comfort. We do not wish to harm you, but you must realize this: there is no pure pleasure without pain. You must let the pain become your pleasure."

"Just don't hurt me for real," Baraka replied in a voice that crackled. "And that means no whips drawing blood either."

"Please forgive me for that," Henri asked of her. "I shall restrain myself this time, but our little film here is ready to begin. Please, *ma chérie*, scream freely if you so desire. These walls are designed to keep sound within so however loudly you cry, you need not worry about anyone outside hearing you."

Henri then stepped from Baraka and returned to the camera. He repositioned the camera behind Baraka's head so that view focused upon her stomach and legs.

"Another quite beautiful actress has joined you now in the theater," Henri revealed as a naked woman with bulbous breasts and red flowing hair suddenly appeared in front of Jared and Frederique. "May I present, Lilith, and her Camazotz masks for our audience."

"How beautiful," Frederique gasped as she released Jared's hand to clap her hands repeatedly.

Jared brought his hand to the mask that the curvaceous red-haired Lilith extended in front of him then surveyed her hour-glass figure as she handed the other mask to Frederique, who immediately placed her mask over her face. Jared then donned his mask and watched the taut halves of Lilith's backside switch in her exit from the theater.

"This is all natural and part of the ritual we must recreate," informed Henri. "This enhances the full Camazotz experience. We shall also play background music from the Camazotz band, starting with the song we performed today at Notre

Dame before those police so rudely interrupted our crucifixion fun."

With their masks in place, Frederique again took Jared's hand. The two watched Henri on the screen as he welcomed Lilith into the room by handing another Camazotz mask to her. She donned the mask before Henri stripped and took another Camazotz mask that he in turn placed over his head. Lilith then took her place to the right of Baraka's feet, lifting her right foot and spreading her leg as she massaged her foot. Henri then took Baraka's other foot and spread her leg before he began to massage her other foot.

"Now, that feels good," Baraka moaned.

Frederique sprang to her feet and stood in front of Jared. The green skeletal design of her dress now glowed and pulsated. She blocked his view of the screen, and when he tried to shift her to the side so that he could see the screen, the touch of her dress shocked him to the point that he had to withdraw his hand from her.

"Azazel," Henri's voice resonated through the theater speaker system, "may I present Baraka to you. She is hereby sacrificed unto you for you to ravish and leave desolated in the name of evil."

As Azazel approached Baraka, he turned his profile slightly toward the camera, revealing that his massive hand covered the end of his enormous erection. Azazel then turned his back to the camera and positioned himself between Baraka's legs, revealing the scaly, feathered texture of his own thighs. Lilith and Henri both shifted their grips to Baraka's ankles as they fully spread her legs apart.

"Oh, my God," Baraka gasped past her mask when she lifted her head enough to see Azazel hovering over her. "You're fucking *HUGE*."

"Turn off the sound in the theater," ordered Azazel. "But leave the film running."

Azazel removed his hand from his erection to take Baraka's ankle from Henri, who then crossed the camera view in his path to the control of the theater sound system.

"Oh, no God!" Baraka cried at the sight of Azazel's fully lengthened and deformed ovipositor appendage. "What is that THING!"

"That's eighteen inches of more pain than pleasure, my dear," said Lilith. "And you're about to experience every last inch of it."

Then the theater fell silent.

ALPHA AND OMEGGA

As soon as Sirena finished reading the alternate history script, the landline phone rang. She and Uriel looked at each other as they both sprang from the sofa. The automated phone voice announced that the call was from The Institute. Uriel handed the script to Sirena then went into the kitchen to answer the phone.

"Uriel here," he said upon his return to the living room.

He motioned for Sirena to sit again on the sofa. He then sat beside her and activated the phone speaker before he set the phone on the coffee table.

"We need for you both to hear this," came the voice of Thoth.

"It's on speaker," said Sirena.

"Look," Thoth sighed, "we've been informed that there's an issue with the timing when your intervention can occur."

"What does that mean, Thoth?" Uriel asked then turned to Sirena and knotted his brow.

"It means you have to stop reading from the script right

now," came Horace's voice. "The La Pagode cinema scene of the script apparently involves an intricate technique of homeopathic magic–a ritualized incantation of sorts–performed by Lilith and Azazel that petrifies the past in such a way that it can't be altered through any time slip we can coordinate. It's creating a fourth dimensional obstruction."

"That's crazy," Sirena muttered as she looked at Uriel and shook her head.

"I know," Thoth acknowledged. "And it could very well be wrong, but our researchers here have concluded that there is a basis in historical text for this type of conversion, if you will."

"So, what do you want us to do?" asked Uriel.

"We need you to time travel right now," O. Cyrus said.

"And stop what's happening to Baraka and Jared before it's permanently too late," added Horace.

"There's only one way I know of," began Sirena, "for us to jaunt through time, and after hearing the sordid business taking place in the script, you'll have to forgive me when I say I'm just not in the mood to do what it takes for me and Uriel to time travel."

"I feel the same way," concurred Uriel.

"Understandable," Thoth said. "But you have to go do this immediately, and we do insist that you perform your own vows for your ritual of transfiguration before you read the script any further."

"I believe you understand where you need to go," remarked Horace.

"But how do we get to the *when*?" Sirena wanted to know.

"The *when* of your time slip is more problematic," Thoth began to explain. "It's not like you're going to have coordinates for place or time that you program somewhere before you two merge yourselves."

"You will both have to think of the time, place, and circumstances before you engage each other," Horace informed them.

"I really don't see how that's going to be possible," countered Sirena. "Everything that Uriel read aloud about what happened to Baraka is such a turn off for me that I think it would make me physically sick to try to engage Uriel sexually right now."

"Again," Thoth began, "that's completely understandable, but we can't stress the urgency behind this if our researchers are indeed correct."

"You see," Horace continued Thoth's thread, "the scene you are reading isn't just some depraved sexual debauchery performed by perverted entities. It's very real in its power of transfiguration about to ossify evil in the very fabric of time by rendering Baraka barren."

"You are already aware," O. Cyrus then spoke, "of the transfiguration implications as they relate to the regeneration of Enoch for his final incarnation. We have his earthly birth parents–Jared and Baraka–together in this scene, but we have them separated by the agency of Lilith, Azazel, and their two Parisian Camazotz."

"And by extension," Thoth's voice returned to resume the explanation, "defiled to the point that this ritualistic seduction leads to an altogether different type of psychogenesis, if you will."

"Wait a minute," Uriel interrupted them. "How did you know where we were at in the script?"

"*Telekiread*," Horace stated.

"*Telikiwhat?*" Sirena laughed.

"It's a technology that researchers at The Institute are developing," O. Cyrus replied matter-of-factly.

"Bullshit!" Uriel erupted. "You're bugging our house again!"

No," refuted Horace. "I can promise you that we've suspended our surveillance of you and Sirena. This really is *telekiread* at work, Uriel."

"What exactly is *telekiread*?" Sirena nearly shouted her question.

"It's simple in a way," O. Cyrus began to explain. "Your reading of the crafted text creates an energy entity that is perceptibly transmitted then received by our researchers through their artifactual equipment."

"That's just preposterous," Uriel blurted. "You're definitely bugging us again."

"How does it work exactly?" Sirena asked as she held her finger up to quiet Uriel. "I mean, is the transmission sound or thought?"

"That's a good question," replied Thoth. "It is not sound, so your concerns about a listening device are unfounded, Uriel."

"Hmmph," grunted Uriel, then Sirena wagged her finger at him to keep him from talking.

"It is telepathy in its purest communicative form," resumed Thoth. "The mental transmission emanates from the reader then travels beyond the constraints of time and space."

"In the case of your reading," Horace began, "the transmission is compounded not by the sound of your voice, Uriel, but rather by Sirena's comprehension of what you were reading."

"Her re-creation of the text in her mind," O. Cyrus jumped in, "synthesized with your own understanding of the text as you read it, Uriel."

"And that doubled the power of the transmission," added Horace, "which facilitated our reception of it through the equipment our researchers have here."

"What equipment?" blared Uriel as he extended his arms and hands in exasperation.

"It's a sophisticated, quartz-based receiver with an inverted amplifier of anti-matter," Thoth started to explain. "None of us here have the technical expertise to fully explicate the process behind how the equipment receives the signal, but suffice to say, it works like a Ouija board in a way."

"At least that's how it was explained to us," Horace qualified Thoth's statement. "It works like a Ouija board—that's actually what they decided to call the piece of equipment that processes the received signal."

"The primary difference, though," qualified O. Cyrus, "between the Ouija board that The Institute has for *telekiread* and the traditional Ouija board is that the transmission is not posed in the form of a question asked. The reading of crafted text generates an actual entity of meaning rather than having some other supposed supernatural entity reply to a question."

"I think I follow this," Sirena said, perking up in her seat as she leaned toward the phone. "You're saying that the way the content is written to convey meaning is how the entity is generated, like a packet of energy that travels without the boundaries of space or time."

"Absolutely!" Horace exclaimed. "It is no different mechanically in the way that you and Uriel are able to liberate yourselves from time and space. The real difference between how this literary meaning travels and the way you two travel is obviously that your travel entails the transmission of your entire consciousness."

"But we also physically travel, don't we?" Uriel asked.

"Yes and no," Thoth answered before he clarified his answer. "You perceive yourself physically elsewhere. That is very true."

"And you are physically perceived by others to the endpoint of your jaunt," added Horace. "That, too, is undisputable."

"You also very much affect physical components in the place you travel," O. Cyrus continued. "But your true physicality–your actual corporeal being–remains stationed at the place of your departure in a kind of suspended animation, like you are on a plane in a holding pattern circling an airport runway just waiting for the clearance to land."

"Even though for all practical purposes," Thoth resumed, "you are physically transported to a different time and place. This process is actually the same as what is referred to in the biblical accounts as *translation*."

"You mean that this is what happened to the biblical Enoch?" Uriel asked.

"Yes," confirmed Thoth. "Only Enoch has figured out much more than that, which is quite beyond us to understand at this time."

"Of course," Horace now spoke, "Enoch's transport wasn't quite actualized the same way as your transport together. It was biblically defined as an act of God, which fundamentally may be true, but it was Enoch who figured out the dynamics behind the jaunt."

"And, of course, the departure flight that Uriel and I take is quite a bit different than Enoch's because ours is triggered by our sexual interaction," Sirena remarked.

"And, this *telekiread* technique of the crafted text," Uriel began to hypothesize, "is much like the specific sexual act that Sirena and I perform together to jaunt from our present and location in a way that defies the constraints of time and space."

"Different dynamics," Thoth replied, "But, yes, very similar in the mechanism of transport."

"In the case of *telekiread*," Horace began to elaborate, "the energy entity that is released travels like a disembodied consciousness consisting of the meaning generated by the content specifically crafted to achieve that effect."

"And that content also alters or preserves," O. Cyrus interjected, "the past in this case or the future in other cases. It is remarkably relevant in this regard but quite as miraculous as the transfiguration that leads to bodily translation like you two and Enoch perform."

"Or the psychogenesis," Horace added, "that enables the incarnation to occur, like that of Enoch's final earthly manifestation."

"For our purposes here," Thoth now firmly stated, "we must remain focused upon one thing: the final incarnation of the translated Enoch through the process of psychogenesis and actual physical birth into this world via the agency of Jared and Baraka."

"And that means stopping the scene we were reading from happening," surmised Uriel aloud.

"Precisely," confirmed Thoth. "You must not read any further. You must travel back in time to save Baraka."

"Very well," Uriel said through a sigh, "tell us exactly what we need to know."

"First off," Horace began. "we need to know that you and Sirena will be able to couple properly for your own jaunt to even transpire."

"Sirena?" Uriel asked her with raised eyebrow. "You feel any better about this?"

"Actually, I do," she replied. "This is all so fascinating that I feel like I can overcome the repulsion that the cinema made me feel with the idea that what we are together, Uriel, is not only historically vital but also quite thrilling both emotionally and intellectually."

"And spiritually, if I might say so myself," Thoth added. "You both will grow stronger and even closer together with this empowering jaunt into a mission unlike any other ever known in human history."

"You'll find, we believe," Horace now spoke, "that your jaunt will land you in the very spot where you finished reading. That's means you'll be in La Pagode in Paris, just as the scene you saw unfolding was about to worsen."

"And I suppose we just have to trust you on this?" Uriel asked.

"There's mathematical modeling behind the *telekiread* theory," Horace resumed in reply, "about how you physically transport to the scene within the text. At that point, you'll experience the events as sentient beings translated into that existing past."

"The mathematical model does get a little shaky at that point," mentioned O. Cyrus.

"And exactly how are we supposed to stop the assault on Baraka?" Sirena asked as she leaned back on the sofa and looked to Uriel.

"That we do not know for sure," admitted O. Cyrus. "But we believe that the jade eggs leftover from your encounter with Azazel and Lilith might have something to do with it."

"How are we supposed to have the jade eggs with us when we consummate our time travel coupling?" asked Uriel.

"We do hate to send you into this without the answers," Thoth continued as he spread his hands apart. "We're just not sure what you can do to stop the assault or how the eggs function exactly, but all that we do know is that it is becoming more and more paramount that this particular episode of the past be altered. The jade eggs seem like they are there for a reason, just like the stone ones were."

Sirena stood. She approached Uriel and put her arm around

him. She looked up to him as he smiled down at her. She tiptoed to meet his lips for their kiss before he put his arm around her and pulled her toward him.

"I guess we'll just see what happens," Uriel said through a sigh.

"Excellent," voiced Thoth. "There is a time element to this in terms of our present here. The intervention for the alternate history version has to occur soon, but you both have an hour or so to prepare yourselves for your intercourse."

"I think we'll be just fine there," Sirena replied before she stroked Uriel's thigh.

"Yep," he added as he began to massage her neck.

Uriel and Sirena then embraced, squeezing each other harder as prolonged silence from the phone filled the room. She nestled her head against his chest, and he rested his chin on the top of her head. The two kept their hands steady in their hug before she shifted her face to meet his eyes. Her pupils seemed to enlarge within their frame of green splintered agate that gleamed with the reflected overhead light of the room. His ocean blue eyes glimmered in return as their wordless exchange instantly engorged him. She felt his arousal against her and encircled his waist with her arms as she brought her moist lips to his. The two slowly swayed as they kissed, gyrating to the frequency between them and letting it guide their bodies in their retreat from the living room to their adjacent bedroom.

"Good night, fellas," Sirena said as she and Uriel crossed the threshold to the bedroom.

"Good night," the three men replied in unison, then the door to the bedroom clicked shut.

Uriel and Sirena again kissed softly, making their way to the foot of their four-poster bed. The two paused from their kiss when he gently dipped her to the mattress, then they resumed their embrace, passionately mouthing each other until he lifted his lips from hers and slid his arms from her back so that he could stand in front of her. He extended his hands for her to take, which she did, then he guided her to stand in front of him.

"Hold out your hands with your fists closed," Uriel instructed her. "Say these words that will pulse within the core of your essence. They are words that are also mine, and I will say them as you say them so that these words become a vow that is ours alone.

"Then after each sentence, hold up one finger and press its tip to mine. Keep each tip pressed until we complete our union. The count of every word that follows will number us, and we will couple in the harmony of our divine love."

Their gaze into each other's eye penetrated them before the words suddenly flowed, and they voiced them in unison as though their thoughts were aligned and merged into one. They then pressed a fingertip together with each line of their incantation:

"EVERY SECOND of breath inside hers
    Slathers him from above.
    Her vines entwined around his mind.
    His heart engorged at the tip of her tongue.
    She is the one he is numbered by.
    She buries him alive inside hers
    At the fulcra where both now come,
    She in her ratio of raw revival,
    He in the instant he fell in love.
    He is the one she is numbered by."

· · ·

WITH THE UTTERANCE of the final word and their finger-tip-pressed hands now interlocked, they swirled into each other like some gear of gyrating flesh meshed together by churning hot blood. Her weight on his face at their opposite ends then melts them together in the exchange of body and soul that gushes its flow through both of them.

Then they are lifted and flying, faster and farther in their ecstasy until their throbbing together slows and they shake in each other's grasp, descending slowly until they softly land still coupled in their reversed embrace.

"One word by one word until we meet in our new time and place at word sixty-nine," Uriel breathes as he turns his face from her flesh. "Our love will transport us over and over again in our soulmate destiny."

"Alpha and Omega," she says to him then kisses his thigh. "Your transfiguration awaits you, my love."

They both then succumbed to the exhaustion from their coupling.

PART III

HALF DOZEN OF THE OTHER

DEVILED SERPENT EGGS

URIEL AND SIRENA REVIVED NAKED TOGETHER AT THEIR opposite ends; his erection climbing past her cheek and her drench slathered across his face. They stirred sleepily within the strange emerald glow that surrounded them until a scream jarred them from the afterglow lag of their time jaunt.

"What was that?" Uriel grumbled as they both pulled each other to their feet.

Sirena then seized Uriel's arm: "What's happening to us?"

The glowing aura that encircled them started to spin. Uriel squeezed Sirena to his chest. The glow churned faster as its force pressed them closer and tighter together until the swirling glow itself clung to their skin, whirling them around each other as its otherworldly fabric shrink-wrapped them into one.

Then a jolt split them apart from each other.

The spinning stopped.

The glow vanished.

"I'm dizzy," Sirena said then swayed into Uriel.

"Goddamnit!" he yelled as he recoiled from her.

"What's wrong?"

"You just shocked the shit out of me!"

The two stood gaping at each other. Their time travel after-glow had transformed into the clothing that they now found themselves wearing. It was the same clothing they just had read about in the scripted version of the *La Pagode* theater scene with Baraka: the identical foxfire-glow skeletal dress that Frederique had worn now gripped Sirena, and Uriel stood clad in the same priest garb worn by the Camazotz Henri. The outfits differed, though, in the egg necklaces that hung from their necks.

"Why are we wearing this?" Sirena asked Uriel as she looked down at the skeletal design that pulsed viridescent along the exposed rib cage. "And what's with these eggs around our necks?"

Uriel touched her waist, only to jerk back his hand when the glowing skeletal design stung his fingertip: "Must be some kind of protection."

"That is correct," a rickety voice ricocheted through the dim corridor. "You are wearing your authority, now that you have transported back in time to La Pagode theater in Paris. You must take the emerald green egg that hangs around your neck, Uriel."

"Who are you?" shot back Uriel.

"I am well known to you both," returned the voice, "but, please, do as I say and pull the egg from the chain and throw it toward my voice. Time is of the essence."

Uriel yanked the egg free from the chain. Sirena stepped closer to him, careful not to graze him with her glowing skeletal dress. The two of them peered closer at the emerald green jade egg within Uriel's palm.

"That's one of Enoch's eggs!" blurted Sirena. "Can this really be?"

"Yes, dear," returned the voice. "Now take the egg you're wearing."

Sirena then realized that the egg hanging from her necklace was the speckled green jade egg that also had been thrown into the downstairs room of her and Uriel's house in Maysville..

"It's the other one of Enoch's jade eggs!" she exclaimed as she pulled it free.

"Indeed," the hoarse voice confirmed. "You need to throw that down the hallway at the same time that Uriel throws his egg."

"Let's throw them, Uriel" Sirena beseeched him.

"All right," he said. "We'll throw them on the count of three."

Uriel and Sirena both cocked their arms, counted to three, then hurled their eggs toward the door at the end of the hallway. The eggs disintegrated into glowing, iridescent dust upon impact.

"Well done," the voice resumed as Enoch stepped through the cloud of rainbow dust. "You two make quite the power couple."

"It is Enoch!" gasped Sirena as she surveyed his ancient face and denim bib overalls. "But you vanished into the storm at Serpent Mound. How did the eggs we just threw get here, and what about the other eggs? I mean you, you left your eggs at that farm before you vanished, didn't you?"

"*Vanished* smacks of too much finality," Enoch smiled and nodded. "More like *translated*, which is how the two jade eggs you just threw attached to both of you, but you're right about the other eggs—I did leave them there at that farm."

"But we can reminiscence about that future happening later

if we're lucky. Right now, we have to save my earthly mother before it's too late and none of my future can happen."

Enoch then reached into one pocket of his overalls and retrieved a stone egg that he extended toward Uriel.

"This is the Camazotz egg," informed Enoch as Uriel took the egg from him. "On one side of the egg, you see the scene of the bat-like Camazotz demon about to bite off the head of one of the Hero Twins in the sacred Mayan narrative, the Popol Vuh."

Uriel and Sirena both studied the depiction on the egg before Sirena spoke: "That's exactly the same Camazotz egg I saw near Serpent Mound."

"Yes," Enoch confirmed. "And on the other side of the egg is the woman tied to a bondage cross as she is giving birth to the serpent-headed demon."

Uriel turned the egg to the other side, revealing the depiction of the horrific scene.

"As you can see," resumed Enoch, "the cross itself is a Roman crucifixion cross, only the cross is horizontal like a cruciform table surface supported by legs beneath the post. This woman is being crucified through her bondage and the birth of this unholy spawn inside of her instead of being crucified upright like Jesus."

"That's just like what we were reading from The Institute script," Sirena remarked as she and Uriel studied the hideous birthing scene on the egg. "The cross is, like you say, the same kind used to crucify Jesus, but it's horizontal to the floor, instead, and supported by table legs. It's not the X-shaped St. Andrew's cross that you normally see as bondage crosses for sexual sadism."

"So, you know about sadistic bondage crosses, do you?" Uriel asked Sirena as he looked at her with raised eyebrows.

"I did some dabbling in my time," Sirena smirked at him.

"I'll bet," said Uriel before he turned to address Enoch. "What am I supposed to do with this egg?"

"You hit the giant Nephilim creature Azazel in the Camazotz mask he is wearing," answered Enoch. "The impact will spark hellfire."

Sirena then asked: "What about me?"

"You take this," Enoch replied as he reached into another bib pocket of his overalls, revealing the translucent white jade egg and handing it to Sirena. "The demonic Lilith is also in there with Azazel. You throw your egg at the Camazotz mask covering the face of that rotten whore, and she will catch fire, too."

Enoch grabbed Uriel by the arm and ushered him down the hallway toward the door with Sirena following them.

"We're in the underground part of the theater now, where the demons hold..." but before Enoch could finish, Baraka's horrific scream detonated behind the closed door at the end of the hallway.

Enoch rushed to the door with Uriel and Sirena in pursuit, then he kicked it open:

Inside, they confronted the scaly and feathered backside of the giant figure Azazel. He concealed Baraka from their view as he straddled the post of the cross positioned horizontal to the floor. Beside him stood a naked masked woman on one side and a naked masked man on the other, each of them holding one of Baraka's legs apart by the ankles so that Azazel could maneuver himself between her spread legs.

"Unhand her, you rotten filth!" shouted Enoch.

The masked Azazel then lifted his leg over the post, turning around to face his intruders. He exposed his enormous ovipositor phallus that towered fully erect from his scaly groin. He shifted farther from the post to reveal Baraka, masked and bound to the bondage cross with her waist tied to the post and her outstretched arms strapped by the wrists to the beam of the cross.

"Oh, my God," gasped Sirena, "Baraka is the one on the egg giving birth to the demon!"

Azazel then grabbed his massive ovipositor and aimed it toward Enoch as he furiously pumped the unnatural member with his huge hands.

"Throw your egg at him now, Uriel!" yelled Enoch.

Uriel and Sirena jumped past Enoch into the room, then Uriel hurled the Camazotz egg at Azazel's masked head.

"No!" Azazel roared as the egg exploded into flames upon impact.

Azazel howled as he smacked at the mask in his attempt to knock down the flames. He stumbled into the post of the bondage cross before he staggered across the room in his flight for the exit.

"Wait, Azazel!" cried Lilith as she dropped Baraka's leg, but before Lilith could pursue him, Sirena stepped forward with the translucent jade egg in hand and hit Lilith between the eyes of her Camazotz mask.

Her mask burst into flames, sending Lilith screaming in her own escape from the room. The third abductor then backed away from the cross, easing Baraka's other leg down to dangle from the cross post before he released her. He waved his hands in surrender without attempting to escape.

"Please, do not harm me," the masked man pleaded. "I am the Camazotz Henri. We are staging theater here, but the girl is yours for free, if you like."

"Get out of here!" Enoch shouted, then the masked Henri fled the room.

"Help me," Baraka whimpered past the bat-winged Cama-zotz mask that clung to her face like flesh.

Enoch stepped to her: "You are safe now. They have not violated you, have they?"

"No," Baraka managed to voice past a sob. "Just get me out of here."

"All right, honey," Enoch tried to soothe her as he undid the strap from one of her wrists. "Everything will be fine."

Uriel stepped to Baraka's other hand and began to undo the strap from that wrist.

"Sirena," Enoch began, "I need Uriel to help me here, so you must be the one to save Jared from the Camazotz Fred-erique upstairs. Go the way the demons left. That hallway and steps at the end of it will take you to the theater."

"Be careful!" shouted Uriel as Sirena ran from the room. "I'll come to you as soon as I can!"

"You're safe now, Baraka," consoled Enoch, then he freed her face from the grip of the Camozotz mask and flung it to the floor, where it burst into flames that consumed it.

"What just happened?" she sobbed.

"You were assaulted by the demonic spawn of a fallen angel and his filthy whore," explained Enoch as he stroked Baraka's hair. "They are the Alpha and Omega of evil on this earth, but we are here to protect you so that you can fulfill your divine destiny, my dearest woman."

Enoch took Baraka by one arm and Uriel took her by the other as the pair helped her up from her position on the bondage cross. She nearly collapsed when she tried to stand but steadied within their hold.

"I think I'm going to be all right," Baraka shakily told them. "I really need to meet my friends so we can leave for Amster-dam, though. I don't want any police involved in this."

"Would you grab her clothes there?" Enoch said to Uriel as he pointed beneath the top of the cross.

Uriel reached beneath the cross and retrieved Baraka's clothes from the floor. He draped her clothes over the cross post, then he turned to Enoch.

"I have to go after Sirena."

"Go," Enoch said.

Uriel tore down the hallway to the stairs. He raced up the steps in his ascent to the theater. When he reached the partition behind the theater screen, he heard a man's voice that he presumed was Jared's:

"What do you want me to do with her?"

"Stomp her brains out," came a woman's reply, but the voice wasn't Sirena's.

Uriel careened through the corridor for the entry to the theater, realizing that Frederique was the one who had spoken.

"I can't do that," protested Jared as Uriel burst into the theater.

Sirena lay on the floor in a heap with her hair splayed across the carpet. Jared stood above her, gaping at Uriel who bolted past them to pursue Frederique as she fled from him. Uriel stopped his pursuit once Frederique disappeared past the side exit door then turned his attention to Jared.

"Hey, Father," Jared began, "I didn't do anything, and I have no idea what kind of kinky shit is going on here."

"Sit down right there," Uriel ordered Jared, who instantly complied. "And I'm not a priest."

When Sirena moaned and stirred on the floor, Uriel dropped to his knees beside her.

"Sirena!" he cried. "Are you all right?"

Sirena groaned when she lifted her face from the carpet. Uriel placed his palm beneath her cheek until she propped her elbows against the carpeted floor and rolled to her side toward him.

"I think so," Sirena mumbled then rubbed her jaw. "That bitch really belted me."

Uriel placed his arm around her waist as he caressed her cheek with his other hand.

"I don't think my jaw is broke or anything," she remarked before she shifted her weight beneath her knees in her attempt to stand. "But the back of my head must've hit the floor hard. Pull me up."

Uriel helped her to her feet then embraced her.

"Quickly," Enoch began, panting as he lurched into the theater. "Uriel must help Baraka back to her hotel. She needs to get on the train bound for Amsterdam. I'll take care of Sirena and Jared, and we'll catch up with you."

"I want to make sure Sirena is fine first," Uriel said as he knotted his brow and grazed her reddened cheek with his fingertips. "I'm not leaving her side until I know that for sure."

"She just dazed me," Sirena said, nudging him from their embrace. "I'm fine. Go do what Enoch says to do. The sooner this is all over, the sooner we can be together again at home."

"She's fine, Uriel," Enoch affirmed. "We'll meet you on the same train. We're all going to Amsterdam. I already have tickets for us, but you need to get out of here right now to help Baraka."

Enoch then reached into a bib pocket of his overalls and pulled out an envelope that he extended toward Uriel.

"Here's your train ticket," Enoch said as Uriel took the envelope, "and money in guilders, francs, and dollars. I'll have a change of clothes for both you and Sirena on the train so that neither of you have to travel in what you're wearing now."

"Good," Uriel replied then turned his attention to Sirena,

gripping her forearms as he searched her eyes. "How can you be sure you'll be all right without me?"

"I really am fine," Sirena replied, patting the underside of Uriel's forearms. "Enoch is with me now. I feel safe with him. You go take care of Baraka. Like he said, we'll meet you on the train."

Uriel lifted his eyes from Sirena to glare at Jared, who visibly shook when Uriel scowled at him.

"Listen to me," Uriel snarled at Jared. "So help me God, if anything happens to her because of you, I'll hunt you down. Do you understand me?"

"I do," Jared's voice quivered as he squirmed in his seat. "I just want to go back to my hotel now. I'm supposed to meet my friends to go to Amsterdam, too."

"Please go before you're too late, Uriel," Enoch urged him. "We might be able to meet you before we all board the train if we quickly get these two rejoined with their friends."

Uriel drew Sirena to him and kissed her. She squeezed him before he released her and hurried away from her in his return toward the lower level. When Uriel reached the basement, Baraka was propped fully clothed against the post of the bondage cross, scribbling into a small notepad.

"Sorry to interrupt you, Baraka," Uriel said. "My name is Uriel, and we need to get you on your way to Amsterdam immediately."

"I'll be putting all of this in my fanzine," Baraka told him. "Especially how this priest showed up out of nowhere to save me from my abductors, which included a giant freak with some kind of deformed horse cock."

"Sorry to say this," Uriel began," but I'm not really a priest. I'm just dressed up like one. You can call me Uriel."

"And how do you spell your name?" Sirena asked, then

Uriel grabbed her by the arm, forcing her to clutch her notepad to her chest as he pulled her along with him in his rush to leave.

When Uriel opened the door, the two of them ran up another flight of stairs until they reached a door that opened into an outside stairwell. They climbed the steps to the edge of the courtyard garden between the street and the cinema building. The two of them made their way to the iron gate, then Uriel shoved it open. Once at the sidewalk outside of the theater entry, he turned to Baraka.

"Do you know where we are going?" he asked her.

"Follow me," she said, wincing before she hobbled off into a hurried gait down the Rue de Babylone.

Uriel kept pace with her as she started to move more fluidly. He then addressed her from behind:

"I'm going on the same train with you to Amsterdam. I have to make sure that you travel safely."

"Thank you, Father," she called back to him.

Uriel opted not to repeat to her that he was not a priest as the two hustled down and across streets in their haste to reach Baraka's hotel. He silently pursued her, impressed by her agility and quickness given her recent bondage. She dodged both pedestrians and vehicles without seeming to second guess her sense of direction even once.

When they did reach their destination, Uriel once again told her that he was not really a priest, but that he was nevertheless a spiritual guide who she could trust. He told her how to spell his name, then Baraka hugged him and thanked him for his intervention. She asked him if he would accompany her to her room, also mentioning that her friend who shared the room with her might still be there, waiting for Baraka to arrive before leaving for the train station.

"I'll walk you up," Uriel replied. "Just to make sure your safe. After that, I'll wait for you outside."

Uriel followed Baraka into the hotel and up the stairs to her room on the second floor. Once Baraka unlocked the door, Uriel stepped in front of her and guided the door open as he peered into the unlit room.

"Doesn't look like anyone is here," he said then stepped aside for Baraka to enter.

"You sure you don't want to come in and wait while I get ready?" she offered. "I'd like to clean up a little before we leave for the station."

"I'd rather wait outside just to make sure there are no more surprises headed this way," Uriel told her. "I can take your bags down, if you like."

"That's all right," Baraka declined his offer. "I only have the one suitcase, and I'll need stuff out of it to get ready."

"Very well," said Uriel. "Just lock the door behind me and freshen up as quickly as you can. How much time do we have anyway before we have to catch the train?"

"Less than an hour," Baraka said as she glanced at the clock atop the nightstand. "The station isn't that far from here, though."

"That's good," replied Uriel. "I'll wait outside for you. Take your time, but just don't take too long, all right?"

"All right," she smiled at him, then he turned toward the stairs as she shut the door behind him.

Once Uriel descended the stairs and stepped outside, he tugged at the collar of the cassock he found himself wearing, wondering how much longer before he could shed his glaring garb for something more inconspicuous. He deliberated about the reason why he was dressed like a priest, only to decide that he was dressed this way to replace the Camazotz Henri who had lured Baraka into her den of perversion in the costume of a priest. Even though he was no more of a priest than the fake priest who was complicit in the attempt to destroy her destiny, he sensed that he had functioned like an actual emissary of Christian belief through his rescue of her from the torture and desecration that awaited her.

Uriel realized his role was to help Baraka restore her faith, which was a responsibility that filled him with the contradictions of his own plight to be the agent of divinity on the one hand and this adulterous homewrecker on the other, who had burdened his own family and Sirena's with the distress of their infidelity and ultimately their decision to forsake their previous lives for their soulmate destiny together.

"Perhaps this is the path to our redemption," he mumbled to himself.

Uriel instinctively turned toward the direction he had arrived. His heart pounded within him when he saw Sirena waving at him as she hurried along the sidewalk.

"Uriel!" Sirena shouted, her voice rippling with joy.

Uriel waved and smiled in return, unable to contain his elation at the sight of her as he started toward her. He noticed the tote bag that she clutched to her side, then he realized she had replaced the green glowing skeletal dress she had worn with a creamy blouse and dark brown slacks. He stopped when Sirena turned her attention from him to address the person next to her: it was Enoch, who was about to enter a neighboring hotel with Jared.

Uriel cast a glance back at Baraka's hotel. When he turned back around toward Sirena, he stood still as he watched her rush toward him. She dropped the tote to the sidewalk when she reached him and leapt into his opened arms. He kept her above the ground, twirling her as they kissed in their tight embrace.

"I'm surprised to see you this soon," Uriel said, once he pulled his lips from hers. "It sounded like we were going to meet on the train at some point."

"Enoch said I needed to join you now," Sirena told him. "Good thing I changed clothes, huh?"

"Yes," Uriel laughed in reply. "Your natural beauty is shocking enough for my poor heart as it is without an electric dress to ramp up the voltage."

The two continued their passionate embrace, merging their mouths and tongues again as Uriel returned Sirena's feet to the sidewalk.

"Get a room," a pedestrian passerby said in broken English.

"That's actually a good idea," Sirena said, once she broke their kiss. "We are in the city of love, after all."

"That's right," Uriel agreed. "It would be such a shame to travel all of this way and not make love here in Paris, wouldn't it?"

"But what about our precious Baraka cargo?" Sirena asked. "Enoch said we're supposed to travel with her. Our seats are apparently in the same compartment of the train as hers."

"What about Enoch?" Uriel posed to her.

"He's going to follow Jared and his entourage," Sirena informed him. "Apparently, Enoch bought an extra ticket beside your seat in case he needed it, and Jared's seat with his friends are in a different section than ours."

"Hopefully," Uriel sighed, "we won't have any more demonic encounters. I'm quite sure I don't want to deal with Azazel or Lilith again."

"Me either," replied Sirena. "I just want to sit beside you with your arm around me as we watch the scenery zoom by."

"I like that," Uriel said smiling. "We'll be together, *ma chérie*, and that is all that truly matters."

Baraka finally reappeared from the hotel. She spotted Sirena and Uriel and approached them, trying to smile. Sirena and Uriel unclasped each other as the young woman neared them.

"Are you okay?" Sirena asked her through a wince as she leaned toward Baraka with her arms extended.

"I'll make it," Baraka said, returning Sirena's hug. "The whip marks still sting a lot worse than the dread of that giant freak who almost assaulted me. I had no idea what I was getting myself in for, did I?"

"How could you know?" returned Sirena as she disengaged the hug between her and Baraka. "There's nothing that really can prepare somebody to face anything like this. You thought you were having fun and doing something that you could write about. Don't blame yourself for any of what happened. You were up against pure, ancient evil that tried to harm you."

"Well," Baraka began, "I suppose I know you're ultimately right about that. I feel better knowing that I was up against forces beyond my control, I guess, but I still have to blame myself for agreeing to accept money for sex. I thought it would be with the Camazotz singer. I understood they were going to film it, and I still agreed to do it because they weren't going to show my face."

"Never underestimate the power of money," Uriel told her. "They say that the love of money is the root of all evil, and I'm inclined to believe that for the most part, except when it's the sheer need for money that is the evil itself."

"I just got greedy, didn't I?" cringed Baraka. "I believe I've learned my lesson."

"There's also the power of influence," Sirena added. "Trust me, I know all about this one. We as young women—and I'll say desirous young women at that—sometimes fall under this spell that we have to sexually perform to gain the control that we often crave above all else. We know our physical appeal is an advantage for us, and it really is only natural for us to want to showcase our beauty and reap its full benefits."

"But I see now how misguided that is," Baraka remarked. "When I saw that enormous *THING* between those awful legs of that freak, I knew that everything I thought I was trying to do by basically whoring myself like that was dangerously stupid. There are much larger spiritual forces at work here in all of this, aren't there? I mean, what I saw was not of this world, was it?"

"This is Biblical stuff you're in the middle of now," replied Uriel. "And it is outright spiritual warfare that pits angels against demons, and good against evil. Never doubt that again."

Baraka covered her mouth with her hand and closed her eyes as she shook her head. Sirena reached to her, lowering Baraka's hand from her mouth, then Baraka opened her eyes to see the smiling face of Sirena beam in front of her.

"Everything is all right now," Sirena reassured her. "We just have to get you to Amsterdam in one piece so that your true destiny of happiness can unfold."

"I don't know about all of that," Baraka tried to laugh, then she turned toward the hotel entrance. "But I do know that I'm Amsterdam bound. There are my friends now, and our taxi just pulled up. They were in the other room down the hallway when you were upstairs, Uriel."

"Both Sirena and I will be on your train," Uriel told her. "We are going to spend time in Amsterdam, too, but I won't let you out of my sight for very long until I'm sure you're safe."

"I appreciate all that you've done for me," Baraka began, "but I would rather you guys don't approach me on the train. When I went to my friends' room after you left, Uriel, I didn't tell them anything about what happened at the theater. I just don't want to have to try to explain any of this to them. They just want to have fun on our trip, and so do I, if I'm still capable of having fun right now."

That's all understandable," replied Sirena. "Just know that we'll be nearby should you need us, okay?"

"Come on, Baraka!" one of her friends called to her. "We got to go!"

"I'm coming!" Baraka answered before she turned to address Uriel and Sirena. "Our train leaves from the Gare Du Nord train station. Get a cab, and you guys can follow us there."

"Here comes a taxi now," Uriel said as he stepped toward the curb and hailed the driver.

"I really do appreciate what you did for me," Baraka said to them. "You guys and that old man, whoever he was."

"You're most certainly welcome, my dear," Uriel replied with a soft smile. "But, trust me, no one is happier about the way all of this ended than that old man."

"Bye for now," Baraka said as she walked away.

When the taxi pulled to the curb, Uriel peered into the open passenger window and said, *Gare Du Nord train station*. The driver nodded then popped the trunk before he exited the taxi. He walked around to Uriel and Sirena, but Uriel held his hand out and announced in English that they had no luggage.

"*Oui, pere*," the driver acknowledged, cocking his head slightly as he studied them, then he shrugged and opened the back passenger-side door for the two of them.

Sirena ducked into the cab and scooted across the seat. Uriel lowered himself into the cab beside her. The driver shut the door and returned to the driver's side of the taxi.

"Enoch put your change of clothes in this bag," Sirena told him.

"I hope he found something a little more low-key for me to

wear," Uriel remarked before he reached into the tote that Sirena held open for him.

"Don't get too excited," Sirena chuckled, then Uriel pulled a black tee shirt from the bag and unfolded it, revealing the rendering of a giant green marijuana leaf on the front of the shirt and the logo of a bulldog on the back.

"Good God," groaned Uriel as the taxi lurched forward. "What next?"

BARAKA'S BIG BUZZ

During the hours of the train ride to Amsterdam, Uriel and Sirena dozed in and out of sleep in each other's arms as they tried to recover from their frenzied thrust into the spiritual warfare within which the two of them now found themselves entrenched. They both periodically glanced toward Baraka, who was seated at the back of their compartment.

Upon their arrival in Amsterdam, the two remained lethargic, shuffling their feet and mumbling more than talking to each other as they followed Baraka and her friends from the train. The itinerary Enoch provided for them included a reservation at a hotel near the hostel where Baraka and her friends would be staying. The note he included with the hotel information also stated for them to avoid eating any type of baked goods that strangers in the streets offered to them.

"Drugs, I suppose," Uriel remarked when he read the note. "But we're going to have to eat something somewhere. Enoch gave me enough money for that, I suppose."

"He gave me some, too," said Sirena, then she nudged Uriel

and pointed as Baraka and her three girlfriends turned a corner ahead of them.

Uriel nodded and offered the crook of his arm for Sirena to take. They followed Baraka and her friends within earshot.

"The luggage lockers should just be around the corner here," announced one of Baraka's friends.

Sirena and Uriel followed the group to the locker location but did not enter the corridor that led to the separate section. Instead, they lingered near the entrance to the storage area. Uriel leaned against the wall, wrapping his arms across Sirena's chest as he pulled her to him. She covered his arms with hers and gripped his forearms as she rested her back against his chest. The two drowsily awaited the reemergence of Baraka and her friends when Sirena's stomach loudly grumbled.

"You must be famished," Uriel said then kissed her on top of her head

"I am," she said. "You have to be hungry, too."

"I could definitely eat about now."

Baraka and her friends reappeared in the main corridor of the station. Baraka made eye contact with Sirena and Uriel without gesturing toward them. One of Baraka's friend separated herself from the group. She held her hands on her hips as she surveyed the different directions available to them for departure from the station.

"Where to, Myrtle?" one of the other young women in the group asked her.

"There's a McDonald's this way!" Myrtle exclaimed with a point in a direction she immediately pursued ahead of the pack. "Let's go there. I'm starving.

"That does sound good," Uriel whispered to Sirena. "I could use a normal everyday cheeseburger with fries about now."

"I guess that will do," Sirena muttered. "I just hope I don't wind up with heartburn."

Arm in arm, Uriel and Sirena silently followed Baraka and her friends to the nearby McDonald's. Once inside of the restaurant, they maintained their distance from Baraka, who finally did notice them behind her. She made eye contact with them, then slightly nodded before turning back around in line.

Baraka's friends chatted constantly in line and at their table once they received their food. Between mouthfuls of bites from their burgers, they detailed their itinerary for their Amsterdam excursion. The De Wallen Red Light District topped their list of discussion due to their proximity to it from the restaurant.

"We're so close to it now," said one of Baraka's friends, "that we ought to walk through it, especially since it's daylight. I'm not sure I'd want to see what was going on there once it's night, though."

"That's probably when all the live sex acts take place," Myrtle blurted, drawing laughter from the other two young woman, but not Baraka, who shakily smiled instead.

The woman then volleyed their suggestions for activities and sightseeing, which included one stop that perked the attention of Sirena enough for her to nudge Uriel with her elbow and say, "I want to go there."

That destination mentioned was the Ann Frank House.

"I suppose we could go if they go there," Uriel speculated aloud. "I'm really not sure what we should do, except for keep an eye on Baraka."

"I suppose," sighed Sirena. "But I'd still like to do something on our own together if we can."

"Maybe we can ask Enoch about it," Uriel said. "I just don't want to fail Baraka at this point. I feel like the forces we're up against are thriving in the overall wanton debauchery of this place. As beautiful and historic as Amsterdam is, I can't help but feel that true evil lurks here."

"I sense that, too,"

Once Baraka and her friends had finished their meals, they left the restaurant. Uriel and Sirena kept their distance in following the group, holding hands as they silently observed their surroundings.

"That's the oldest building in Amsterdam!" blurted one of Baraka's friends once they reached view of the Oude De Kerk church in the Red Light District.

"It says here," said another of Baraka's friends who was reading a brochure, "that this church is 800-years old."

"Do you want to go inside?" Baraka asked her friends.

"Let's go see all of the sex stuff first," replied the young woman with the brochure. "Then maybe we'll visit the church to feel a little cleaner."

Baraka forced her laughter to match that of her friends. She glanced back toward Uriel and Sirena, who now followed arm in arm at their distance. Baraka then lifted her head slightly to acknowledge that she noticed them. They both nodded in return.

"So, are we going to go inside the sex shops and dope cafés with them?" Sirena asked.

"Not unless you really want to," Uriel said. "Let's just follow them and see what they do. Sooner or later Enoch will contact us."

"How is Enoch going to manage to keep track of Jared?" Sirena asked him. "I mean, Jared will be running around with all of his guy friends. I can't imagine Enoch being able to keep up with them if Jared decides to cut loose on all the prostitution and drugs here."

"That's a good question," acknowledged Uriel. "But I would

think Jared may have underwent a change of perspective after what he witnessed in Paris. If you were an impressionable young man in your early twenties and had that happen to you, I'd think you'd be a little gun shy to try out another improvised tryst."

"Probably, but look at that," replied Sirena before she gestured to a window across the street where a prostitute in red lace lingerie stood on display with arms at hips and breasts torpedoed to the glass. "How can he resist that kind of temptation when it's made so easy and presented like it's normal and nothing is wrong with it."

"That's true," conceded Uriel. "I'm not sure that we're here to prevent Jared from having sex with an Amsterdam Red Light District prostitute, though. Probably not what Enoch would want for his future father to do, but probably not the end of the world either, as long as Jared takes the appropriate precautions."

"You men disgust me," Sirena muttered at him, twisting her arm from his. "It's all right for Jared to show up and have at it with that poor young woman over there. For all we know, she's been sex trafficked to set herself up here to prostitute herself, and even if she wasn't trafficked, she's still reduced to this deplorable state of letting herself hang out of that window for all these men pricks to pass by until one decides to pay to use her."

"I understand your point," Uriel tried to sound conciliatory. "I really am on your side, you know. I don't agree with what this place is either, but sex is offered freely and legally for sale here in a way that hopefully does take out the worst elements of what prostitution brings to the women who find themselves involved in it."

"God, look at that!" Sirena said loud enough that Uriel noticed Baraka turn ahead of them to look toward them. "Advertising live sex on a marquee! That really is disgusting, Uriel, whether it's legal and controlled or not. This whole avenue is nothing but the Champs Elyssey of carnal sin."

"I agree," Uriel said before he reached to her shoulders and pulled her to him. "That's why it might be important for Baraka to see what true love is in an environment like this. Kiss me, my eternal soulmate."

Sirena resisted at first, tossing her shoulder to dislodge Uriel's hand from it, but relented once she met his eyes.

"You know I love you more than life itself," he smiled to her. "Always have. Always will."

"I know," she smiled in return, parting her lips as he lowered his mouth to hers and the two kissed in their deepening embrace.

"Whoops," Uriel said once he disengaged their kiss. "Looks like Baraka and her buddies are on the move. Let's try not to get hit by one of these trams, what do you say?"

"Sounds like a plan," Sirena said, then she took his hand as they crossed the street together.

Uriel and Sirena maintained their distance in their effort to keep pace with Baraka's group. The bustle of the Amsterdam streets kept them alert, and the sights of the shops and cafés furnished focal points for their ongoing conversation as they continued toward the unknown destination Baraka and her friends might choose. Finally, at the urging of one of the young women, the group stopped outside of a café with a large marijuana leaf sign and a bulldog logo that matched Uriel's shirt.

"Look at that," Uriel said to Sirena, pointing to the storefront. "Just like my shirt. Guess Enoch knew what he was doing when he packed this for me."

Two of Baraka's friends entered, but Baraka and Myrtle paused at the entrance. Baraka looked at Uriel and Sirena until Myrtle pulled her by the arm into the café.

"Let's just go in and see what happens," Sirena suggested. "We'll keep our distance."

"All right," replied Uriel before the two of them walked toward the café entrance. "I just don't want you smoking any ganja while we're in there."

"Not even a little?" Sirena prodded him. "I haven't been stoned since yesterday."

"You got stoned yesterday!" Uriel feigned his shock. "And you didn't even share with me."

"Ha!" Sirena laughed. "You wish."

"You're right, I do wish," Uriel admitted. "You know how high I like to fly."

"Maybe we could buy some hash instead?" jested Sirena as she pointed to another sign below the cannabis leaf sign.

"Black Lebanese or blonde Afghani?" he joked in return as he held the door open for her.

"I'm quite sure that I wouldn't know, would I?" Sirena posed before she entered the café.

"Probably not," Uriel said, following her. "More of a European thing, I suppose."

Cannabis aroma and incense filled the café. Once inside, Uriel and Sirena stopped to watch the group of young women addressing the bartender at the counter. He explained that they should have a seat at the table and a menu would be provided for them to review.

"But we just ate," one of them protested. "We don't need a menu."

"It's not that kind of menu," Myrtle replied. "This is a menu for smoking."

Baraka nervously joined in the laughter of her friends. She then noticed that Uriel and Sirena were also in the café and nodded almost imperceptibly before she followed her friends to a table. Uriel and Sirena stepped to the bar. Uriel quietly asked the man if he and Sirena could just order coffee and sit at one of the tables on the other side of the café away from Baraka and her friends. The bartender accommodated their request and pointed toward a smaller round table in the corner of the room for them to take.

As Uriel and Sirena walked toward their table, they were startled by the sudden exclamation from Baraka:

"No way!" she blared as she held up a flyer that had been placed on the table. "The Violet Phlegm are playing here tonight!"

"Oh, God, Baraka," Myrtle bellowed. "Don't drag us out tonight to go see them. We have tickets in London to see them already."

"But they're such a great band!" boomed Baraka's voice. "It's incredible that they're even here! I obviously knew they were playing in London next Saturday, but for them to be here, too. I can't hardly believe it. I didn't see any kind of notice about it."

"Let's see what else is going on," said one of Baraka's other friends. "I wouldn't mind seeing them now and later in London, but there might be other stuff here that we want to do instead."

"All right," Baraka relented. "But I'm going to go see them tonight. This would be perfect material for my fanzine. I mean, here we are, and my favorite band is playing a surprise gig in Amsterdam! That's just insane."

"So, we're your favorite band," came the voice of a man with his back to them at a nearby table. "That's good to know."

Baraka turned to face the man, but he did not turn around. Instead, he inhaled from a small pipe, setting adrift striations of smoke that wafted above him.

"What do you mean by *we* exactly?" Baraka asked before

she loudly scooted her chair from the table to half turn around toward the man.

"What I mean is," the man began as he did the same with his chair and met Baraka's stare. "that I am in the Violet Phlegm band."

"Oh, my God!" Baraka yelped before she brought her hands to her face. "You're the sax player, Steve Mackay!"

"Yours truly," the man said then extended the pipe for her to take.

Baraka declined the offer with a wave of her hand but continued to address the man: "I can't believe Violet Phlegm is playing here tonight. I'm set for London but had no idea about here."

"We go on at eight at the Milky Way," the man informed her, then he toked the pipe.

"Is that far from here?" Baraka asked him then waited for him to blow the smoke through his nose.

"Just down the way," he said. "You can ask anyone. They all know where it is."

"Hey," Baraka began as she fingered through her handbag, "I do a fanzine about alternative music and musicians called, *Baraka's Big Buzz*, and I'd absolutely love to pop a few quotes from you. Not a lot of bands have sax players, obviously, and your stuff is just crazy huge."

"Wow," he chuckled, "not sure I've ever been called *crazy huge* before. Sure, I'd be honored. I'm guessing that you're Baraka."

"She is," blurted Myrtle. "And she likes to detail some of her sexcapades in her fanzine, too."

"Shut up, Myrtle!" Baraka blasted her friend.

"If it's sexcapades you're after," the musician began, "then Amsterdam is definitely the place for you. I'm almost afraid to walk out of the door here. There's so much that's just right up in your face here that it's really quite overwhelming."

"I'm really not interested in sex," Baraka countered before she waved her hand toward her friend. "I mean, the fanzine is about music and the experiences that come with it. My friends just don't always get it."

"Hey!" Myrtle protested above the laughter of the other two at the table. "I do too *get* sex."

"I see," the man said before he stood and stepped to the table, offering the pipe to Myrtle.

"Thanks," Myrtle said then took the pipe.

"You know," the musician began as he returned to his seat and addressed Baraka," I can probably arrange for you to meet the band after the show. Last I heard, they were planning on sticking around the Milky Way just to chill out for the night before we all have to hit the road again tomorrow."

"That would be killer," Baraka flashed her smile at him as she tossed her wavy hair to the side. "I would love to do interviews with them."

"The Milky Way is a small place," the man remarked. "It might get a little tight if the floor gets full but make sure to ease your way up to the stage toward the end of the show."

"Most definitely," she smiled at him. "While I have you here, maybe you could answer a question for me."

"Shoot," he said as he stood and stepped toward the table to take the pipe from one of Baraka's friends, who was passing it back to him.

"Like I mentioned," Baraka began, "you don't often find a sax player in a band that plays any kind of alternative music, really, especially one that kind of tests the boundaries between punk, folk, jazz, and rock like the Violet Phlegm do."

"That's true," he remarked then inhaled from the pipe.

"So, my question is," she resumed, "how did the Violet Phlegm find you and what was it about them that drew you to play for them."

"I saw them early on back in the states," he began then clanked the ash from the pipe into an ashtray at his table. "I dug what they were doing. Hard not to, you know? Nobody else really has that weird blend of electric guitar, standup acoustic bass, and fan-brushed drums."

"Right," agreed Baraka. "I don't think anyone else sounds at all like them. They really do produce a unique sound."

"Of course," the man resumed, "there's an ongoing mix of different instruments–like my sax–and I think that's the thing that keeps them fresh and creative, you know. They like the experimentation to see where the fusion of sounds takes them."

"How are your sax parts conceived?" she asked him as the bartender arrived to hand menus to Baraka and her friends.

"They just let me free flow jam with them on certain songs," he explained. "Most of the time, one of them will tell me they hear a sax at a certain point in a song they're working on, and I'll sit in with them on those songs and kind of blend in to what I think they're doing."

"Cool," she said before she glanced at the menu.

"I would recommend the East Indies sinsemilia," he suggested to Baraka. "That's what your friends just smoked."

"I'm actually good," she replied then set the menu on the table.

"I want hash," Myrtle announced.

"Then I'd recommend the black Lebanese," he smiled when he addressed Myrtle. "It's quite the buzz."

"Oh, thanks," Myrtle smiled in reply as she met his gaze. "And thanks, too, for sharing your pipe with us."

"Any time," he replied before he turned his eyes from hers to take the glass of beer on his table.

Baraka returned to her notepad to write. The musician sipped his beer before he leaned toward her and peered at the notepad.

"So, what did you decide to write?" he asked her.

"I'm writing about what a gentleman you are," she said without looking up. "I mean, here we are–four chicks from the states–just hanging out in an Amsterdam café with Violet Phlegm sax player Steve Mackay who is gracious enough to share his weed and thoughts with us."

The bartender returned to take the order from Baraka's group. The three women discussed their options without input from Baraka, who continued to write in her notepad while the sax player leaned toward her. Finally, Myrtle told the others to put down their menus because they were ready to place their order.

"Is a gram enough for all of us to smoke right here?" Myrtle asked the bartender.

"I think so," he replied with Dutch accent. "If you want more, we have more."

"Then give us a gram of the black Lebanese, please," she requested as she batted her eyes at him.

"Certainly," the bartender said before he left the table.

"How long will you ladies be here?" the musician asked Baraka.

"We're just here two nights," Baraka answered without pause in her writing. "Then we're off to London."

"That's cool," he remarked. "I'm going to have to meet up with the band here in a few, but I'll be sure to tell them about you."

"I appreciate it," Baraka said as she finally tore herself from her notepad to look up at him.

"Do you ladies have a pipe to smoke your hash in?" he asked them as he scooted his chair from the table and stood.

"No," came the consensus answer from the trio.

"Here's an extra one you can have," he said then set the pipe in front of them on the table. "There's a screen in it. Just light your chunk on fire then blow out the flame before you toke the hash. You ladies have fun in Amsterdam. Hope to see you all tonight at the show."

"Bye," Myrtle said first before the others joined in.

"You'll definitely see me there," Baraka declared as she stood and held her hand for him to shake. "I'm really excited about the show. Thanks so much for talking with me here."

"Your welcome, Baraka," he smiled at her as he shook her hand. "I think it's cool what you're doing."

"Thanks," she replied once they released their handshake.

Baraka remained standing. The sax player nodded his head on his way to the exit at the front of the café. She peered down at her friends at the table then looked toward Sirena and Uriel at the other end of the room. She turned toward a television in the front of the café beside the exit. Once the musician had left the café, she motioned with her head for Sirena and Uriel to meet her by the TV. As she walked away from the table, Myrtle asked her where she was going.

"I just want to see what's on the TV up there," Baraka said pointing to it.

"Just make sure you come back to smoke with us," Myrtle said. "We all have to get tore up together."

"Okay," Baraka said before she continued to the front of the café.

Sirena and Uriel followed her to the sitting area at the café entrance where the wide-screen television hovered. Baraka stood in front of the screen, then Sirena and Uriel came to her side. All three watched and listened to the video, which features a band performing with a lead singer who suddenly pulled down his pants to expose himself while he sang.

"That's *The Boobs*," Baraka informed them. "No better way to get welcomed to Amsterdam than with the flopping penis of a clearly deranged lead singer, I suppose."

"You really don't have to stay here like this," Uriel told her. "We can arrange for you to meet with Jared, who is supposed to fulfill your destiny and vice versa. Everything would probably be a lot easier that way."

"I don't know anything about this *Jared* guy," Baraka began. "But I've been thinking about what happened in Paris, and I'm not sure I want to have the future mapped out for me to avoid things, even if that choice puts me in real danger like I was in back there. Living too safe makes everything seem so robotic and manufactured without any poetry, I guess."

"Poetry?" balked Sirena. "Trust me, there's poetry involved. Without poetry, Uriel and I wouldn't be here at all. It's poetry that binds me with him. If it's poetry you want, you'll have to author it yourself. We know that you are a talented creative. You find that your true being can expand within the parameters that destiny sets."

"And if I refuse to comply?" Baraka posed, still focused upon the television screen with the singer parading around exposed on stage.

"We really don't know the answer to the question for sure," Uriel admitted. "But we have seen an episode of yours in the future. It was not very pretty and definitely a fate worse than death, something I can assure you that you would like to avoid."

"Tell me about it," she started to say then changed her mind. "No. Wait. I don't want to know what my future is. I want it to unravel however organically it must. It should be spontaneous and self-fulfilling, not a contrived alternative to doom, or whatever, that is rendered out of fear."

"We do appreciate your independence," Sirena remarked. "It is admirable and certainly a strength of yours. However, the forces all of us are up against are brutal and cunning. They are truly demonic. You may think that some free-flowing future can happen by the seat of the pants, but not in your case and not by your pants."

"She's right," concurred Uriel. "The future may reveal itself more fluidly for others but not you because the significance of your fate marks you as a target for evil forces. They want to stop you from fulfilling your destiny because of the threat you and Jared represent to their control over this world."

"I'm still going to do the things I want to do," Baraka replied, scowling as she turned to them. "I will not live my life in fear. Besides, I don't know who in the hell this *Jared* is that you keep mentioning."

"You don't know him yet, at least," Sirena said. "But you will. You must."

"What?" Baraka barked back at Sirena before her friends summoned her to rejoin them at the table. "I've got to go now. I'm going to a concert tonight at eight o'clock at a place called the 'Milky Way' to see the band, the Violet Phlegm."

"Sounds colorful," quipped Sirena.

"They are," Baraka glared at her before she turned from the pair in her return to the table with her friends.

Sirena and Uriel remained standing below the television until Uriel motioned for her to take a seat at the two-top table nearest them. He pulled out the chair for her. She sat down, then he sat beside her, propping his forearms against the table edge.

"What do you think we should do?" Uriel asked.

"What can we do?" Sirena answered with a question of her own.

"I really don't know," Uriel sighed before he rubbed his eyes. "It seems like the longer we wait to unite Baraka and Jared, the more she will pull away from the idea based upon her belief in the future, regardless of how misdirected it is."

"If only she could see the footage of herself in the future that we saw," Sirena remarked. "That would change her mind."

"That would," agreed Uriel. "Not sure how to pull that off, though. I mean, here we are now, and that footage is in the distant future. Just trying to describe it to her without actual video to corroborate our depiction of events is likely to just drive her farther away from us."

Sirena and Uriel both turned their attention to Baraka, who took the pipe from Myrtle and laughed, then she put her lips to it and drew hashish smoke. She puffed out her cheeks in her suppression of the cough that audibly churned in her throat. She then passed the pipe back to Myrtle before she blew a cloud of smoke across the table. The young women all laughed before Baraka turned toward Sirena and Uriel to flash an upturned eyebrow that smacked of disdain and rebellion.

"Even after what she went through in Paris at La Pagode," Sirena muttered. "She was almost torn apart by Azazel. Now, she's ready to put herself out there on another limb. I just wonder what the other side is planning.

"Surely, torching the Camazotz masks of those perverse predators with Enoch's eggs won't stop them from revealing themselves again here, will it?"

"I would guess that there's much more in store," Uriel sighed before he turned from Baraka and her friends to glance out the window below the television. "And I'd say it's coming sooner rather than later."

Uriel gaped at the sight of a tram passing by with an older man and younger one seated together. He squinted as he watched their faces passing by, then the older man motioned for him to follow them. He was sure that the two were Enoch and Jared.

"There they just went!" he exclaimed, which prompted a shush from Sirena as she gripped his forearm. "That was Enoch and Jared in that tram, and Enoch wants us to follow them."

"But what about Baraka?" implored Sirena. "I'm not going to stay here without you, Uriel."

"No," agreed Uriel. "I don't want you to leave my side. We'll go after Enoch together. Why would he wave for us to go after him if he didn't think it was all right for us to leave?"

"But what about Baraka?" Sirena again implored in her whisper. "We can't just turn her loose, can we?"

"We know where she'll be tonight at eight o'clock, don't we?" countered Uriel.

"We do," Sirena perked up. "She'll be at the Milky Way listening to that Violet Phlegm band, right?"

"That sure sounded like the plan to me," Uriel added. "But I think we should get out of here and chase that tram down.

"Enoch wants something."

AMSTERDAMNATION

URIEL SPRANG TO HIS FEET, GRABBING SIRENA'S ARM. He pulled her along as he scrambled for the exit. Once he flung open the door, he took Sirena's hand in his and trotted off at a jog.

"You're going to have to keep up with me," he told Sirena. "I assume they're headed to Jared's hotel, but I don't know that."

"Where were Jared's friends?" Sirena panted her question as she struggled to keep up with him.

"I don't know," Uriel replied. "I didn't notice if they were all on the tram or if it was just Enoch and Jared."

Uriel led Sirena on their chase through the streets of Amsterdam. He maintained visual contact with the tram throughout and finally slowed once he saw Enoch (still clad in his bib overalls) and Jared (along with his friends) disembark from the tram. Jared and his friends traveled in one direction after that and Enoch in the other. Uriel led Sirena across the street then stopped between Jared's group and Enoch.

"We should tell Enoch what's happening," Uriel said then ushered Sirena in that direction.

Enoch ambled along the sidewalk to a hotel entrance. Before Enoch reached the door to the hotel, Uriel shouted his name. Enoch turned and waved for Uriel and Sirena to come to him, which they did. Uriel held his hand out for Enoch to shake.

"Thank God you made it," Sirena sighed. "We were wondering what we should do."

"Where's Baraka?" asked Enoch as he disengaged the handshake between himself and Uriel.

"She's in a café with her friends not too far from here," informed Uriel.

"It's not a good idea to leave her on her own," Enoch stated, positioning his thumbs beneath his overall suspenders. "She's a real wild child."

"Then why did you wave for us to follow you?" asked Uriel.

"I didn't wave at you," Enoch replied.

"Yes, you did," insisted Uriel.

"I didn't even know you saw me," Enoch said then removed his thumbs from beneath his suspenders. "Maybe that's when I was swatting at a fly in the tram."

"Should we go back to Baraka, then?" Sirena asked. "I'm sure she's still at the café."

"Yes," advised Enoch. "You really should stay within eye contact with her at all times. She's very vulnerable right now, and, as you have seen, the forces in pursuit of her are depravity personified."

"What are you going to do?" Uriel asked him.

"I'll stay on the trail of young Jared," Enoch replied. "This is our hotel. I've made reservations for all of us here. The hostel where Jared and his group are staying is down the street. It also happens to be the same place where Baraka and her friends are staying. Hard to believe they didn't somehow bump into each other in the past when they were this close to each other."

"When are we supposed to sleep?" Sirena asked. "I've noticed that our time travel ability does nothing to curtail our need for sleep."

"I think that once we are sure," Enoch began, "that Jared and Baraka are tucked in safely at the hostel down the street, we can all get some shut eye. Until then, we have to maintain constant vigilance or else suffer potentially devastating consequences, not just for me, but for all of humanity in the future."

"Geez," muttered Sirena, "You're really putting a lot of pressure on us."

"Well," Enoch began with outstretched arms. "You two are the only ones who can do this. It's either you or no one."

"We understand, Enoch," Uriel said as he placed his arm around Sirena. "She just gets a little cranky when she's tired."

Sirena smacked his chest then smiled toward Enoch.

"I know how important this is," she emphasized with a nod.

"Go then," Enoch waved them off. "Protect Baraka, especially from herself. I'll take care of Jared."

Uriel nodded then escorted Sirena back toward the café where they left Baraka. The two held hands as they walked briskly, pausing occasionally to regain their bearings and remember the direction they should take. Finally, the pair reached the café and reentered only to find the group of Baraka's friends still seated at the table but without Baraka.

"Do you see her anywhere?" Uriel whispered to Sirena as the bartender nodded toward them.

"I don't," replied Sirena. "I'll check the restroom for her. Get us a seat."

Uriel released Sirena as she stepped to the bar to ask the bartender where the restroom was located. He pointed toward the back of the building before he turned to nod and smile at Uriel, who pointed toward the table for two at the front of the café. The bartender tipped his hand in a gesture asking if Uriel wanted a drink, but Uriel shook his head no. Uriel sat then waited. After a couple of minutes, Sirena returned, shaking her head as she approached Uriel.

"No Baraka," she informed him.

"Where could she be?" Uriel asked.

"I have no idea," replied Sirena. "But we're going to have to find out. We're going to have to ask her friends where she went."

"But what do we say?" Uriel asked as he rubbed his chin.

"I have no idea," she sighed. "This whole thing is getting complicated fast."

"I know," Uriel said, lowering his hands. "How about this? I can say I heard that the sax player from the Violet Phlegm mentioned she was in here. What was the name she called her fanzine?"

"*Baraka's Big Buzz*, I believe," answered Sirena.

"Yes," remembered Uriel. "That was it. So, I'll go up to them and say that I'm a friend of the sax player's and I was hoping to talk to Baraka about the band."

"Maybe you could say you're a roadie or something," suggested Sirena.

"I don't know about that," Uriel said. "Roadie might be a little too sketchy for them to tell me anything. Maybe I should introduce myself as their publicist."

"But that's not going to work either," countered Sirena. "They'll recognize you from being in here earlier. They'll wonder why you didn't say anything then."

"You're right," groaned Uriel. "How about this, then: we caught up with the sax player on the tram and started talking. He mentioned the Violet Phlegm show and Baraka's fanzine.

We mentioned that we are publicists for the Milky Way where the concert is being held and would like to invite Baraka to a pre-concert party at the venue?"

"That's sounds much more...inviting," Sirena confirmed. "And plausible."

"That's it then," Uriel said as he scooted back the chair and stood. "Maybe you should come with me. That way we're even more believable."

"I'll come," Sirena replied before she also stood. "But you do the talking. I never was very good about trying to keep stories straight."

Uriel held his arm for her to take. She locked her arm into the crook of his and the two of them walked to Baraka's friends. Once the pair reached the group, Uriel spoke.

"Pardon me," he began, "But there was a young lady named Baraka who was here earlier. We're wondering where we might find her."

"Wow," Myrtle blurted in reply as she spun around to face Uriel and Sirena. "Baraka sure is the most popular girl in school today."

The two other young women guffawed at this remark, slapping each other on the arms as their laughter continued without abatement.

"We ran into the saxophone player from the Violet Phlegm," Uriel continued, now directly addressing Myrtle. "He mentioned she produces her own fanzine that covers alternative music. My wife and I are publicists for the Milky Way venue where the Violet Phlegm concert will be held tonight. We were hoping to invite her to a party before the concert at the club so that she can interview the Milky Way manager and maybe even a couple of musicians from other bands."

"Can we come, too?" one of the other women blurted before both returned to their giggling laughter.

"Absolutely," smiled Sirena. "But we really need to talk with Baraka first."

"Why is it so important to talk to her now?" asked Myrtle.

Sirena began to speak but stopped and turned toward Uriel, who removed his arm from Sirena's and extended his hand for Myrtle to shake.

"I'm Uriel," he introduced himself as Myrtle took his hand. "And my much better half is Sirena."

"Myrtle," Baraka's friend replied. "Pleased to meet you both."

"We're stoned," babbled one of the other women at the table before both of them erupted into laughter.

"Don't mind them," Myrtle said with a wave of her hand. "I have to say, though, I find it really weird that we get here in Amsterdam and all of the sudden everybody wants a piece of Baraka."

"What do you mean by *everybody*?" Uriel asked her.

"Well," began Myrtle, "there's you two, of course, but there's also the saxophone player and the other dude with his chick who both beelined straight for Baraka after we started getting high."

"Other musicians, perhaps?" posed Sirena.

"That's what's making this seem even weirder to me," Myrtle began as she rubbed her eyes. "They said they were the exact same type of people as you–music publicists."

"What!" shouted Uriel. "That's impossible! They're impostors then."

"No," Myrtle began to clarify as she lowered her hands from her eyes. "They didn't say your names. They said other names, and they said that they were publicists for a different place–the Paradiso–I think the woman called it. Something like that."

"What were their names?" pursued Sirena.

"The chick's name was Lilith," revealed Myrtle. "And the dude had a name like Azzmazazz or some foreign junk like that."

"Azazel," gasped Uriel.

"Yeah," Myrtle said with a snap of her fingers. "That's exactly what his name way. Huge giant of a dude. Biggest guy I think I've ever seen up close, actually."

"They're actually competitors of ours from the other big music venue here in Amsterdam," Sirena lied. "We're all good friends, though."

"Any idea where they were headed?" Uriel asked. "Maybe we can catch up with them."

"They wanted to take Baraka to meet some people at a place near the Moulin Rouge, I think they said," revealed Myrtle. "Supposed to be across the canal from the big church up the street from here. They literally left like two minutes before you two showed up. The chick told us to head up there when we finish here."

"Good," Uriel said as he grabbed Sirena by the arm. "Maybe we can catch up."

"Thanks, Myrtle," Sirena managed to say before Uriel whisked her away in their hurried exit from the café.

Once Uriel and Sirena hit the sidewalk, they ran side by side toward the towering Oude Kerk church until Sirena started to lag behind him, still gripping his hand.

"We have to go faster," Uriel urged Sirena.

"I'm running as fast as I can," she panted.

Uriel led the way across the canal before the two encountered gathering foot traffic. They finally slowed to a fast walk as they weaved their way among the pedestrians.

"Look, Uriel!" Sirena pointed and yelled as she halted, jerking Uriel's hand to prompt him to heed her.

Uriel stopped, turning to look in the direction Sirena pointed and noticed the sight that had caught her attention: a woman was struggling to resist the advance of a large man and a red-haired woman trying to secure their victim by her arms.

"Oh, my God, it's Baraka," voiced Uriel. "And the demons!"

When Baraka screamed, Uriel bolted toward her with Sirena behind him.

"Let her go!" yelled Uriel.

Azazel and Lilith turned toward Uriel and Sirena.

"She must not have recognized them because of the masks!" shrieked Sirena.

As Uriel and Sirena both bolted into a sprint, Azazel lifted Baraka and flung her over his shoulder. Lilith sprang to the door at the building beside them and pushed it open. She held the door for Azazel to enter with Baraka flailing in her attempt to escape. Lilith then slammed the door shut.

Once Uriel and Sirena reached the building entrance, a familiar voice prompted them to turn around. Enoch–still dressed in his bib overalls–motioned for Jared to cross the street with him before he waved to Uriel and Sirena.

"Enoch!" they both exclaimed.

"We had better hurry," Enoch said once he reached the sidewalk. "They won't waste any time defiling her."

Uriel ran to the door and tried to turn its knob.

"It's locked," he informed them.

"Try to kick the door in, Jared," Enoch said.

Jared took a running leap at the door and kicked its center

but was knocked backwards to the sidewalk without the door budging.

"We've got to get in there fast," Enoch said before he pulled Jared up by his arm. "Quickly, go around the side and find another way in."

Uriel led the way down the alley beside the building. A stairwell descended to the foundation, leading to an underground door with an unlit neon sign that read "LIVE SEX" above it.

"Oh, no," Sirena gasped when she saw it. "We've got to get in there right now."

Uriel descended the steps with the others behind him. He reached the door but could not open it. He rammed his shoulder into it repeatedly without budging the door. A voice yelling in a foreign language then boomed from the building interior before the door flung open.

A large mustachioed man wearing a turtleneck sweater emerged into the stairwell with his hands clenched into fists. Uriel stood to face him, but Enoch stepped between the two.

"We want to come inside and watch the show that's about to go on," Enoch told the man, extending a wad of currency for him to take.

"Come inside," the man said in English as he took the money.

The group filed in behind Enoch, then the man shut the door behind them.

"Wait," he told them before he moved past them to walk ahead of them. "Follow me."

The group followed the man up steps to a large furnished room without anyone present. When the man stepped to a bar at the far corner of the room, Enoch pursued him and tapped him on the shoulder before he reached the telephone situated on the bar.

"I hear there's quite a show about to go on," Enoch said, smiling at the man.

"I'm not sure," the man replied before he motioned for the others to enter the room. "Please sit so I can find out what is happening now. I heard the people come in, and they went straight to the upstairs club, but no one told me about any of this."

"That's where we were told to go," Enoch lied to the man before he pointed to the staircase on the other side of the room. "Is it up the stairs this way?"

"Yes," the man answered. "But the sex acts for the public are usually done in the basement club, not upstairs."

"They said this was more of a VIP thing," Enoch lied again before he sprung toward the steps, motioning for the others to follow him.

"Wait!" the man hollered. "I must ask the owner what is happening here first!"

Enoch and the others did not heed the man, who took the telephone from its base instead of pursuing the group up the steps. Before they reached the top of the stairs, Baraka's scream resounded from an interior room down the hallway.

"Hurry!" Uriel shouted as he elbowed his way past the others toward the room from which the scream came.

Uriel seized the door knob but could not turn it. He then slammed his shoulder into the door before Baraka screamed again.

"Hold on!" the mustachioed man yelled as he ran up the steps. "Do not break the door down!"

"We paid good money to see this!" Enoch feigned his anger

at the man, who scowled at the group as he passed them to reach the locked door.

"I know that!" snapped the man as he retrieved a set of keys from his pocket. "I can't contact the owner, so I will let you enter.'

The man then keyed the door knob lock first and the deadbolt second. Once he flung open the door, he stepped back and gaped at what he saw.

"What is this?" he gasped as he back pedaled from the threshold.

"Jared and I must enter first!" Enoch yelled as he elbowed his way into the room then retrieved two eggs from the bib pocket of his overalls.

Enoch handed the stone egg to Jared and kept the jade egg as the two entered the room ahead of the group.

"What are you doing?" Uriel shouted his question as the entire group entered the room to see a scene similar to the rescue of Baraka in Paris.

Baraka lay naked, limp, gagged, and strapped to a Latin cross positioned horizontally above the floor. Lilith held one of Baraka legs to the side by her ankle and Azazel held the other as he hovered over her, straddling the post of the cross.

"Get out of here!" Azazel yelled as he stepped over the post and turned toward the trio, revealing the engorged ovipositor towering erect from his scaly and feathered groin.

"Throw your egg at him, Jared!" commanded Enoch.

Jared instantly slung the stone egg at Azazel, whose chest burst into flames upon the egg's impact. Azazel screamed and smacked his chest to extinguish the flames. Lilith lunged at Jared, who sidestepped her advance just as Enoch threw a jade egg that ignited her hair upon impact.

Uriel pulled Sirena out of the way as Azazel and Lilith

lurched past them, screaming in their flight from the room. The couple crashed into the man at the threshold, knocking him over in their escape. Uriel released Sirena and started after Azazel and Lilith until Enoch yelled for him to stop and help free Baraka from the cross.

"That's too close a call," Enoch remarked as he unstrapped one of Baraka's wrists from the cross beam. "I just hope the third time isn't their charm if there is a third time, which I pray there isn't."

"I know what you mean," said Uriel before he unstrapped Baraka's other wrist.

Jared approached Baraka and removed her panties from her mouth. He gently lifted the back of her head from the cross post and cradled her neck. As he stroked her hair with his other hand, she opened her eyes and steadied them upon him.

"Hi, Baraka," he whispered his greeting. "I'm Jared. You're safe now."

"So, you're Jared." sputtered Baraka's faint voice.

"Let's sit her up, gentlemen," Sirena said then helped guide Baraka's legs to the floor. "We need to get her dressed and get her out of here."

Once Baraka was upright, she covered her breasts with her arms.

"Time for you guys to leave the room," Sirena told them. "I'll help her dress."

"We'll be right outside the door if you need us for any reason," Uriel told her before he stroked Sirena's arm on his way past her.

"Okay," said Sirena. "Just leave the door cracked open a little when you leave."

Enoch and Jared followed Uriel from the room. The three

of them watched the man stumble down the stairway when they stepped into the hallway.

"Do you think she is all right?" Uriel asked Enoch.

"I think she just fainted," Enoch replied. "She seems to be intact."

"So, she is my Baraka," Jared sought confirmation from Enoch. "My beautiful soulmate on this earth."

"Yes, indeed," Enoch said, smiling at the sight of Jared peering past the ajar door.

"I'm just so glad we weren't too late," commented Uriel.

"I bet I'm even gladder about that," Enoch chuckled gruffly. "We were just lucky to all show up here at the same time."

"How did you know to come here?" Uriel knotted his brow when he asked Enoch.

"I didn't," claimed Enoch. "After you tracked me down, I decided to get Jared and head toward the café where you said Baraka and her friends were. I wanted to introduce the two of them. We were on our way there when we stumbled upon you here. We really were just that lucky."

"But you had the eggs?" pursued Uriel. "Why, and which ones did you have?"

"Somehow, I ended up with the stone egg of Enoch and the Olmec Blue jade egg in my possession after my time jaunt," Enoch explained. "It just dawned upon me to use them when we ran into the trouble here."

"You mean the egg of Enoch," Uriel began his question, "that depicted your parents at this age on the other side?"

"Eggs-actly!" quipped Enoch. "When I showed the egg to Jared, he nearly passed out. He couldn't believe that the egg portrayed him exactly how he appears right at this moment in time. Now that he has seen Baraka for himself, he is a believer in their destiny."

"And you two threw the eggs," Uriel surmised, "that actualized their destiny together?"

"Yes," confirmed Enoch. "Jared threw my egg with him and Baraka depicted on it at Azazel, and I threw the protective Olmec Blue jade egg to ward off Lilith."

"And the rest is history, as they say," Uriel smiled at Enoch before he reached out to shake the old man's hand.

"It's looking that way," Enoch said, then he gripped Uriel's hand and met his eyes. "I do appreciate what you've done for me."

Enoch and Uriel released their handshake when Sirena opened the door for the clothed Baraka to enter the hallway. Jared immediately went to her with his arms outstretched. She met his embrace and found his lips when he brought his to hers.

"You and I are destined to be together." Jared said to her once he pulled his lips from hers.

"That's what I keep hearing," came Baraka's groggy reply past her wisp of a smile.

"What exactly have you heard about me?" Jared replied before he blushed.

"That we're soulmates destined to be together," answered Baraka as she searched his eyes for the truth in her statement. "That we will live important lives together."

"Yes," he proclaimed. "I am that Jared. I am your Jared."

The two buried their faces into each other as they again embraced.

"Does this mean our work is done here?" Sirena asked Enoch. "You know, Uriel and I didn't get the chance to enjoy each other's company in the City of Love. Maybe we can do some sightseeing in Sin City while we're here?"

"I don't see why not," Enoch laughed. "After everything you two have been through, you're certainly due for a real vacation."

"You sure you got everything from here?" Uriel asked Enoch as he patted him on the back.

"I do believe I'm all set," Enoch answered then nodded toward Jared and Baraka still engaged in their embrace. "They appear to have finally met."

"Ready to head back to the hotel, Uriel?" Sirena asked him, bringing the palm of her hand to his chest.

"Are you sure you don't want to watch one of these live sex acts first," Uriel joked as he brought his hand to hers and interlocked their fingers.

"I'd much rather perform our own in private," Sirena said with a wink and grin.

"It's a date," Uriel laughed.

"You two take care now, you hear," Enoch said to them, then he stepped to Baraka and Jared to address them. "How about you two come with me for a while. We need to sit down properly and powwow."

Uriel released Sirena's hand as he put his arm around her, guiding her to turn with him in their descent down the steps. Sirena in turn put her arm around him as the two led the way for Enoch and his future parents to follow.

"You know there really are some fun things we could do while we're here in Amsterdam," Uriel said to Sirena.

"Like what?" Sirena asked him.

"Visit the Ann Frank House?" Uriel suggested.

"That would be a powerful experience," Sirena replied. "But just doesn't sound like my idea of fun right now after what we just experienced."

"How about the Vincent Van Goh Museum then?" posed Uriel once he reached the front door of the building and unlocked the knob lock first then the deadbolt.

"Lovely and all, I'm quite sure," Sirena began before Uriel

opened the door and she stepped past the threshold, "but the renderings of an insane artist aren't exactly pulling me in right now either."

"I see your point," laughed Uriel as he waited for the other three to exit the building. "I hear the Violet Phlegm are playing tonight at the Milky Way. How's that sound?"

"Too noisy for me," remarked Sirena, then he closed the front door and stepped to her.

"I heard that," Uriel replied. "The hotel it is, then."

"But I think my new friend Jared and I have a concert date tonight," chimed Baraka as she took Jared by the hand.

"I can't conceive of anything better," Enoch smiled at his parents then winked at Sirena and Uriel. "Now, you two couples go on about your separate ways, and I'll catch up to you all at some point in the future."

"Good luck," Uriel wished Jared and Baraka.

"You, too," Baraka smiled in return. "Thanks for everything."

"You bet," Sirena replied before she took Uriel's arm and the two of them crossed the street, leaving Enoch and his future parents.

THE AMSTERMATH

URIEL AND SIRENA FLUNG THEMSELVES INTO EACH OTHER'S arms when they reached their hotel room. They groped and mouthed each other as he backed her to the bed, then he pulled her blouse over her head and unhooked her bra from behind, freeing her breasts across her chest for him to fondle and thumb her nipples. She groaned before she yanked down the side zipper of her slacks and tugged the pants over her hips.

"Oh, Sirena," Uriel moaned as he handled her bare backside.

"Take me right now," she moaned back.

Uriel cradled her behind and lifted her, then he heaved her to the sheet-covered mattress. He lunged to her, cramming his chest between her spread legs as he tongued her nipples and clenched her waist.

"I want you inside of me," groaned Sirena.

Uriel pushed himself from the side of the bed then stood, wrenching himself free of his shirt. Sirena sat up and scooched herself to the side of the bed, lowering her feet to the carpet before she unbuttoned and unzipped his jeans. They both tugged at his pants until Uriel was able to push them down his thighs to his knees. Sirena then jerked down his briefs before she grabbed his erection with both hands and mouthed him.

"That is divine," he said, then groaned as she guided her mouth back and forth along his length.

Uriel gripped both sides of her head as he took control of the speed and depth of his penetration into her mouth and throat. She hummed her groan and wriggled her tongue against him.

"Wait," he said, pulling himself from her mouth. "As great as you're making me feel, maybe we should recite our sixty-nine vow and join at opposite ends right now. We really need to make sure we jaunt back home again."

"Okay, my love," Sirena managed to say before she gripped him with both hands. "But I want on bottom this time and you on top. I want you down my throat."

Uriel pried her fingers from him then pulled Sirena up by her hands to a stance in front of him.

"Now make your fists," Uriel began his instruction for her, "and say these words that will pulse within the core of your essence. They are words that are also mine, and I will say them as you say them so that these words become a vow that is ours alone.

"Then after each sentence, hold up one finger and press its tip to mine. Keep each tip pressed until we complete our union. The count of every word that follows will number us, and we will couple in the harmony of our divine love."

Their gaze into each other's eye penetrated them before the words suddenly flowed, and they voiced them in unison as though their thoughts were aligned and merged into one conscious entity. They then pressed a fingertip together with each line of their incantation:

"EVERY SECOND of breath inside hers
  Slathers him from above.
  Her vines entwined around his mind.
  His heart engorged at the tip of her tongue.
  She is the one he is numbered by.
  She buries him alive inside hers
  At the fulcra where both now come,
  She in her ratio of raw revival,
  He in the instant he fell in love.
  He is the one she is numbered by."

WITH THE UTTERANCE of the final word and their finger-tip-pressed hands now once again interlocked, they swirl into each other like some gear of gyrating flesh meshed together by churning hot blood. His weight on her at their opposite ends then welds them together in the exchange of body and soul that gushes its flow through both of them.

They are lifted and flying, faster and farther in an ecstasy that bursts into bliss beyond thought. As their consummation concludes, they shake in each other's grasp, drifting down until they find themselves conscious again but still coupled in their reversed embrace.

"One word by one word until we meet in our new time and place at the sixty-ninth word," Uriel wheezes as he turns his face from her drenched flesh. "Our love will transport us over and over again in our soulmate destiny."

"Alpha and Omega," she pronounces, once she pulls her mouth from him. "Your transfiguration awaits you, my love."

PART IV

YOLK YOKED

OVA VU

THE RINGTONE FOR THE INSTITUTE ON URIEL'S MOBILE phone heralded the dawn of a new work day for Uriel and Sirena, but neither moved to answer his phone on the dresser as they remained pretzeled together atop the comforter of their king size bed.

The ringtone paused for voice mail pickup, only to resume almost immediately with another call from The Institute.

"Guess they don't want to leave a message," Sirena griped without budging. "Wish they could give us a little more time to come down from our jaunt lag."

"No such luck," sighed Uriel, then he began to unravel himself from Sirena.

The ringtone stopped then began again with another call just as Uriel had separated himself from her. He dropped his feet to the floor and sat at the edge of the bed as he surveyed her curvaceous side profile with her taut bottom half aimed toward him.

"Maybe I should just put the phone in the other room," he yawned then gripped half of her heart-shaped behind.

"They'd probably just send somebody over to bang on the door," remarked Sirena without turning toward him.

The ringtone stopped, only to begin yet again.

"Pushy bastards," muttered Uriel, then he stood and stepped to the dresser to take his phone.

"The Uriel and Sirena Time Traveling Circus," he bellowed. "How may we service your past, present, and future needs yesterday, today, and tomorrow?"

"Funny," grunted Thoth at the other end. "You should've been a standup comedian instead of an archangel, my boy."

"Too late for a career change?" joked Uriel before he put the phone on speaker.

"I'm afraid so," guffawed Thoth until Sirena's groan halted his laughter. "Was that Sirena?"

"I'm afraid so," Uriel mocked Thoth with his reply. "She's no where nearly as happy as I am to hear the jarring gruff of your voice."

"I'm hurt," Thoth feigned offense. "I thought I'd be the highlight of her week."

"Oh, you are the highlight," Sirena voiced past a yawn as she rolled to the edge of the bed. "Uriel is just jealous."

"Now, now, you two," Thoth replied. "I know you'd like to relax a little longer, but we really do have important work to do. For starters, we're going to need you two to file reports of the events overseas, in addition to what led to your departure. One of contingencies that you two might find difficult in adjusting to is the fact that the present you've returned to is different than the past you left—at least in some ways."

"I see the beautiful Sirena sitting in front of me," Uriel

began, "looking at me like she knows who I am, so is our situation really any different?"

"No," Thoth answered. "Not in essence, although you will discover some differences that might cause instances of déjà vu or jamais vu, for that matter."

"And here I was hoping that what happened in Paris stayed in Paris," responded Uriel before he grabbed a pair of sweat pants from the dresser with his free hand and tossed them to Sirena.

"C'est la vie," sighed Sirena once she caught the sweat pants. "Just an occupational hazard, I suppose."

"More or less," acknowledged Thoth. "We do not have the knowledge that you have about what the present was like for you before you went back in time and altered fate. As far as we know, what you fixed was never broken, so the clock of today would be the time that we have deduced as the day Sirena left to meet Enoch at Serpent Mound to view his clutch of cosmic eggs."

"I'm on an Alpha and Omega merry-go-round," grumbled Sirena. "That day was so much fun the first time around."

"So if you already know about that Serpent Mound date, Thoth," Uriel began as he set the phone on the dresser and maneuvered himself into a pair of gym shorts, "then surely you must also know that we went to Paris and Amsterdam in 1987 to save the biblical Enoch's parents from Azazel and Lilith in their attempt to defile Baraka, leaving her barren, and prevent her from meeting her future husband, Jared?"

"Yes," came the voice of O. Cyrus. "We do know that, and here's how: we have an alternate history chronometer that has recorded our communications about events and actions that occurred before your departure."

"But how?" Sirena blurted then grabbed one of Uriel's Tshirts from the corner chair and guided her head through its opening.

"We work with a particle physicist who is affiliated with CERN," Horace disclosed to them. "She has apprised us of the results of your trip based on data that resulted from the spray of particle collision rearranged on our behalf."

"Do what?" laughed Uriel before he took a T-shirt from the top dresser drawer and put it on. "Do you mean *CERN* as in the European nuclear research group?"

"Indeed," O. Cyrus said. "We can..."

"Wait a minute," interrupted Sirena. "Either this is déjà vu is or you already said there was a CERN connection involved in our trip to Paris before we had our jaunt there to rescue Baraka."

"Or is it jamais vu," asked Uriel, "because I got this eerie feeling that I know I've been in this exact same situation before even though it seems like it's just now happening for the first time?"

"Well," resume O. Cyrus, "however you want to describe it, we do have the math to share with you at some point if you're really interested in knowing exactly how this data is transmitted and collected."

"But just not now," interceded Thoth. "We need your reports first, then we'd like for you two to meet some folks."

"Oh?" responded Sirena. "Who are we meeting?"

"Enoch and his parents," answered O. Cyrus.

"Seems like we just saw them," Uriel bristled in reply. "Do we really have to reunite so soon?"

"Yes," said Thoth. "Only this time the Enoch you will see with his parents won't seem older than Methuselah."

"He'll be the age of our kids," Sirena reckoned aloud.

That's right," confirmed O. Cyrus. "And we need for you two to give them the egg of Uriel."

"But wait a minute," Sirena began to question the request. "I thought you said to me originally that the egg Enoch gave to me at the Serpent Mound was for The Institute. If that's true, then why are we giving it back?"

"We don't have direct knowledge about those instructions," Horace admitted. "Unfortunately, all of the details about Enoch's clutch of cosmic eggs were lost in translation, if you will."

"We know about this now," resumed Thoth, "because we believe Enoch contacted us requesting that you two bring the egg to him and his parents."

"But you do know about the eggs," Uriel began his inquiry, "and how they've been used to this point?"

"Yes," Thoth confirmed. "We do have some of that narrative already, but we don't remember it like you do. You see, because the past was altered, those eggs were never actually uncovered by Enoch."

"But we have been advised," Horace then proceeded, "that Enoch must have the egg of Uriel to perform his next translation."

"What about the swirling gray egg of jade," added Sirena. "I have both of them here."

"So, let me get this straight," Uriel said. "You mean we have two eggs that never really existed?"

"Never found, is perhaps the better way of phrasing it," O. Cyrus replied. "We believe that's why the egg needs to be returned to Enoch, so he can regain the knowledge through the agency of Uriel that his current incarnation has yet to remember."

"Very well," said Uriel. "When and where do we meet them?"

"The Great Serpent Mound in Adams County, Ohio," Thoth informed them.

"You mean the Serpent Mound is there again?" asked Sirena.

"What's that supposed to mean?" Horace asked in return.

"I mean the Serpent Mound itself was stripped from the site when Enoch was launched up into the storm," Sirena explained. "The effigy is not there anymore."

"Perhaps that's what happened in the past," began O. Cyrus, "that you experienced before you changed the future. I can assure you that the Serpent Mound is there now."

"All right then," Uriel interjected, "we'll meet Enoch and his parents at the Serpent Mound and give the egg to him."

"Why don't you take both eggs?" suggested Thoth. "The gray jade egg also might have something to do with the triggering of Enoch's memory."

"Fine," Uriel replied. "We'll give him both of the eggs. When do you want us to go?"

"Please send us your reports first," instructed Thoth. "Start with Sirena going to meet Enoch about the eggs. Like we've said, we've pieced some of what happened together, but that meeting really seems to be the starting point for what happened afterwards."

"And once you're finished with the reports," O. Cyrus chimed in, "drive to Seaman, Ohio near the Serpent Mound. We have made hotel reservations for you there tonight and tomorrow night. If you don't get there today, don't worry about it, but you do need to meet Enoch tomorrow at noon. We've taken great measure to ensure that he'll be there with his parents."

"Wait a minute!" Sirena exclaimed. "We have the script you guys sent to us that detailed what we were supposed to do when we traveled back in time to Paris and Amsterdam."

"If we sent such information to you," Horace began, "I seriously doubt that the files are still there based on the time reset that has taken place since you altered the past."

"I'll check on the laptop as soon as our call is finished," Uriel said as he nodded toward Sirena.

"So, you guys are going to start your day today," Thoth summarized for them, "like you started your day a few days ago according to your sense of time."

"Beginning with me driving alone to Serpent Mound?" Sirena asked as she looked at Uriel and knotted her brow.

"Maybe you won't repeat exactly what you did," explained O. Cyrus. "There may be similarities, but the experiences are now completely different because the time has been reset."

"Weird," remarked Sirena as she stood and stepped across the room to Uriel.

"If that's all, fellas," Uriel began then draped his arm over Sirena's shoulder, "then we'll finish up with you guys."

"Very well," Thoth said. "Just get those reports to us before you leave for Serpent Mound."

"Will do," Uriel replied, then he released Sirena and retrieved his phone from the dresser.

"Bye now," Sirena said.

"Bye," the three men replied before Uriel ended the call and returned his phone to the dresser.

"So, let's go see what the laptop has for us," Uriel said to Sirena, then he put his hands on her waist and drew her to him.

"The script would be great, wouldn't it?" Sirena smiled at him. "We wouldn't even have to write anything down if those files are already there."

"I doubt we'll be that lucky," Uriel answered her with a frown. "Go put on some coffee while I get us ready to write."

"I'll grab the eggs first," Sirena said as Uriel released her.

Sirena squatted to the bottom dresser drawer and opened it. She shifted a couple pairs of shorts aside and retrieved the two eggs from the drawer, then she followed Uriel from the bedroom into the living room. She set the eggs beside the laptop on the coffee table before she went into the kitchen to start the coffee.

Uriel powered the laptop then sat on the couch in front of the table.

"We're going to have to mention the awful videos of Baraka and Jared that we saw," Uriel raised his voice for Sirena to hear him in the kitchen.

"Yeah," she raised her voice in return, "the videos and events that led up to us traveling to Paris."

"I don't see any files on the desktop here from before, so I'll just start hammering away about our European vacation," Uriel told her, then he opened a document and began to type everything he could remember about the events.

By the time Sirena arrived in the living room with two cups of coffee, Uriel was well into a narrative that described the return of a distraught Sirena from the Serpent Mound and the viewing of the disturbing videos of Baraka and Jared that The Institute had provided them.

"How's it going?" she asked him once she had set the cups on the table.

"Fine," he said. "I'll let you relate the whole account of meeting Enoch and viewing all of the eggs."

"Yeah," Sirena began as she plopped down beside him on the couch, "I had the file that Enoch gave to me with the eggs, but the file that Enoch gave to me wasn't there with eggs in the dresser drawer. That's where I put them all together before."

"So, I really wonder how it is even possible for us to have these two eggs," Uriel said then touched the stone egg that depicted him with gold-flecked wings. "I mean, if nothing else is here from your visit with Enoch and our interaction with The Institute, then how are these impossible eggs actually here?"

"Maybe only the great Salvador Dali knows," Sirena replied as she bumped Uriel with her hip, scooching him over until she could view the entire computer screen. "Maybe they're his phantom eggs from some other dimension."

"Sounds about as reasonable as anything else," Uriel said, then his phone rang with a different ringtone. "Why would my daughter be calling me now?"

Sirena lifted her eyes from the screen to meet his gaze. She shrugged before he answered the phone.

"Hello, Julia," Uriel greeted his daughter. "Hold on! Calm down! Where are you?"

Sirena kept her attention on Uriel, who sat beside her before he spoke again:

"What exactly is wrong with your mother?"

"Put the phone on speaker," Sirena whispered to him.

Uriel activated the speaker phone then set the phone on the table.

"Mom's going crazy, and we can't stop her!" Julia cried while the shouts of Uriel's other two children and their mother blasted in the background. "She's not making any sense!"

"What do you want me to do?" Uriel yelled his question.

"Help us!" Julia screamed.

"It will take me two hours before I can even get there," Uriel said with some measure of calm restored to his voice. "Can you put your mom on the phone?"

"Talk to Dad, Mom!" Julia pleaded with her mother as her voiced turned away from the phone.

"Fuck that evil bastard!" Uriel heard his ex-wife scream.

"We might have to call the police if she doesn't stop throwing stuff and screaming," Julia managed to say through her sobbing, "We'll be waiting for you! Just hurry!"

Julia disconnected the phone call, and Uriel stared at the phone until Sirena placed her hand on his forearm.

"I can do these reports," Sirena told him. "You go do what you have to do to take care of them. Sounds like they really need you right now. Or would you rather that I go with you?"

"I really don't think you should go with me for this," Uriel answered her.

"Then I'll wait for you."

"But I don't see how I'll be back in time for us to make it to our hotel in Ohio tonight," Uriel told her. "This does sound really bad."

"Don't worry about me or Enoch's eggs," Sirena tried to comfort him. "You can come back here when you're able to, and we'll leave then. Maybe you can just meet me at Serpent Mound tomorrow. You might not even need to go with me at all. It sounded like The Institute just wants the eggs given to Enoch. I can do that by myself."

"I don't want you to do anything alone right now without me," Uriel said as he turned toward her and held her hand in his. "I want us to do all of this together. I'd never forgive myself if something happened to you."

"Nothing is going to happen to me," she smiled at him as she freed her hand from his and patted him on his thigh. "We've defeated the forces of evil at their own game. It's all good. I'm more worried about what you'll be headed into. It does sound like an awful mess."

"I'll throw on some jeans and a shirt and get out of here,"

Uriel said before he returned to the bedroom and stepped into the walk-in closet.

"There's a clean pair of socks on the ottoman in here," Sirena informed him. "And your gym shoes are under the table."

"I wonder what happened to her," Uriel posed upon his return to the living room. "She seemed fine before we went to Paris. I mean, she seemed stable after the divorce was finalized and even purposeful in how she told me she intended to take care of what the kids needed in all of this."

"Maybe something changed with her because of our intervention in Paris and Amsterdam," suggested Sirena. "There's no telling what else has changed because we went back and altered fate."

Uriel climbed into his jeans and pulled his shirt over his head. He then stepped to the ottoman and took the pair of socks before he returned to the couch to sit beside Sirena.

"It will all be straightened out," Sirena said to him then watched him yank the socks over his feet and cram his socked feet into his untied gym shoes.

"I sure hope so," Uriel sighed as he stood, "because if it isn't straightened out, I'll be leaving it all behind. The future is all about you and me. I won't let anyone interfere with our destiny."

"Good," she said with a smile before she approached him, wrapping her arms around his waist and pulling him to her.

Sirena tiptoed to mouth Uriel's lips. He gripped her shoulders and massaged them as the two brought their tongues together and kissed within their tightened embrace.

"I better go right now," Uriel said, once he ended their kiss. "Or else I won't be going at all."

"Get out of here," Sirena grinned at him then patted his backside.

Uriel returned to the bedroom to retrieve his wallet and keys from the dresser. He stuffed the wallet into the back pocket of his jeans and the keys in a front pocket before he returned to the coffee table and took his phone.

"Want me to get a travel mug for your coffee?" Sirena asked Uriel as she stood and pried his phone into his other back pocket.

"I'll grab some coffee on the road," Uriel informed her then proceeded to the stairwell and hustled down the steps.

He turned once he reached the bottom of the stairs and looked up at Sirena:

"I love you."

"And I love you," she replied then blew a kiss to him.

Uriel smiled as he went to the front door, unlocking it and opening the screen door. Sirena sighed then propped herself against the stairway wall. She heard Uriel pull the front door shut then let the screen door clack closed behind him.

"Great," Sirena muttered, then she returned to the living room and sat on the couch in front of the coffee table. "Might as well get these reports done. Let's see how far he got."

Sirena began to review the document. She sighed before she gripped the handle of her coffee mug and sipped from its brim.

"Looks like I should start with my trip to see Enoch," she said then smacked her lips and returned her mug to the table. "I'll write this like the script that The Institute had us read."

Sirena shifted to the edge of the couch and steadily typed without stopping to review what she had written or stumble over word choice. Her narrative began with her improvised meeting with Enoch, then she detailed their adventure at the Serpent Mound. She continued her narrative with her account of the events that transpired upon her return home, from the viewing of the videos of Baraka and Jared to the eggs thrown through the downstairs windows and the arrival of Azazel and Lilith. She realized that she included details that Uriel had described in his rendering but continued without pause to compare her account with his.

"They will get whatever we give them," Sirena said then sipped more coffee from her mug. "And they can make whatever sense out of it that they want."

Sirena proceeded to describe her and Uriel's time in Paris and Amsterdam, more or less listing as much as she could remember without struggling to recall all of the details. She described the truck with the band at Notre Dame and the mayhem at La Pagode theater, but as she began to describe the scene that unfolded inside of the building in Amsterdam, one commonality of their European excursion dawned upon her: three times Baraka was placed upon a cross during her ordeal. The first atop the truck at Notre Dame, where she was whipped by the faux priest and then the other two times on crosses that were cruciform platforms like bondage cross tables to which she was bound in preparation for the violation of her body.

"The cross itself is crucial in all of this," Sirena mentioned to herself, pausing just long enough to sip some of her cooled coffee before she resumed her furious pace of writing.

Sirena added information and scenes that occurred to her out of sequence, listing them with notation about their correspondence to events that she had previously described. As she continued with her deluge of words, her mobile phone rang from the bedroom dresser, but the ringtone was not that of Uriel's phone or The Institute's number.

"Is that Raegan's ring?" Sirena asked herself aloud then sprang to her feet and hustled into the bedroom to answer the phone. "Hello."

"Mom!" greeted the voice on the other side.

"Raegan?" Sirena sought confirmation. "Is that you?"

"Yes, Mom!" came the reply. "It's me! It's so great to hear your voice again!"

"Well, yours, too," skeptically voiced Sirena. "But you do sound a little scratchy. Is everything all right? I mean, it's been a really long time since we last talked."

"Things couldn't be any better, Mom!"

"That's great, honey," Sirena said as she knotted her brow. "It's just that I really didn't expect to hear from you so soon, or ever again for that matter. You were absolutely furious with me before."

"I'm so sorry. I hope you can forgive me for being so angry with you, Mom. It was just so hard to see you and Daddy torn apart like that. I never saw any of that coming."

"I know," Sirena said consolingly as she stepped back into the living room. "I never meant to hurt any of you. It's just that the feelings that Uriel and I have for each other are so powerful."

"I understand," Raegan said. "I mean, I really understand now. You see, I met somebody, and I love him like he's the only one in the world. I really understand now how you feel!"

"Really?" Sirena crooned in return. "That's great, honey! I'm so happy for you. Tell me all about him."

"He's brilliant and so handsome, but I really want you to see for yourself. Is there any way you could meet us today? We're not too far from where you are."

"Where are you?" Sirena asked.

"We're visiting the Serpent Mound up in Ohio about an hour or so from Maysville."

Sirena remained silent, wondering if the fate that she and Uriel altered had somehow produced this profound change of heart in her daughter, who she figured would hate her for the rest of her life for leaving her father.

"His parents are here, too. Bring Uriel. We'll have a great time. I think this might be the guy!"

"Oh, Raegan," Sirena nearly cried. "That's just wonderful."

"So, can you meet us up here today?"

"Well," Sirena began as she returned to the living room, "Uriel probably is out for the rest of the day, but I think I can come up on my own, if that's okay."

"That's great, Mom! It would be nice to meet Uriel under better circumstances like this and have him with us, but I really want to see you. You know what I mean?"

"I do, sweetie," Sirena said as she felt the tears swelling in her eyes. "I really do."

"Oh, Mom, how soon can you get here?"

"I have some work correspondence I have to finish up here first," Sirena answered, throttling her tears, "then I have to discuss some issues with my employer, but I would think I can leave within the hour. Where did you want to meet?"

When Sirena heard the name of the hotel, she realized that she hadn't included its name in the report she was preparing for The Institute, then she felt her stomach churn when the coincidence dawned upon.

"I know where that hotel is," Sirena remarked before she sat on the sofa and tilted the laptop screen upward. "I spent a little time up there recently. I think I can be there by two o'clock. Does that work for you?"

"Yes. Can't wait for you to get here, Mom!"

"Me either, Raegan," Sirena said in return. "I'll let you know when I leave Maysville, okay?"

"Great! Bye, Mom."

"What's your friend's name?" Sirena asked, but her daughter had disconnected the phone call.

When Sirena tapped the end button for the call, she realized something that had escaped her mind following her whirlwind jaunt with Uriel in Paris and Amsterdam: she had not checked her phone to see if the video she took of Enoch at Serpent Mound was still there.

"Enoch," she mumbled.

Sirena maneuvered through phone screens to access the videos she had taken, but when she surveyed the videos on file, none were of Enoch.

"It's not there," she said to herself. "That's got to be because it hasn't happened yet. Today is the day it was supposed to happen. Now, it never will."

Sirena sighed as she set her phone on the table then returned her attention to the laptop.

She reread the last two paragraphs of copy before she resumed typing text. She rendered her narrative of events as fast as she could without filtering them. Her words flowed unabated until the familiar ringtone of The Institute sounded.

"Hey, there," she greeted the caller.

"Hey there, yourself," came the graveled voice of Thoth. "We just received confirmation of your meeting with Enoch and his parents today."

"Oh?" Sirena replied as she saved her work on the laptop.

"We need for you to leave right now," Horace blurted.

"But Uriel isn't here," Sirena informed them. "And he won't be back for a few hours."

"Then you'll have to go by yourself," Thoth said. "Apparently Enoch and his parents have other plans this evening that will require you to meet him as soon as possible."

When O. Cyrus said that Enoch's girlfriend and her mother were meeting Enoch and his parents, Sirena sprang to her feet.

"What?" her question blared.

"O. Cyrus said," began Thoth, "that Enoch and his parents are meeting his girlfriend and her mother."

"I don't understand," Sirena's voice shook. "I'm supposed to meet my daughter, her boyfriend, and his parents at the Serpent Mound in a couple hours."

"Now, we don't understand," Thoth replied.

"Do you think my daughter's boyfriend is Enoch?" Sirena asked as she returned to the couch.

"Sounds possible," said Horace. "Or else it's an unusual coincidence."

"Too much happening," O. Cyrus chimed in, "for this to be coincidental."

"More like synchronicity, maybe?" posed Thoth.

"Or maybe Enoch is trying to help me," Sirena surmised aloud.

"How so?" asked Thoth.

"My daughter sounded so happy," Sirena started to explain. "She wants me to meet her boyfriend so much that she was willing to break her silence with me. Maybe Enoch is trying to help me reconnect with my children."

"I suppose that's possible," O. Cyrus began his response, "but we're not even sure at this point that Enoch knows who he is or why you'll be giving him these two eggs you have."

"You said he asked for us to bring the eggs to him," Sirena snapped. "And now you're saying he doesn't know who he is?"

"We said we believe that it was Enoch who contacted us," began Thoth, "but not necessarily the Enoch of our present time."

"You mean a different version of Enoch?" Sirena asked in return.

"Yes," replied Thoth, then Horace spoke:

"His anamnesis may not have started yet for the Enoch of this present time."

"What does that mean?" Sirena inquired.

"It means he may not have started to remember who he is yet," explained O. Cyrus. "Or who he was and will be again, rather."

"How can he not know who he is?" pursued Sirena. "And I thought you all were in contact with him directing all of the interaction with him?"

"Actually," began Thoth, "we rely on the analysis we received from our particle physicist with the CERN connection. She provides us with our information about Enoch and his parents through a process called…"

"Stop, Thoth," demanded Horace. "It is definitely not appropriate at this time to divulge how our colleague operates. Besides, we can't really explain how it works anyway."

"True," concurred O. Cyrus. "The premise is so unbelievable that only the mathematical model can effectively describe the process, and prerequisite knowledge is definitely required to comprehend that."

"So, what were you going to have me do?" Sirena began to rebuke them, "throw the eggs at him then wave and say 'bye' as I run away."

"We were in the process of determination for that," Horace began, "before we were notified about the need to meet Enoch sooner rather than later."

"This is starting to make less and less sense," grumbled Sirena. "So, you're telling me that Enoch doesn't know who I am and isn't expecting me to give him the eggs?"

"Correct," affirmed Thoth. "This younger version of Enoch, in any event."

"At least as far as we know," added O. Cyrus.

"But if he's your daughter's boyfriend," Horace remarked but didn't finish his comment.

"Then I can come up with some kind of explanation as to why I'm giving him these eggs," Sirena finished the implication by O. Cyrus.

"That's sounds like something," replied Thoth. "Maybe a gift?"

"A gift!" laughed Sirena. "I'll gush about how glad I am to meet him then tell him that I have some heartwarming gifts to show my appreciation–a couple of rock eggs!"

"Tell him that they're like Faberge eggs," suggested Horace.

"Or maybe eggs related to the history of Serpent Mound?" posed O. Cyrus.

"I know!" Thoth's hoarse voice boomed. "Tell him you picked them up at a roadside stand on your drive up, and that the seller told you that they're related to the Serpent Mound somehow."

"Yes," concurred Horace. "Do that."

"That sounds plausible and interesting," added O. Cyrus.

"But what if he declines to take them?" asked Sirena.

"You'll have to use your charm," Thoth told her.

"Great," muttered Sirena. "I can hear him tell my daughter now what a nutjob her mother is for insisting he take these eggs from me."

"There could be worse things," replied O. Cyrus.

"Like him not receiving the eggs?" speculated Sirena. "I mean, what if I keep the eggs instead of giving them to Enoch? What harm would that cause?"

"That we don't know," admitted Thoth. "But we better follow the advice we're receiving at this point."

"Fate can be a real fickle bitch," O. Cyrus joked.

"Watch that," Horace reproached him. "You can't just sling a word like that around nowadays."

"What, *fickle*?" O. Cyrus joked further.

"You know what he means," Thoth said to O. Cyrus. "Hope you don't take offense at that, Sirena."

"Are you kidding me?" Sirena nearly yelled. "None of that matters right now! I need to know what I'm supposed to do!"

"Go to Serpent Mound," Thoth instructed her. "Give the eggs to Enoch. Tell him that you just bought them and thought they were interesting."

"Good God," muttered Sirena. "Maybe I should just cancel all of this and wait for Uriel to get back."

"You can't wait for four hours," countered Horace. "Where is Uriel anyways? I thought he was working on the report with you?"

"I'm finishing my part of the report," said Sirena. "Uriel went to meet his kids. Apparently, his ex-wife is having a hard time right now, and his daughter asked him to drive down there to see if he can help out."

"That doesn't sound promising," Horace remarked.

"No, it doesn't," agreed Sirena. "I should be there with him instead of here."

"Hopefully, he'll work things out there for the best," Thoth replied. "But we really need for you to go conduct this business for us today. I understand developments have complicated this for you, but don't worry yourself too much over it."

"Try to enjoy yourself," suggested O. Cyrus.

"Yeah, right," Sirena snapped, then she returned her attention to the computer. "I'm going to attach the report in an e-mail to you guys. I'm as done with it as I'm going to get."

"Very well," Thoth acknowledged her.

"Now, if you gentlemen will excuse me," Sirena began her farewell to them. "I need to get dressed in a hurry so that I can get out of here."

"Remember," Thoth said to her. "You're going straight to the hotel to meet Enoch and his parents."

"Which is the same hotel where I'm meeting my daughter," added Sirena.

"We just received the email with your report," Horace informed her.

"All right, guys," Sirena sighed. "Talk with you all later."

Sirena disconnected the call and began to call Uriel but stopped.

"I better get dressed first," she said to herself, then she set the phone on the table and hurried into the bedroom.

Sirena yanked a pair of jeans from a hanger in the closet. She peeled the sweatpants from her body, leaving them in a pile on the closet floor, then tugged herself into the tight jeans. She grabbed a sweater and pulled herself into it, covering her T-shirt beneath the collar of the sweater.

"I do need to call Uriel," she said to herself.

Sirena took a pair of his tube socks from the top dresser drawer and gathered her tennis shoes to take with her to the living room. She covered her feet with the socks then pried her feet into her shoes before the phone rang with Uriel's ringtone.

"Thank God," she sighed then retrieved the phone from the table. "Uriel! Are you all right?"

"I'm fine, baby," he said to her. "Just closing in on ground zero here."

"I hope it goes well for you with them," she said. "I need to let you know that The Institute asked me to leave for Serpent Mound now, and also that Raegan called me, asking me to meet with her and her new boyfriend and his parents."

"What?" Uriel asked, half-laughingly.

"Yeah, right?" Sirena replied then continued. "And, get this, it sounds like Raegan's boyfriend is Enoch."

Sirena waited for Uriel to respond, but as his silence prolonged, she offered a segue for him. "How do you like them eggs?"

"I don't know what to make of that," admitted Uriel. "Does The Institute know all of this?"

"They do now," Sirena replied. "And they shared a little piece of helpful information with me."

"Oh?" came Uriel's uncertain voice.

"Enoch doesn't know who I am or that he's about to receive a pair of eggs from me," Sirena related then began to giggle so genuinely that Uriel soon found himself joining her laughter.

"That's all crazy," Uriel managed to say. "But Raegan calling you out of the blue like that is really bizarre, isn't it?"

"That's what I thought," Sirena agreed. "But she explained it to me, and she made sense. I think she's in love with this boyfriend of hers."

"Your daughter is in love with Enoch," Uriel paraphrased.

"That's who we think it is, anyway," Sirena said. "Raegan didn't exactly say his name was Enoch, but I'm inclined to believe that none of this is coincidence."

"And Enoch won't know who you are?" Uriel questioned her further.

"Nope," Sirena replied. "I'll be on some weird incognito mission, I guess."

"Be careful driving up there," Uriel said to her. "I don't want you to get too distracted by all of this mess going on now, but it's great that Raegan wants to reconnect with you. I know how sad all of that made you."

"If I glean nothing else out of this," Sirena began, "at least it has led me to be on speaking terms with my daughter again. For that I am truly grateful."

"Well," Uriel began in reply, "I hope my dealings leave me grateful, too, but I can't imagine exactly how right now. I can't get through to any of the kids, so I guess I'll just have to find out what's going on when I get there."

"I'll be thinking of you," Sirena tried to console him. "Together, we be all right in what we do separately."

"That's absolutely right," Uriel declared. "It's our love that matters first and foremost."

"Always, baby," chimed Sirena. "Always."

"Then go do your thing," Uriel said. "And I'll go do mine. Then together we will meet again to do our thing."

"Ooh," Sirena throatily replied. "I like the sound of that."

"Love you," he said.

"Love you, too. Bye."

SERPENTRIPETAL

Déjà vu flooded Sirena as she traveled along the same scenic byway from Maysville that she had taken just three days ago when she met Enoch and witnessed the havoc at Serpent Mound. Anxiety surged through her when the fundamental unreality of her situation struck her, and she questioned whether her current trip was any more real than her first one.

This time it has to be different, Sirena told herself in her resolve to thwart a panic attack. *And it's personal now with my daughter involved.*

Sirena pondered Raegan's change of heart in regard to their relationship. As much as she wanted to believe that Raegan had finally accepted the reality of her mother's new life with a different man than her father at its center, Sirena remained somewhat dubious about the reversal because of the intense hatred for her that her daughter had conveyed from the outset of her split with Earl. She tried to convince herself that the arrival of a young man in Raegan's life actually could quell any rancor Raegan had for her. After all, Sirena reminded herself, she understood too well that unadulterated love had the power to trump all other factors in one's life, like her love for Uriel had done.

Sirena caught herself glancing into the rearview mirror to check for traffic behind her. She squirmed knowing that she still feared Earl, which by extension also made her doubt the authenticity of her daughter's feelings toward her.

But why? she asked herself. *Why can't I let this fear go?*

Sirena's mobile phone apprised her of an upcoming turn. She followed the instruction, then the ringtone of The Institute resounded. She took the phone from the console and swiped to accept the call, which she then tapped to broadcast over speaker.

"Hi there, guys," she greeted them.

"Hi," the three men returned her greeting in unison.

"What's up?" she asked as she returned her phone to the console.

"We have a slight modification in your itinerary," Thoth informed her.

"Oh?" she replied.

"Yes," Thoth resumed. "We've been apprised that Enoch and his parents won't be at the hotel to meet you. They'll be at another location where I believe you've been before."

"The Serpent Mound?" she speculated.

"No," Thoth said. "But it's on the way there."

"Remember where Enoch wanted to meet you because his car wouldn't start?" Horace blurted his question.

"I do," answered Sirena. "But that never actually happened, right?"

"It did in your mind," replied O. Cyrus. "And that's where you need to go now. They'll be waiting for you there."

"But my daughter hasn't said anything about this?" countered Sirena.

"Perhaps Enoch is not your daughter's boyfriend," ventured Horace.

The ringtone of another call signaled that her daughter was calling. She slowed on the two-lane highway then steered to a stop within a gravel pullout beside the road.

"Raegan's calling me," Sirena told the men. "I've just pulled over off the road here."

"Take it," Thoth said. "We'll text the map link for your new destination to you."

"Okay, thanks," Sirena said before she disconnected with The Institute and took Raegan's call.

"Hello," greeted Sirena.

"Hi, Mom!" came her daughter's staticky voice. "We've got a change of meeting location if you don't mind."

"Oh?" Sirena feigned surprise.

"Yeah," began Raegan, "we have a chance to meet with an artifact collector who has some things my boyfriend and his parents are interested in buying."

"That sounds neat," acknowledged Sirena. "What things?"

"Apparently they're some kind of valuable art eggs."

"Art eggs?"

"Yes," continued Raegan. "Enoch says they're very important eggs historically."

"So, your guy's name is Enoch," Sirena nearly stuttered from the chill that shook her. "I don't think you mentioned that before. That is an unusual name."

"It's biblical, I think," replied her daughter. "Even his parents' names are biblical–Baraka and Jared. Supposedly these eggs they're all interested in have some biblical significance, too, which is weird because they were found near the Serpent

Mound and have all these Mayan Indian symbols and images on them."

"Is that so?" Sirena swallowed hard in reply, swarmed by the surreal immediacy of Enoch, Baraka, Jared, and the cosmic eggs of the Serpent Mound.

"Yes," returned Raegan. "Enoch said that these eggs somehow represent portals for people to move back and forth between the past and the future. Apparently, this was a thing some time back in history."

Sirena fought the fear that swarmed her. Dread left her speechless for too long, then her daughter's staticky voice returned.

"Mom?"

"I'm here," Sirena replied, resisting the urge to tell her daughter that something came up and she couldn't meet with her. "I'm listening."

"Good," sighed Raegan. "I thought I lost you for a minute. The reception out here is kind of dicey. Let me text the link to the address before I lose you."

"Okay, dear," Sirena's voice quivered in reply. "I'm pulled over on the side of the road. Hopefully, the reception will stay good enough here for a little longer."

"Are you all right, Mom?" Raegan asked.

"I'm fine," managed Sirena. "Go ahead and send the link to me. I don't think I'm too far away from where you are. I look forward to seeing you again and meeting Enoch and his parents, too. I'm so excited for you, Raegan, and I'm so happy we're on speaking terms again."

"I'm sorry I was such a bitch," apologized Raegan. "I didn't mean to be so nasty to you."

"I know, honey," Sirena tried to console her daughter. "It's hard for all of us. I'm just glad you've had a change of heart."

"Love you, Mom," Raegan said.

"Love you, too," Sirena nearly wept.

"I just sent the link," Raegan informed her mother. "Can't wait to see you!"

"Me, too," replied Sirena. "Got the link. Thanks, sweetie."

"Bye, Mom."

Once Sirena disconnected the call with her daughter, she stared blankly into the rearview mirror, oblivious to the lack of traffic behind her as she struggled to assimilate not only the change of venue for her upcoming meeting, but all of the details and circumstances that were now suddenly in play and forcing her to feel like she was starting to lose some measure of control over her destiny again.

The idea that Enoch was her daughter's boyfriend numbed her. She also felt stunned by the fact that she was about to meet Baraka and Jared, whose destiny together she had helped save. As much as she felt aligned with Enoch and his parents, she knew in the cosmic scheme of things that this twist of fate somehow threatened her, like her very life and soul were about to undergo such upheaval that all of the normalcy she and Uriel had started to establish together was on the verge of disintegration.

I need to call Uriel, Sirena told herself as she picked up the phone and noticed the battery level of her phone already had dipped under fifty-percent. She connected her phone to the car charger then tapped the button to call Uriel.

"Seems like my battery is draining way too fast," she muttered before Uriel frantically answered.

"Jesus Christ, Sirena!" Uriel's voice blared above the yells and cries surrounding him. "They're all going nuts here!"

"What's wrong?" Sirena shrieked.

"My daughters are trying to restrain their mother!" Uriel managed to voice above the others.

"Oh, God, Uriel!" Sirena shrieked again.

"I'm going to have to call the police if you don't stop this right now!" Uriel yelled away from the phone before he addressed Sirena again. "I don't know if I'm going to be able to make it back in time, honey."

"Don't worry about that," she tried to reassure him. "They need you there. Help them. I'll take care of our business on this end."

The bawling of Uriel's ex-wife and the shouts of his children drowned his response to Sirena.

"Just call me if you need me!" Sirena tried to yell above the commotion.

"I will!" Uriel blared. "I love you!"

"I love you, too!" Sirena managed to tell Uriel before he disconnected the call.

Sirena tapped the button to end the call then returned to the home screen of her phone. She tapped the text messaging icon, which revealed the last two texts sent to her at the top of her message list. The top message was the directions link her daughter had sent her. The directions link sent by The Institute appeared below that. Sirena moved her fingertip toward the link sent by The Institute when a horn blast behind her jarred her.

"Shit!" Sirena shouted as she glared toward the pickup truck that passed her.

With the truck vanishing from her view around a bend in the road, Sirena returned her attention to the phone still in her hand, which shook when she pressed her fingertip on the directions link her daughter had sent to her. She then shakily opened the link for directions and downloaded the map to her phone before she tapped the button to begin the voice guided directions.

"Head northeast on State Route 770 for one mile," came the female voice for map directions as she restarted her SUV.

Sirena felt the sweat bead from an uneasiness fraught with sickening déjà vu. Paranoia seized her as both of her eyes began to twitch and her heartbeat quickened. The surrounding canopy from trees crowding the road hovered ominously–it now seemed to her–with every twist and turn in the narrow path ahead of her. She gulped repeatedly to thwart the nausea rising within her. She felt dizzied from her jangled sense of time to the extent that she slowed the speed of the SUV in her attempt to regain enough composure to continue without stopping in the lane she traveled.

"Uriel," she gasped.

Since Sirena left her husband of twenty-two years for Uriel last summer, she dreaded separation from her newfound soul-mate. The consummation of their coupled destiny had so enraptured her that every second they were apart felt like the universe was collapsing inside of her.

"Turn left in five hundred feet," instructed the female voice of her phone map app. "Take Church Road for one-point-three miles to your destination."

Sirena slowed on the two-lane state highway and signaled when she saw the street sign posted ahead. She glanced into the rearview mirror then turned onto the gravel road that was too narrow for two cars traveling in opposite directions.

This can't be right, she thought.

Her glance into the mirror reminded her of the other reason why she dreaded separation from Uriel: fear of retaliation by her ex-husband Earl. Even though their recently finalized divorce seemed amicable enough, Sirena knew too well of the volatility that lurked behind her ex's middle-aged veneer of dutiful Christian family man. She feared that his suppressed hatred for her might compel him to exact revenge.

Sirena ensured she wasn't followed during the hour drive from her home in Maysville, Kentucky to this destination near Great Serpent Mound, but she felt a different dread spike through her as she found herself alone in such a remote location instead of a hotel lobby about to reunite with her daughter and meet her mysterious boyfriend and his parents.

What if this is a set up to lure me out here to the middle of nowhere? she imagined.

"Stop it," she scolded herself aloud. "This is all legit. The meeting place has just been changed. The Institute confirmed it. That's all."

Sirena breathed easier with the knowledge that The Institute knew of her whereabouts, but as she ventured farther and slower along the potholed, narrow road that snaked between a creek ravine to her left and treed, hilly terrain on her right, she wanted to update The Institute about her progress. She braked to a stop then retrieved her phone from the console beside her, only to find the screen black.

"Damn it," she sighed aloud when she realized her phone battery had died.

Sirena set her phone down before she glanced in the rearview mirror again. With no one behind her, she pulled forward, steering around a pothole that consumed nearly half the right side of the road.

It's less than two miles on this road, she told herself. *It can't be too much farther.*

Sirena was already perturbed by the change in meeting location, and now this aggravation of the dead phone battery irked her further. She hoped that the meeting with her daughter, Enoch, and his parents would be brief but understood that The Institute expected her to return the cosmic eggs in her possession to Enoch.

Once Sirena cleared two switchback curves that coiled through the surrounding forest, a dirt driveway opened to her right. She skidded to a stop in the gravel then peered down the drive. She saw Raegan facing her and a red-haired woman beside her with her back toward Sirena. She noticed what appeared to be two men, kneeling but eclipsed from full view by her daughter and the other woman. They were gathered in front of a pickup truck parked between a small ranch house and a shed at the end of the driveway and surrounded by pecking chickens. Her daughter waved to her first then motioned for her to drive toward the group.

Sirena smiled at Raegan as she neared the group. She parked in front of them then stepped out of the SUV. Her daughter approached her as Sirena shut the driver's door, but a multi-colored item on the floorboard of the backseat caught her attention.

"What the hell?" Sirena voiced then stepped to the back door

Sirena opened the door and gaped at the colorful garment on the floorboard. It was the huipil that Enoch had given to her before the two of them had went to Serpent Mound.

"How is that possible?" gasped Sirena as she stooped to touch the garment.

"Get her now!" a man's voice roared from the group.

When Sirena turned toward the outburst, Raegan tackled her, knocking her to gravel and pinning her to the ground by her arms.

"What are you doing?" Sirena asked, stunned.

"I'm paying you back, bitch," her daughter glared at her

before she shifted her forearm to Sirena's throat. "Don't you even open your whore mouth."

Sirena choked from her daughter's restraint, but she could see the other people approach them.

"No," she gurgled.

"Oh, yes," replied the red haired woman standing beside Raegan, who Sirena now recognized was the demonic Lilith. "We're going to have some seriously sick fun with your whore ass. Aren't we?"

"Wicked fun," the towering Azazel began his reply. "We're going to have so much fun that I'm quite sure it's criminal. And we're going to watch Earl finally get to administer the justice that you've dodged for far too long with that homewrecking adulterer of yours, Uriel."

"He's going to be next," came the voice of Sirena's ex-husband Earl before he stepped around Azazel to squat beside Sirena. "But I do believe your daughter here is going to enjoy what we do to you more than anyone else here. Ain't that so, Raegan?"

"That's right, Daddy," Raegan said before she spit into Sirena's face and pushed harder against her throat with her forearm.

"Don't kill her so quick," laughed Lilith. "Get your money's worth first. Torture her. We've got this place all to ourselves for a while. The house is all set up with the tools of our trade."

"You know I want to watch you writhe in agony, don't you?" Raegan smiled at Sirena before she eased the pressure of her forearm against her mother's throat. "They're going to tear your rotten ass apart, Mommy."

"No, Raegan," Sirena wheezed then coughed until her face turned flush and she spat blood.

"Why don't you get up off your dear mother?" Earl suggested as he placed his hand on his daughter's shoulder and raised himself to a stance between Azazel and Lilith. "Let's get her to the house where we can chat with her in private."

Raegan shoved her mother's chest when she stood. She then moved beside her father, both of them watching Sirena spitting more blood in her attempt to roll to her side. Before Sirena could kneel, Lilith kicked her in the backside, knocking her forward until her face impacted the bottom of the SUV door. She dropped her car keys to the ground then hit the gravel facefirst.

"Your lovely Mayan wardrobe won't help you now," laughed Lilith before she stepped over Sirena and retrieved the huipil from the floorboard. "It really is miraculous that this thing is even here. It just shows you how close you were to getting out of all of this free as a bird without properly paying your debts for all of the damage you've done."

"So close," began Azazel before he grabbed Sirena by her hair and yanked her to her feet, "and yet so far. Why don't you show Sirena here just how much you love her now, Earl?"

"Love to," Earl said with a smile, then he grabbed Sirena by her throat and spit in her face.

"Don't do this, Earl?" Sirena pleaded past Earl's grip around her throat. "You don't know what you're doing."

"Don't know what I'm doing?" Earl laughed then released her throat. "I know exactly what I'm doing. I'm making sure you get everything you deserve."

"No, Earl," gasped Sirena as she staggered within Azazel's restraint of her. "You have no idea what's really happening here."

"We both know what's happening," intervened Raegan, then she slapped Sirena across the face. "And we're going to love every second of this."

"Where are the eggs, Sirena?" Lilith asked then stepped in

front of Sirena and peered into her eyes. "If you tell me where they are, we'll set you free."

"No, you won't," Sirena whimpered as she slumped in Azazel's hold.

"You're right," laughed Lilith. "We won't set you free until the damage we inflict is irreversible. I suppose that I'll just have to find the eggs myself then, no thanks to you, and here we all thought you were such a well-intentioned soul who only wanted to do the right thing."

"A real do-gooder," mocked Azazel, "But all of us here know you're nothing but a lying, psycho Christian cunt. Thanks for that."

"That gives me an excellent idea!" exclaimed Lilith as she snapped her fingers. "We'll brand your forehead with the word, WHORE, so that no one who comes across your disfigured corpse has any doubt what you really were."

"That's funny!" laughed Raegan. "Can I do it to her?"

"Of course, you can," replied Lilith, then she turned to Earl and addressed him. "And we'll tie her up for you to do whatever you want to her before my man and I get down to the business we have with her."

"I'm going to rip her ass apart," Earl said with a nod.

"Get the eggs," Azazel told Lilith. "They're probably in her purse."

"Yes, dear," replied Lilith, then she stepped around the SUV and opened the front passenger door to reach into Sirena's purse on the seat.

"Don't let them do this," Sirena struggled to raise her head to address her daughter and ex-husband. "I'm sorry."

"Too late for sorry, honey," Earl scowled at her in reply.

"Here we are!" Lilith proclaimed then slammed the door shut and stepped around the front of the SUV to join the group.

"We have our stone egg of Uriel and our jade egg of misty swirling gray."

"But wait," Azazel said then jerked Sirena by her hair, "weren't you supposed to deliver these eggs to somebody else? Surely you didn't intend for us to have them?"

"Raegan," began Sirena, "stop this. You have no idea what this about. Get in my car and get out of here right now. They're going to kill you and your dad."

"Cunt," growled Raegan, "don't tell me what to do. Besides, I wouldn't miss what's about to happen to you for the world. I want to carry the horror on your face with me for the rest of my life. I hate your guts, you fucking whore."

"Ditto," added Earl. "But I must confess that I'm looking even more forward to seeing that pain on your boyfriend's face when I finally get ahold of him."

"Well," Lilith began then clapped her hands together, "let's get this party started, shall we?"

Azazel swooped Sirena from her feet and flung her over his shoulder before he followed Lilith toward the house. Earl and Raegan followed them. As they stepped to the porch and Lilith opened the door, Sirena tried to lift her head to see the front of the house.

"This isn't the trailer where I met Enoch," Sirena wheezed aloud.

"No, it isn't," Lilith said to her smiling as she bent down to view Sirena's upside-down face. "We tricked you. The place you went to meet Enoch is just a little farther down the road. You were so close. If you scream loud enough, maybe Enoch and his parents can hear you from here."

Azazel proceeded into the front room of the house, which featured a horizontal Roman cross supported by wood legs.

"Look familiar," Azazel whispered to Sirena before he

pulled her from his shoulder and sat her on the post. "Just like the ones we had set up for Baraka in Paris and Amsterdam, isn't it?"

"Oh, my God," Sirena gasped.

Azazel seized her shoulders and pinned her to the cross.

"There's no God here," Lilith remarked from the threshold. "He's gone fishing."

"Earl and Raegan," Azazel began as he held Sirena in place, "the straps for her wrists are underneath the crossbeam. I hear this whore really likes to be tied up with her new boyfriend. You just loved every last sordid second of it, don't you slut?"

Earl and Raegan went to opposite sides of the beam then retrieved the straps below them. They each strapped one of Sirena's wrists to the bondage cross then stepped around the beam to stand at Sirena's feet. Azazel tore the sweater from Sirena chest then ripped the shirt and bra beneath it from her, exposing her breasts. Sirena began to flail her feet in her attempt to kick Azazel, but Lilith grabbed her legs and held them as Azazel undid the button of her jeans and jerked them from her body.

"Earl," Azazel said, turning as he pointed to Sirena's panties, "would you like the honors."

Earl stepped around Lilith, who had pinned Sirena's legs to the cross post. He then turned to his daughter and motioned for her to approach him. Azazel stepped aside to allow Earl and Raegan reach Sirena, then he moved toward the duffel bag positioned on the floor against the wall.

"Too bad it's come to this," Earl told his daughter. "But she has every awful thing about to happen to her coming for what she did to our family."

"You're damn right she does," Raegan said, sneering at her mother. "Plus, the insurance money is going to come in handy."

Sirena was about to yell for them to stop what they were doing and leave before it was too late, but instead, she could only scream when she saw Azazel raise a metal club in each one of his huge hands and hit Earl and Raegan on their heads with such force that both of them collapsed to the floor.

Sirena screamed again when Azazel leaned over the limp bodies and again bashed their heads with the clubs, spraying blood into the air. Sirena could only sob when Azazel repeated the blows and the blood again sprayed into the room.

"What a couple of ingrates," remarked Lilith. "After all you did for them, and this is how they wanted to repay you? Just a pair of truly rotten souls."

"Why?" cried Sirena. "Why did you have to kill them?"

"Don't fret, Sirena," Lilith tried to console her. "These two just didn't have your best interests at heart, not like your brother and I do."

"What?" Sirena managed to ask past her sobbing.

"There's a lot you don't know," Azazel said before he dropped the clubs to the floor beside the bodies. "Or that you don't remember yet."

"We're not going to kill you," Lilith said soothingly before she released Sirena's legs and stepped forward to run her finger through Sirena's hair. "We're here to reunite you with your family so that you can perpetuate our legacy for victory in the final reckoning."

"What?" Sirena spewed, glaring at Lilith.

"The Rapture, dear," Lilith said with a smile, "with your brother and me here to shape your destiny, there will be no stopping us when The Rapture finally arrives. You see, Sirena, I'm your real mother. You already remembered that you are a Siren Nephilim begat from the unholy tryst between angel and human, but what you haven't remembered yet is that the angel in that tryst was your father, Samyaza, and the human was me, although I am also as much demonic as I am human."

"No!" screamed Sirena. "No!"

"Oh, yes," Lilith whispered into her ear as she held Sirena's head still. "I am your mother, and you are the spawn of evil."

"It gets better, sis," Azazel chimed before he peeled the shirt from his body and removed his shoes and pants, exposing the enormous ovipositor that hung pendant down the length of his scaly groin and feathered thighs. "You and I are going to be proud parents of the greatest evil of all."

"What?" Sirena gasped as Lilith tilted her face so that she could see the ovipositor as it hardened and lengthened in its rise.

"Yes," Lilith resumed, "you and Azazel are going to give birth to the crown prince of all darkness, whose soul will be a light in this world for all of the downtrodden and diseased to worship and follow into a new era of depravity and debauchery that will overwhelm The Rapture and do to those Christians what their God did to us through the Great Flood."

"Uriel!" Sirena cried with her remaining strength.

"Well," Lilith began, "there's him, too, only he's not on our side, now, is he, dear? You're here obviously to fertilize the eggs that Azazel will deposit deep inside of you, but also to lure your archangel boyfriend to his demise. We couldn't have pulled this off, though, if we hadn't been able to create a diversion of demonic possession with his ex-wife. I believe you're familiar with our use of the Camazotz, aren't you, Sirena?"

"Yes," wheezed Sirena.

"Well," Lilith replied past a chuckle, "your boyfriend is there fighting one of them right now. He'll win that battle soon enough but won't be able to win the war and rescue you in time, I'm afraid."

"I'm ready," Azazel informed Lilith as he gripped his massive, erect ovipositor with both hands.

"You most certainly are," agreed Lilith, ogling the sight of Azazel before she released Sirena's face. "Just make sure you clean this mess up after you're done with her. Bury poor Earl and Raegan in the pit out back and try to clean up Sirena the best you can. She needs to be presentable enough to Uriel for him to believe there's still enough of her left to try to rescue. Otherwise, we might never be able to lure him into our design."

"I'll take care of it all," Azazel said as he lifted his leg over the cross post to straddle it in his approach of Sirena. "Just please leave, now. I'm about to gush all over the place."

"I can see," Lilith chuckled then stepped to Azazel, rubbing his throbbing ovipositor. "You come from the mightiest of genes between mine and those angelic ones of your father, Samyaza. He'll be here shortly to perform a little video interaction of his own with Sirena to entice Uriel further into our intrigue."

Lilith removed her hand from Azazel, who then took Sirena by her ankles and pinned her feet against her outstretched forearms.

"Just remember that you can't mess her up too bad her," Lilith reminded him, then she stepped across the floor toward the front door. "Samyaza has to have her presentable enough, so we can use her to snare Uriel."

"But what if the intercourse causes her to bleed to death?" Azazel asked as he turned toward Lilith. "Once I start, I'm not going to be able to stop."

"You won't kill her," Lilith told him then opened the front door. "She really is quite a gifted whore who loves it huge and rough. Now, I've got to drive her SUV back to Maysville so that it looks like she's missing somewhere there, and then I've got to wait for Uriel to get home before I can throw his eggs through his window so that he can see for himself what has happened to his beloved soulmate."

"Just get out of here!" Azazel shouted. "I have to take her right now before I bust!"

Lilith crossed the threshold then shut the door behind her. She removed the eggs from the back pockets of her jeans then put both eggs in one hand before she opened the driver's door of Sirena's SUV. She removed Sirena's phone from the console then set it on the passenger seat. She placed the eggs into the console cupholder then retrieved the keys from the gravel and stepped into the SUV.

Sirena's wailing scream from the house caused her to pause before she positioned herself in the seat and inserted the key into the ignition. She then adjusted the rearview mirror to view her reflection.

"Eternally gorgeous," she said to herself, smiling as she started the SUV for her drive to Maysville.

SERPENTIZED

"Sirena!" Uriel shouted as he slammed the front door behind him.

He awaited her reply at the bottom of the stairs, but none came. Instead, the landline phone rang from upstairs. The automated phone announcement identified the caller as The Institute. Uriel hurried up the steps. He grabbed the phone from the coffee table and pressed the button for the speaker phone.

"Hello," he greeted the callers then returned the phone to the tabletop.

"Uriel," fired the voice of Thoth, "sit down, please. We have urgent news to convey to you."

"Wait a minute," Uriel replied. "I just walked in the door, and I need to talk with Sirena first."

"That's what we need to talk about," came the frantic voice of Horace. "You have to listen to us."

"What is it?" Uriel asked.

"We're fairly certain that she's been abducted," explained O. Cyrus.

"Why do you think that?" Uriel barked in reply then sat on the couch.

"We've lost contact with her," began Thoth, "plus, we've received some disturbing news from our friend at CERN about an apparent dimensional portal that has opened."

"What in the hell does that mean?" asked Uriel. "And where is Sirena? Her car is parked outside."

"Thoth," came Horace's quivering voice, "I think we need to tell him all of this in person."

"Too late," snapped Uriel. "Tell me right now what's going on."

"You tell him, O. Cyrus," Thoth said then sighed.

"Very well," came the voice of O. Cyrus. "Are you seated?"

"I am!" shouted Uriel. "Now just tell me where Sirena is!"

"She's been kidnapped by Azazel and Lilith," informed O. Cyrus.

"What?" Uriel yelled.

"She was tricked," O. Cyrus resumed. "We found out that she never met Enoch and his parents but, instead, was somehow detoured into a trap by her daughter then captured by Azazel and Lilith."

"Why?" Uriel again yelled his question.

"They want you, for starters," O. Cyrus replied. "But I'm afraid they also want her to fulfill a certain function."

"Just tell me what's going on!" blared Uriel.

"They're going to impregnate her with the demon seed of the Antichrist," Horace shakily conveyed.

Uriel sat stunned and speechless.

"I'm afraid that's probably true," O. Cyrus broke the silence. "Azazel is going to defile her so that the two of them will conceive that unholy offspring together."

"Where is she?" Uriel demanded to know as he sprang to his feet. "I have to rescue her!"

The silence between the three men of The Institute grew as Uriel awaited his answer.

"Well?" he shouted. "Where is Sirena?"

Thoth sighed before he spoke: "We're just not sure yet, Uriel. I'm afraid she is captured, and it's probably too late to stop Azazel and Lilith from having their way with her."

"Find out where she is!" erupted Uriel.

"We're working on that," returned the voice of Horace. "But first we need for you to tell us about your experience with your ex-wife. This may prove important to us as we continue to research the situation with Sirena."

"How can that make any difference?" Uriel shouted.

"It may be crucial," Thoth said. "You see, we believe that there may have been another force at work through your ex-wife."

"Like a possession," added O. Cyrus.

"Like a demonic possession, you mean?" probed Uriel.

"More like angelic possession," Horace said.

"Angelic?" questioned Uriel.

"Yes," Thoth answered. "We think that one of the leaders of The Watchers–the fallen angel, Samyaza–may have entered through the CERN portal we mentioned and returned from his imprisonment in the darkness of the Dudael. We believe he was the one who overtook your wife with the agency of a Camazotz at his command."

"So, you think the Fallen Angels are starting to escape?" Uriel posed.

"At least Samayza," Horace confirmed, "We obviously already know about Lilith and her offspring on the loose."

"What offspring?" Uriel barked his question.

"We now understand that Azazel is actually the son of Samyaza and Lilith," began Horace, "conceived after Lilith left the archangel Samael."

"Lilith coupled with Samael after she left Adam," added Thoth. "Then Eve was created for Adam. We had always thought that Azazel himself was one of the Watchers, but now we have reason to believe he is this very unique Nephilim produced by Samyaza and Lilith."

"That's the first I've ever heard of this," Uriel shot back.

"We mentioned before," Horace resumed, "that we would research how both Azazel and Lilith had managed to escape the oubliette of the Dudael confinement. They were supposed to remain imprisoned until they are cast into fire on the Judgement Day. Now, we're inclined to believe that they were somehow freed to travel back into time from the moment of their rescue in the *future* by the son he will soon have with Sirena."

"What son with Sirena?" Uriel gasped as he sat back down on the sofa.

"The Antichrist they are going to conceive, if they haven't conceived him already," Horace replied. "That's what's happening here right now, and I'm afraid this is something we can't stop."

"I have to stop it," Uriel cried. "Sirena is my soulmate! We've sacrificed everything for each other!"

"We understand," Thoth tried to console him. "This is going to be very hard to accept, and we don't expect you to take this without fighting back."

"We're counting on you fighting back," added O. Cyrus. "You must fight back and win."

"How?" came Uriel's reply of exasperation.

"You might have to kill Sirena before it's too late," O. Cyrus said.

"Kill her!" shrieked Uriel. "I can't kill her!"

"Hold on just a second," pleaded Thoth. "We don't know that her death is what will be required just yet."

"That's what it sounds like to me," maintained O. Cyrus. "Urile, you must kill Sirena to save her and the rest of humanity. There doesn't seem to be any other way at this point to prevent them from destroying the effect of The Rapture. Sirena must die before her child from Azazel lives."

"I can't kill her!" Uriel blared. "I love her! You all are crazy!"

"Nobody is going to kill anybody," Horace intervened. "We're still trying to compile all of the facts and process them into a working theory about what is actually happening. Our hypothesis is that the Antichrist born from the unholy union between Azazel and Sirena opened the portal that has allowed him to rescue both Azazel and Lilith from their imprisonment, who have in turn somehow freed Samyaza."

"I don't understand how this Antichrist can do something when he couldn't have existed in the first place with Azazel and Lilith both imprisoned," began Uriel. "But if Sirena is doomed, I don't want to live. I can't survive without her. We are each other together forever."

"We appreciate your passion for Sirena, Uriel," Thoth said to him. "But you have to understand the larger forces at work here. There are other signs and interstellar phenomena that we are just now starting to piece together that suggest the beginning of the end is upon all of us—earthly and divine."

"I don't care about any of that," Uriel nearly wept. "I only care about Sirena. She is all I care about. I knew that as soon as I saw her. She is my soulmate. The only thing that matters to me is that we're together."

"Unfortunately," came the abrupt response from O. Cyrus,"

your eternal consummation with her just isn't going to happen. If she lives you die, and the only way for you to live now probably is to kill her."

"I won't believe it!" Uriel fired back. "We're destined to be together forever!"

"They also know how you feel about Sirena, Uriel," Thoth informed him. "It's how they'll lure you to your demise unless you're prepared to face them."

"So, prepare me!" shouted Uriel. "Tell me what I need to do to get Sirena back!"

"We're working on it," Horace tried to reassure him. "We're hoping that Enoch can provide us with more information, but the Enoch that is among us now is not the same one that Sirena met during her first visit to the Serpent Mound. He's much, much younger and still yet to regain the memory he'll need to understand who he is and why he's here."

"So, if he can't help, who can?" Uriel asked them.

"We have a team in the field working on that right now," replied Horace. "They're trying to track Sirena's movement from the time she left Maysville until the time of her return, but so far they haven't discovered anything definite."

"They've already been in your house, Uriel," Thoth informed him.

"What!"

"We had no choice," O. Cyrus remarked. "Time is of the essence and after the scene that they found at the house near Serpent Mound, well, we just needed to act fast with the hope of somehow finding Sirena."

"What scene are you talking about?" Uriel growled in reply.

"They found the Roman cross like the one that was used in Paris and Amsterdam by Azazel and Lilith in their attempted abduction of Baraka," Thoth said. "This cross had straps for bondage and there was blood splattered all over the room."

"Did somebody call the police?" blared Uriel.

"We communicated the information to the authorities through indirect channels," Horace stated. "But we can't risk direct involvement with the police at this point, not if we hope to find Sirena before it's too late."

"The police don't know Sirena is missing," Uriel surmised aloud.

"Correct," Horace confirmed. "We could never explain to the police what is happening. It would only slow us down."

Uriel stood, rubbing his head before he started to pace the floor.

"I thought she was supposed to go to a hotel," Uriel said then paused before he resumed. "Did she go somewhere else after that?"

"She never went to the hotel," O. Cyrus answered him. "She was on her way to an alternate location to meet Enoch and his parents, but, apparently, she was diverted to the other location where the bondage cross was found. We were able to approximate her transmission signal through her phone and car, but the signal was interrupted too often for an exact location. We were lucky that our team stumbled across a witness in a pickup truck who had actually seen Sirena parked roadside near the location where they found the bondage cross."

"But we didn't pursue that information at first," O. Cyrus began to explain, "because we had her signal tracked back to Maysville where her SUV is now."

"We had no doubt that she had returned to Maysville," added Thoth. "Her car is there, after all."

"But now you're not sure she came back here," speculated Uriel.

"Correct," said Horace. "We suspect someone drove her car back to Maysville and that she never returned home."

"And you really don't think they'll kill her?" Uriel nearly sobbed his question.

"Because of you," Horace began, "and because of the demon they want her to deliver. We're as certain as we can be that they'll keep her alive."

"Have they contacted you?" Uriel asked them.

"Not yet," Thoth said before the breaking of glass in the downstairs room froze Uriel in his stance.

"What was that noise?" asked O. Cyrus, then the squeal of tire tread tore from the street.

"I think that's our message!" Uriel yelled before he sprang for the stairway and barreled down the steps to the front room downstairs.

When Uriel reached the room, his eyes found the two eggs side-by-side in the middle of the room. He recognized that they were part of Enoch's cluster of cosmic eggs: one of the eggs was stone and the other its jade counterpart. Shards of glass crunched beneath him as he stepped to the eggs. He stooped to retrieve the stone egg first, which displayed his own angelic self, fit with gold-flecked wings and serene countenance. He then turned the egg as he straightened into his stance, shuddering at the image that had replaced the gray swirling mist there before.

The red-eyed, winged entity stared directly at him, sneering past a mouthful of fangs. Its clawed feet clung to a pedestal that bore the name, *Samyaza*.

Uriel studied the serpent renderings snaking along the four wings attached to Samyaza until he peripherally detected movement from the gray jade egg still on the carpet. He stooped again, retrieving the jade egg to bring it closer to his eyes. He gasped as he beheld the image of a person with their back to him, standing in a swirled gray robe in front of a kitchen sink. Uriel nearly dropped the egg when the splattering of water from the faucet resounded against the kitchen sink and the person started scrubbing something within the sink.

"Sirena?" Uriel nearly cried, amazed that the gray jade egg somehow acted as an audiovisual stream. "Is that you?"

The person paused from scrubbing to untuck their hair from beneath the collar of the robe but did not turn around to address Uriel. The flow of shoulder length wavy hair suggested that the person was indeed a woman. She then resumed scrubbing with even more effort.

"What are you cleaning?" Uriel asked aloud before he realized he was watching the scene he and Sirena had watched of Baraka's Camazotz possession from the video that The Institute had streamed for them. "Oh, my God, no. You're not cleaning anything. You're cleansing yourself, aren't you?"

A gray spiral of light twisted its way from the ceiling to the woman then surrounded her, casting a peculiar shadow that enclosed her features within an oval egg shape. The woman then jerked at the sink–shocked by something unseen.

"Noooooooo!" the scream exploded as she groped for the kitchen counter in her collapse to the floor, where she retched and convulsed.

"Is that you, Sirena?" Uriel yelled at the scene portrayed within the egg. "Tell me where you are!"

The woman struggled to kneel on the floor then gripped the edge of the counter to pull herself to her feet. Her hand shook as she took a flat mirror from the countertop, then she held the mirror in front of her face.

"Honey!" screamed Uriel, turning the egg to try to see if the woman was actually Sirena, but her position in front of the sink blocked his view of her reflection.

The woman then retrieved a paring knife from the sink. She brought the knife in front of her face and leaned toward the mirror she now held in her other hand, appearing to drive the point of the knife into her forehead.

"Ahhhhhhhh," she wailed as her head jerked from the knife apparently carving into her forehead.

"Oh, my God!" Uriel yelled, turning the egg again to try to see the woman's concealed face. "Stop it right now!"

When the woman dropped the knife into the sink, Uriel bolted from the room, still holding the eggs as he scaled the steps two at a time in his haste to reach the upstairs living room.

"Thoth!" Uriel shouted once he reached the top of the steps, then he lunged for the phone on the coffee table. "There's a woman inside of the gray jade egg cutting her face with a knife! I think it's Sirena!"

"What?" the voice of Thoth exploded above the others. "Tell me what's going on?"

The woman then turned around within the egg toward Uriel. Her hands still covered her face and concealed her identity, but her white robe was splattered red with drops of blood.

"Can't let the demon in," trembled her muddled voice. "Can't let the demon in. Please, God, help me keep the demon out."

The woman lowered her bloodied hands from her face, but her face was covered with too much blood for Uriel to see if the woman was Sirena.

"Sirena!" Uriel screamed at the image within the jade egg. "Show me it is you!"

Uriel heard the three men of The Institute imploring him to look away from the egg, but he did not heed their warning. He instead allowed the scene generated within the egg to captivate him.

Water again streamed from the faucet as the woman bent over the sink with cupped hands and repeatedly lowered her face into them. Her long, slender fingers then ran through her hair, wetting it back somewhat, then she undid the sash of the blood-splattered robe and dropped it to the floor.

"That has got to be you!" blared Uriel. "Turn around, Sirena! Please turn around!"

"You are an abomination in the eyes of God," screeched a garbled unnatural voice from the woman, whose naked backside remained within Uriel's view. "You deserve death and eternal torment for your sins against God. Grab your robe and wipe the blood from your face. See for yourself what you truly are regardless of who you try to pretend to be."

The woman stooped to retrieve the robe from the floor then brought it to the sink. She dabbed the robe against her face until stopping to peer into the mirror on the counter.

"Noooooo!" she shrieked, then she covered her face with her hands and bawled. "Nooooooo!"

The woman finally turned from the sink with her hands still covering her face, but she exposed her large breasts within the mist of the egg. Her body heaved as she continued to sob.

"Sirena," Uriel whimpered. "My poor Sirena. This body is yours."

The woman then lowered her hands from her face and cast her heartbroken eyes directly toward Uriel: it was Sirena, and she had carved the word WHORE into her forehead.

"Sirena!" cried Uriel. "What have they done to you?"

Sirena recoiled from the egg-shaped shadow surrounding her, as webbed appendages unfolded from the oval. Uriel gaped in horror at the sight of the winged entity separating itself from Sirena as she convulsed with her eyes rolled back into her head and foam spilling from her mouth.

"Hold on, baby," Uriel anguished aloud, tightening his clench of the jade egg as he watched Sirena collapse to the floor.

Uriel shook at the sight of the shadowed entity within the egg extract itself from her motionless body. The shadow sharpened into the image of a winged being with scaled and feathered body that enlarged as its definition increased. Once fully formed, the entity turned directly toward Uriel with its glowing red eyes glaring at him and his smile revealing a mouthful of gleaming fangs.

"Samyaza!" Uriel spewed through clenched teeth as he glared in return at the figure.

"Hello again, Uriel," the growling voice of Samyaza boomed in reply. "Looks like things have changed a little since you last bid me farewell."

"What do you want from her?" Uriel trembled as he yelled.

"What we want from her," Samyaza began before he turned toward Sirena and grabbed her by her hair to fully expose her face to Uriel, "is transfiguration. She is the WHORE OF BABYLON, after all, but we want to see her transfigured into the fifty-year-old mother of unholy divinity."

Sirena lowered her eyes to look at herself as she held her visibly shaking hands and arms out to her side and surveyed them. She then brought her hands to cover her mouth and stifle her sobs.

"Sirena!" shouted Uriel. "Please hear me!"

"She can't hear you," came Samyaza's grating laughter, then he flung Sirena by her hair, toppling her to the floor. "That's because she's mine now, just like she's always been, really. You see, your Sirena soulmate here is a vile whore who has been so defiled so many times by so many men, women, angels, demons, and beasts, that there could be no more suitably debauched vessel than this filthy whore body to beget the most depraved soul ever to curse this universe."

"Please don't hurt me anymore," Sirena's voice quivered as she struggled to lift herself to sit upon the floor. "Whatever you are."

"She can't see or hear you either," Uriel gasped in amazement as he held the jade egg even closer to his eyes.

"No, she can't," Samyaza replied then stepped back from Sirena. "Watch what she does now in her vain effort to escape her wretched fate."

Before Uriel could respond, Sirena struggled to her feet then staggered as she began to pace in the kitchen, mumbling and rubbing her hands together. She then stopped pacing to unseeingly pass Samyaza in her path toward an adjacent room. Uriel continued to stare at the jade egg in anticipation of her return to the kitchen until the voices of the men from The Institute snapped him from his reverie.

"Where is she!" Uriel heard Thoth shout above his reverie. "Tell us where she is!"

"She's where Baraka was possessed in the video you had Sirena and me watch," Uriel told Thoth. "Do you know where that is?"

"Whatever you do," Thoth yelled his reply without answering Uriel, "do not put your lips to that egg! Do you hear me!"

"I hear you," acknowledged Uriel as he glanced from the phone to the jade egg then back to the phone. "What would happen to Sirena if I did?"

"Nothing would happen to her," Horace said. "It's what would happen to you: you would turn to stone from the contact."

"Now, that really is a shame," Samyaza replied, snapping

his fingers to redirect Uriel's attention. "This is going to be a whole lot more work for everybody now, thanks to your friends there."

"What the hell is that supposed to mean?" Uriel snapped back at Samyaza.

"That means," Samyaza began but then paused at the sound of noises like thrown objects crashing within the room where Sirena had entered, "that we could have killed you quickly instead of luring you somewhere to kill you there."

Sirena returned, still naked and carrying a white, lidless five-gallon bucket. She placed it on the floor beside the sink before she opened a cabinet beside the sink and retrieved a shaker of salt. She then took the mirror from the counter and flung it across the kitchen. The mirror shattered against the wall, scattering its shards across the floor.

"Got to keep the demon out," Sirena said as she shook salt from the shaker along the seam where the window met the sill.

"What are you doing, Sirena?" Uriel screamed.

"I believe she's spreading salt to keep evil spirits away," replied Samyaza. "It's an old wives' tale that salt repels us from entering a house to possess the people living there."

Sirena then stepped to the kitchen door that led to the outside of the house, now chanting: "Keep the demon out. Keep the demon out. Keep the demon out."

Sirena stooped to the kitchen door and shook the salt shaker along the threshold, still chanting but louder now with a voice that started to crack and garble. She stood and desperately began to shake the salt all over herself. She poured salt into her cupped hand, then she dropped the shaker to the floor and winced as she rubbed the salt against her crotch.

"Oh, noooooooo!" Sirena screamed when Samyaza grazed

against her then encircled her with his four, serpent-tattooed wings. "Stop! Stop! Stop!"

Sirena crouched to her knees in her attempt to drop to the floor, but her body remained suspended within Samyaza's winged grip. She tried to pull her arms to her chest, but his shadow overpowered her and kept her afloat with outstretched arms. Only when the phone rang did Samyaza retract his wings, then Sirena collapsed to the floor, curling into a ball and sobbing. The phone continued to ring without answer.

"Somebody is trying to help her," Uriel blurted. "Answer the phone!"

"It's us calling her Uriel!" Thoth shouted. "We know where she is! The police are on their way there now!"

The phone rang an abbreviated fifth time then rang no more. Sirena stopped her sobbing and shakily lifted her head from the floor.

"This is my last chance," Sirena managed to say before she clambered to the five-gallon bucket on the floor.

Sirena squatted over the bucket and grunted. The splatter of loose fecal matter resonated below her first, then the splatter of urine followed. She stood above the bucket and peered into it. She retched at the sight of her bodily fluid then knelt beside the bucket and lowered her trembling hands into the mixture gathered at the bottom. She scooped the urine and feces from the bottom, lifting the foul murk from the bucket.

"Keep the demon out," Sirena cried as she smeared the excrement over her chest and along her arms.

Uriel gagged as he watched Sirena apply the waste to her legs, chanting her cry of *Keep the demon out*. He then retched when Sirena scooped more filth from the bucket. He wept as she applied it to her face then crammed it into the orifices of her lower body.

"Keep the demon out," Sirena's repeated cry turned increasingly less intelligible as her sobbing overtook her and her body heaved with each utterance.

Sirena then grabbed the bucket and held it over her head before she flipped it, holding the bucket there until all of its contents spilled onto her head. She then flung the bucket across the room before she smeared the waste into her hair.

"Keep the demon out," she repeated with restored pronunciation, then brought her hands to her mouth and inserted her fingers, gagging as she smeared the waste across her tongue and against her teeth and guns.

Sirena removed her fingers from her mouth. She looked at her soiled hands and legs. A knock pounded against the kitchen door.

"Police!" came the shout. "Open up!"

"Keep the demon out," Sirena managed to utter one last time before she again collapsed to the kitchen floor, where her motionless body sprawled.

The first kick from outside shattered the door window glass and cracked the wood jambs. The second kick split the door in two with half remaining on its hinges and the other half splintering as pieces of it flew across the kitchen.

Samyaza turned toward Uriel and scrunched his face into mock surprise before he said, "Wonder if they're too late?"

Azazel stepped into the kitchen with Lilith behind him, both of them laughing as they pointed at Sirena then waved toward Uriel.

"So very nice of you to come for Sirena's little housewarming party here," Samyaza greeted Azazel and Lilith before he turned back to address Uriel:

"Uriel, I know how impossible all of this must seem to you, especially when you were just starting to settle in with your crap-covered whore of a soulmate here. But we got plans for her now. Before too much longer she'll bear the demonic seed of Lilith and my son, Azazel."

"Looks like somebody can't hold their past," scoffed Lilith before she kicked Sirena in back of the head. "And she always seemed like such a shrewd, competent whore, so organized and capable of doing anything and everything just to survive."

"The demon is here, Uriel!" Sirena managed to yell. "The egg of Azazel is inside me! Destroy them both before it's too late!"

"Whatever," grunted Azazel before he addressed Samyaza. "We need to get her out of here now before the police really do arrive."

"Very well," said Lilith, then he stepped to Sirena and lifted her from the floor by her hair. "Come on whore, time for you to go now. We have more fun and games planned for your psycho Christian ass, sister."

"So long for now," Samyaza said with a wave toward Uriel as Azazel and Lilith dragged Sirena by her arms from the house. "We'll contact you shortly with instructions, now that we know we have your attention and you have our eggs again. Just make sure you don't bring your friends from The Institute with you then."

Samyaza then followed his accomplices and their captive from the house, and the jade egg returned to its static state of gray, swirled mist within Uriel's hand as he shook from his sobs.

"Uriel," O. Cyrus gently called to him. "You must let Sirena go now. If you meet with them, they will kill you. Her fate is sealed either way until we can find an alternate way out."

"And we will find that way out," added Horace. "Our liaison with CERN informs us that the quantum processor for parallel universe capability has nearly assimilated the wormhole in suspension from the collider conduit. Once that junction is constructed, we can redirect Sirena from the point of her capture. Just be patient."

"I can't risk waiting," Uriel managed to tell them past his suppressed sobbing. "I have to rescue Sirena."

"I know this is hard, Uriel," Thoth now commented, "But you really have to wait before you act. We have our researchers working on everything they can right now to help find Sirena and get her back."

"Where do you think they're taking her?" Uriel asked them.

"I don't think it's prudent for us to disclose that," Horace replied.

"Maybe we should tell him," countered O. Cyrus. "We don't exactly have our agents in range yet to track Sirena. He actually might find her first."

"Or he might get himself actually killed," rebutted Thoth. "Can we really risk that?"

"Let me be the judge of that," voiced Uriel. "You three understand how tied together Sirena and I are. We are soulmates and can't be separated or we both will die. You have to tell me what you know."

"Perhaps so," Horace replied. "But is that enough to withstand the forces of evil that seek your destruction. This is no time to become overly sentimental."

"Sentimental!" shouted Uriel as he sprang from the sofa. "What are you talking about, *Sentimental*! They were making her torture herself in the vilest way, just like they did to Baraka in the video we watched before. I have to do everything I can do to try to rescue Sirena! Tell me where she is!"

"All right, Uriel," relented Thoth. "I'll tell you where we think they might be headed. I agree with you that we need to do whatever it takes to try to spare Sirena from the fate that awaits her. But we'll provide the location to you on one condition."

"What condition?" snapped Uriel.

"That you don't do anything drastic if you locate Sirena before our agents arrive," qualified Thoth. "We will know your location so that we can get to you as quickly as possible in the event that you are captured and taken somewhere."

"It's your car," responded Uriel, "and you've got the GPS tracker in it. Of course, that didn't seem to help keep track of Sirena, now, did it?"

"That was our fault," Horace acknowledged. "We didn't know where she was located exactly. Unfortunately, the difference of less than a mile between locations made all of the difference in the world."

"We won't make that mistake again," Thoth tried to reassure Uriel. "But you have to promise us that you won't do anything drastic because if they capture you...."

"They will definitely kill you, Uriel," O. Cyrus finished Thoth's warning.

"Whatever you want," Uriel agreed to their condition. "Just tell me where to go!"

"We don't know that exactly just yet," stated Thoth, "But we'll send the link with directions directly to your phone once we think we know precisely where she is."

"I'm leaving now," Uriel told them. "At least tell me what direction I'll be travelling."

"Go toward the Serpent Mound," Horace directed him. "Then you'll know for sure where to go as soon as we know."

"Thank you," Uriel said.

He disconnected the call and hustled down the steps then out of his house with his phone and the eggs in his hands. He darted across the street to his parked SUV. He struggled to open the driver's side door, but once he managed to push it all the way open with his foot, he reached across the driver's seat to place the two eggs in the passenger seat. He then set his mobile phone on the console between the seats and climbed into the car.

Don't fly, he told himself as he turned the ignition. *This is no time to get pulled over.*

PART V

SERPENT MOUNDED

OUROBOROS

Since Uriel left his wife of twenty-two years for Sirena last summer, he dreaded separation from his newfound soulmate. The consummation of their coupled destiny had so enraptured him that every second they were apart felt like the universe was collapsing within him.

Now that Sirena had been abducted, he felt like his mounting grief was about to suck his heart into a black hole of despair. The deeper he sank into it, the more he remembered about the entities he now found himself facing. It was as though his sense of looming loss created the anti-matter of memories beyond his earthly grasp in a sequence of fleeting images that depicted his previous encounters with Azazel, Lilith, and Samyaza.

"Turn left in five hundred feet," instructed the male voice of his phone map app. "Take Church Road for one-point-three miles to your destination."

Uriel slowed on the two-lane state highway and signaled when he saw the street sign posted ahead.

Can this be right? he asked himself before he glanced into the rearview mirror and made the turn onto a gravel road that was too narrow for two cars traveling in opposite directions.

Uriel's glance into the mirror reminded him of the other reason why he now dreaded separation from Sirena even more: fear of unimaginable vengeance by the evil forces that now assailed him and Sirena for his part in their capture and imprisonment from which they were now somehow free. Even though his reunion with Sirena across limitless time and space was miraculous beyond belief, Uriel knew too well of the vicious demonic volatility that motivated the entities involved in Sirena's abduction. He feared that their venom for him and Sirena would compel them to devise the most brutal, malicious revenge in their design to annihilate the world and any trace of love that had existed within it.

Uriel had heeded the traffic behind him to ensure he wasn't followed by anyone during the hour drive from Maysville to this location near the Serpent Mound. He periodically glanced at the gray jade egg, hoping for Samyaza to return within its swirled mist to tell him where to find Sirena. He also eyed his mobile phone on the console beside him, waiting for The Institute to provide him with the directions to his destination, which The Institute did nearly halfway during his drive north.

Now that he found himself alone in this remote location about to arrive at an unknown destination to face God knows what in his hope to save Sirena, he felt a different dread spike through him.

What if Samyaza was using The Institute without their knowledge to lure him out here to the middle of nowhere? he thought.

"Stop it," he scolded himself aloud. "The Institute is fully equipped to fight this evil."

Uriel had texted The Institute that he had received their directions. He breathed easier with the knowledge that The Institute knew of his whereabouts, but as he ventured farther and slower along the potholed, narrow road that snaked between a creek ravine to his left and treed, hilly terrain on his right, he wanted to directly phone The Institute about his progress. He braked to a stop then retrieved his phone from the console beside him, only to notice the map was gone from the screen and the signal icon indicated no reception.

"Damn it," Uriel sighed when he realized he hadn't down-loaded the map to his phone.

Uriel set his phone down before he glanced in the rearview mirror again. With no one behind him, he pulled forward, steering around a pothole that consumed much of the right side of the road.

It was less than two miles on this road, he told himself. *It can't be too much farther.*

Uriel was already perturbed by the situation he faced without much in the way of a plan to rescue Sirena, and now this aggravation of losing his directions irked him further. He had hoped during the drive from Maysville that either he or The Institute would figure out some plan of action for him. Those details might have come out if he had been able to call The Institute.

Once Uriel cleared two switchback curves that coiled through the surrounding forest, a dirt driveway opened to his right. He skidded to a stop in the gravel then peered down the drive. A hoary-headed old man clad in denim overalls and surrounded by pecking chickens stood in front of a car parked between a trailer and a shed at the end of the driveway. The man waved first then motioned for Uriel to drive toward him.

"Jesus Christ," Uriel gasped. "It's Enoch."

The chickens scattered when Uriel pulled up beside Enoch, who pulled at the SUV driver's door handle even before the car completely stopped.

"Hurry up!" Enoch wheezed as he flung open the door. "We don't have much time!"

Uriel jumped out of the SUV and followed Enoch to the wrought iron patio table, where Enoch lifted a brilliantly colored huipil to reveal two eggs, one stone and the other of swirled gray jade.

"Notice the first one is a painted stone egg with the ouroboros symbol," Enoch pointed out to Uriel. "It's the snake eating its own tail."

"What do I do with it?" asked Uriel.

"Keep this with you," Enoch told him. "Do not show this egg to them. The other side is the blank swirling gray of future mist, like what you would see when you pass through the clouds during an airplane flight."

"What about that other swirling gray jade egg, like the one I already have with me?" Uriel asked, pointing to that egg.

"Take that one, too," answered Enoch. "They will ask for those other two eggs that you brought with you—the Uriel egg and the original gray jade egg. Give those to them. They will bring Sirena out for you to see but will not let you have her."

"But I have to rescue her," protested Uriel. "I can't let them have her."

"We're too late for that," Enoch told him. "For now, anyway. Perhaps you will find her again, but Sirena belongs to them for now. There's nothing more that can be done about it."

"No!" cried Uriel. "I have to save her!"

"This is the Alpha and Omega of your future," Enoch began as he placed one hand upon Uriel's shoulder and pointed to the ouroboros egg with his other. "Your transfiguration awaits you, but first, you must endure their capture of you. It's the only way."

"No," wept Uriel. "This can't be."

"It is," sighed Enoch before he took the paired ouroboros eggs from the table and closed Uriel's hands around them. "And you have work to do, so listen to me closely. When you hear them summons you, you must meet with them. They will want the paired eggs of Uriel and Samyaza with the gray jade egg you already have for their power to open the portal that leads to your capture. Give those eggs to them. As much as you will want to resist their capture of you, you must let them do it. Do you understand me?"

"No, I don't understand," came Uriel's strained reply. "Why can't I take Sirena from them?"

"I will do everything within my power to reunite you and Sirena soon enough," promised Enoch as he patted Uriel's shoulder. "Just not right now. I will liberate you both once my own transfiguration is complete. I am destined to be like you, Uriel, only the strongest of them all."

"Oh, Uriel," the voice leaked past the open door of the SUV. "Don't you want to see your poor, beloved soulmate Sirena in distress?"

Enoch and Uriel both turned toward the voice emanating from the SUV then looked at each other.

"It's time for you to meet them," Enoch said before Uriel hurried back to the SUV.

Uriel reached across the driver's seat, placing the ouroboros egg and its jade complement in the console cupholder. He then took the jade egg of swirling gray mist from the passenger seat.

"I'm here," Uriel announced as he brought the egg closer to his face. The mist cleared, then the face of Samyaza appeared on the egg.

"Eggscellent," Samyaza quipped past his widening grin of fangs. "Now that you are there, I need you to be here at the Serpent Mound. I know you're close, Uriel, so hurry."

"Where's Sirena?" blared Uriel as he squeezed the jade egg.

"Why she's just off camera here," chuckled Samyaza. "So close but not quite in view. Perhaps you would like to hear from her first?"

"Yes!" shouted Uriel.

"Smack the whore," Samyaza said as he turned his face from Uriel and the sound of a smack resounded before the rip of tape preceded Sirena's scream.

"Stay away, Uriel!" Sirena managed to voice before she was muzzled again and silenced.

"Sirena!" cried Uriel as he met the glare of Samyaza. "I'm coming!"

"Of course you are coming, old friend," Samyaza replied with a sneer. "I can't wait to get you within my sight again."

"I'll be there soon," Uriel proclaimed as he glared at Samyaza within the egg, then he set the egg in the passenger seat and climbed behind the wheel.

Uriel slammed the door shut and started the SUV. As he spun the car around in the drive, he glanced at Enoch, only to see the old man waving the huipil in front of him as he stepped across the front of the SUV. Uriel lowered the window, and Enoch thrust the huipil into the cab.

"Carry their eggs in this sacred huipil," instructed Enoch, "then fling it into the air once they have their eggs. It will fly from there and hopefully will find Sirena when the time comes."

Enoch then dropped the huipil to Uriel's lap and stepped back from the SUV before Uriel turned the rest of the way around.

"Remember, you must be captured!" Uriel heard Enoch's shout wane as he sped toward the road.

Uriel tore from the gravel driveway then careened out into the narrow road, hoping he would remember how to reach the Serpent Mound. When his phone suddenly revived and the voice of his phone map blurted his next direction, he accelerated, driving as fast as he could along the backroads without losing control. He clenched the steering wheel in his desperation to see Sirena again.

When he reached the open two-lane highway with a directional sign posted for the Serpent Mound entrance, he noticed the blackening sky shaped strangely ahead of him. The faster he drove, the faster the approaching squall line seemed to move toward him. When he finally reached the entrance to the Serpent Mound, the bruised sky hovered above him, climbing beyond his vision to see its end.

"Welcome to the Great Serpent Mound, Uriel," Lilith's voice preceded her emergence from the attendant booth at the entrance. "I'll be your park guide on such a lovely day as this."

Uriel wordlessly pulled ahead to park closest to the walkway that led to the earthen effigy. He watched Lilith toss her flowing red hair behind her as she approached him, gripped by the gray dress that rippled in the sudden flow of breeze.

Uriel struggled to stuff an Ouroboros egg into each of the front pockets of his jeans. He then took the huipil from his lap, folded it, and placed the Uriel and Samyaza eggs within it before he climbed from the SUV.

"Let me take those for you," Lilith said, attempting to snatch the eggs from the huipil.

Uriel blocked her reach: "Not until I see Sirena."

"Very well," Lilith said then strode ahead of him to the path that led to the Serpent Mound.

Uriel pursued her, shivering from the chilled infusion of breeze that enveloped him. As he proceeded, he passed the observation tower, and the landscape of the serpent effigy unwound in front of him.

"Walk to the egg at the head of the serpent," instructed Lilith, then she pointed ahead without turning to face him. "And place the eggs you have in the ground shape of the egg at the serpent's mouth. You will be met there."

"By Sirena?"

"Yes," Lilith replied.

Uriel broke into a sprint along the paved path that circled the effigy. The rumble of thunder above shook him, and raindrops pelted him as he neared the head of the serpent. When he reached the turn in the path at the head of the serpent, he stopped and turned toward the way he came, surprised to see someone standing atop the observation tower at the entrance to the path around the effigy.

"Sirena," he breathed before he held his hand in the air for her to see.

Sirena began waving her hands toward him and shaking her head before the hulking figure of Azazel rose from his seated position on the tower deck. He restrained Sirena's arms from behind, then the wind surged into gusts that buffeted Uriel. The downpour shielded Sirena and the tower from his view, but the ground within the egg at the serpent mouth erupted before a glowing egg tore from the earth in front of him.

Uriel took the stone and jade eggs in his hand, then he flung the huipil into the air as far as he could. The wind caught the huipil, launching it over the serpent effigy toward the observation tower.

"Step into the egg," the voice of Samyaza instructed Uriel from the jade egg within his hand.

Uriel brought the egg closer to his eyes and met the stare of Samyaza.

"You must now step into the egg at the mouth of the serpent," Samyaza ordered him. "Or else I'll kill her when we're finished with her."

"Promise me she will live," Uriel pleaded.

"Sure," Samyaza grinned at him. "But only if you step into the egg right now."

Uriel stepped onto the wet grass in front of the glowing egg. He squinted to see if he could glimpse the tower and Sirena in the distance, but the rain shield still obstructed his view.

"Leave your eggs on the ground before you step into the serpent egg," the voice of Samyaza rose from the jade egg amidst the howling of the strengthening gusts.

Uriel dropped the eggs to the ground as he stepped to the glowing egg at the opened mouth of the serpent. He glanced behind him to see the swirling funnel of a tornado twisting its way down from the greenish black sky, then he returned his attention to the glowing egg that had emerged from the ground. He touched the grayish glow in front of him. When he slipped his hand through the gelatinous eggshell, he brought his other hand to the glow and continued forward, feeling the soft, sticky covering of glow pull him farther into the egg itself.

Once he completely entered the egg, its lift from the ground jolted him. He felt the egg wobble within the tornadic grip surrounding it then gaped as the entire egg with him in it shot into the air. He braced himself against the inside of the egg as the head of the serpent tore from the ground in pursuit of him and the egg.

Uriel tried to push against the egg but could not shove his hands past the glob of eggshell. He watched the body of the serpent effigy come to life below him as its coils tore from the earth, then he witnessed the tail whip itself into the air in front of him. He fell to the bottom of the egg as he watched the tail wrap around the egg and push it toward the mouth of the serpent.

"Oh, God, no," Uriel gasped as he helplessly felt the tail of the detached serpent shove him and the egg into the mouth and then down the throat of the airborne snake as it lifted to writhe within the shape of the tornado snaking its way through the sky.

The serpent mouth closed, rendering Uriel in darkness that undulated through the weightless space that encompassed him.

EPILOGUE

MEMO TO ENOCH, AGENT METATRON:
From Thoth, Director of External Affairs for The Institute of Artifactual Research
RE: **Operation Rescue Uriel**

WE'RE unsure about the exact date when we can access the dimension where Uriel remains trapped, but we do understand here at The Institute that we are in a race against time. You already must know that, if we are too late, Uriel will be eaten by the unholy antithesis of this universe, who is due to arrive on this planet in the form of the demonic entity often referred to as *The Antichrist*. That arrival will transpire, as I'm sure you're also aware, through the agency of Uriel's beloved soulmate Sirena, which perfects the treachery of this unholy manifestation because Sirena will be eaten to death from inside by The Antichrist as it develops within her womb. This consumption of its mother will effectively transfer the incarnation capability of

Sirena to him, making him eternal in physical transfiguration at the ultimate expense of Sirena, whose death will be thereafter permanent.

With his transference of Sirena's power to him, The Antichrist will be poised to feed next upon Uriel. We fear that this single anthropophagus act shall forever doom humanity in debauched anarchy by virtue of the essence that it will wipe out from the face of the earth. That essence is, of course, the celestial heart of Uriel, which is what makes him the archangel that he is.

We can't allow that to happen, which is why we've decided to forego any further pursuit of Sirena in the hope of her rescue so that we can apply all of our resources toward saving Uriel. It saddens us deeply, and we're sure you as well, that we must content ourselves with the torturous murder of our beloved Sirena, but that is just how the cruel course of her fate has to unravel.

Sirena will always be regarded by us here at The Institute as an angelic force in her own right in this eternal battle we wage between good and evil. We love her for her youthful heart and her old soul and grieve her loss to us as both an ally and a delightful woman whose rise above her unfortunate circumstances is truly an inspiration for all of us to seek truth and empower ourselves with our own spirit of mind. That travel to true happiness was her purview.

With our mourning for Sirena duly noted, we now wish to inform you of our plan of action. We have proceeded with our search for Uriel through the channels that we believe are available to us, including the Ouroboros egg and its gray jade counterpart that you gave to Uriel before he was captured. We understand based upon your own information, as well as further research through our sources involved in the physics of particle collision, that the Ouroboros egg provides us with the means to communicate with Uriel, even if we can't locate him. We believe we have successfully plotted this communication and will attempt to contact him after completion of a few more tests. If you are still available to us within our dimension, we will apprise you of the results.

However, such communication with Uriel in and of itself will not enable us to free him from his imprisonment. We know that, but we believe we have ascertained the path of inquiry that will enable us to attempt a rescue of Uriel subsequent to our communication with him. For us to actualize that, we've solicited the assistance of experts in the quantum mechanics of artificial intelligence capable of processing the infinite possibilities of parallel worlds so that we can pinpoint not only Uriel's location but also the matrix of his imprisonment.

Calling the prison in which Uriel is bound a *wormhole* really doesn't do justice to the fabric of its design. It is a *snakehole* in time and space; the Alpha and Omega of all possibilities in parallel worlds unseen by the human eye yet clearly defined by its serpentine shape of the Serpent Mound itself in its terrestrial mirroring of its cosmic counterpart.

The actual Serpent Mound was, in fact, stripped from its historic site by the tornado that hit the location last fall. Whether or not this is a temporary condition remains to be seen, pending any developments in the future that might alter our current past within this earthly realm.

Until that day if and when fate is altered again, we must trust our research and our instincts in all of this. Should you be able to provide any further guidance as we proceed, we would must certainly appreciate it. We will do our due diligence in trying to invoke you in ways that might work, but we are limited in our understanding of you at this time in history.

In fact, we are forced to speculate about you in many respects because the historical accounts of you are detailed in Apocrypha, which we can't verify with any more accuracy if the sole accounts of your life were rendered exclusively in the Christian Bible itself.

However, we at The Institute are learned in the accounts about your historical plight as a man who is translated by God into Heaven where he is advised by Archangels–Uriel included among them–for your transfiguration into the Archangel Metatron.

In respect to this conversion of yours from man to Archangel, we share similar awe in your transformation as we do in that of Uriel, whose transfiguration from Archangel to human man through the agency of Sirena is equally a marvel to us.

So please understand our limitations. We have no guidance to follow regarding what will happen to you in the future front that awaits us here on earth during this version of time. All that we do know for sure is that Uriel is now suspended in a cosmic *snakehole* between worlds waiting for us to free him before it's too late. Unfortunately for us, we have no way of knowing what *too late* even means. For all we know, we are already too late, and The Antichrist is among us, having devoured Sirena internally and Uriel, piece by angelic piece.

But we must assume we have more time, which is why we have produced this book, novelizing the course of events that have led to Sirena's abduction, Uriel's capture, and your own flight from our presence. We have to rely on this message reaching you through your reading of this book.

Telikiread is now the last hope for humanity's salvation.

For all we know, you really were the young man that Sirena was supposed to meet with his parents Baraka and Jared before she was abducted. If that's the case, we can only hope that you are a quick learner and fast reader, but we haven't been able to locate your presumed parents. We fear that they and you have met some fate similar to that of Uriel and Sirena met through the agency of Samyaza and his syndicate of evil.

Should you find this, and us as a consequence, we can only hope there is time left. Perhaps the gestation of The Antichrist requires much more time than a normal human one. We just simply don't know.

In any event, find us if you can. We will be searching for you in the meantime, and waiting your triumphant presence within our realm, be it that of a young man or an ancient old one.

We are encouraged that we will meet you soon because of the pair of unusual items we recently received here at The Institute.

The first is stone egg that depicts the sarcophagus lid of the Mayan Snake House–Pacal the Great–in his manifestation of Votan. He appears to be at the controls of some kind of upward launching machine, perhaps like that which carried Uriel away from this dimension. The other side of this stone egg depicts the effigy of Serpent Mound.

The second item is a jade egg that, as best as we can find, is described as Galactic Black.

Both of these eggs were listed among the original clutch of cosmic eggs that you first presented to Sirena, but neither is mentioned again in all of the accounts of the *Serpent Egg Rapture* that transpired afterwards.

We're hoping that this means you have a couple of eggs up your sleeve!

Godspeed Metatron.

ACKNOWLEDGMENTS

Thanks to publisher Tony Acree and the Hydra Publications staff for bringing this book to life. This is my third novel published by Hydra, and I look forward to writing many more!

I also really appreciate the gracious talent involved in the cover design of Serpent Egg Rapture. First and foremost, thank you Emily Billingsley for the magnificent modeling for the book cover. And thanks to photographer Bob Willcutt of Bob Will-cutt Photography for capturing the essence of the book that Emily projects so well. Thanks, as well, to Tom Jones of Bob Willcutt Photography for a superb job with the cover design and layout.

I also want to thank actress and Audio Sorceress audio book narrator, Marnye Young, and author/poet Dr. Suzi Hall for their advanced praise of the book. Thanks, too, to additional advanced readers David Alexander, Britt Hempfling, and Patrick Davis for their valued input during the creation of Serpent Egg Rapture.

ABOUT THE AUTHOR

Robb Hoff is the Hydra Publications author of the Eggsquisite Corpse Thriller series that began with his surrealist, Salvador Dali inspired, Cosmic Egg Rapture (2018) and continues with the release of his horror noir latest, Serpent Egg Rapture. He is also author of the Hydra-published The Lycanthrope Series that began with Contract With The Lycanthrope (2019).

www.ingramcontent.com/pod-product-compliance
Lightning Source LLC
Chambersburg PA
CBHW021209250626

47155CB00008B/2743